TIME CHAIN

A NOVEL

D1454198

STEVEN DECKER

Printed in the United States of America
Published in Hellertown, PA
Cover design by Christina Gaugler and Cassandra Yorke
Cover image by Serferis
Interior design by Leanne Coppola
Map on page 7 by Sarah Neville
Library of Congress 20222911077
ISBN 978-1-952481-99-4
2 4 6 8 10 9 7 5 3 1

For more information or to place bulk orders, contact the publisher at Jennifer@BrightCommunications.net.

BrightCommunications.net

For Cam, Paige, and Colin.
Each of you, my greatest accomplishment.

Author's Note

There's a wonderful map on the next page, done by Sarah Neville, which shows the area where the book opens and which becomes the base of operations for the unlikely fellowship that forms throughout these pages. A few charts also appear in the first half, and while these are not necessary, I thought people who like charts might enjoy them. For those of you who are not "chart people," you may ignore them and rely fully on the prose of the book.

SD

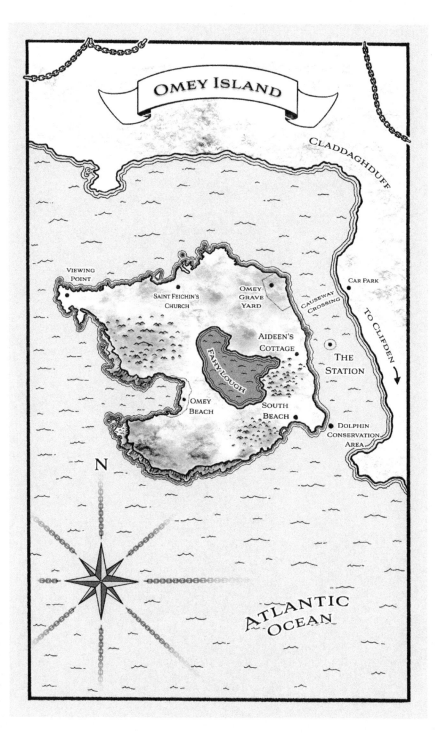

Prologue

Assemble the links
Piece by piece.
Then travel through time
And earn your release.

Found in a stack of papers on the desk of Dr. Charles Burke.
It is assumed that he is the author.

Chapter 1

As Dani approached the water, a rainstorm erupted. She secured the hood of her rain jacket and steeled herself for an uncomfortable delay in her walk to Omey Island. A deluge of raindrops plunged into the channel that separated the Irish mainland from her destination, covering its rippled surface with a blanket of tiny splashes. The sound of a thousand whispering ghosts surrounded her.

A line of signs on posts marked the way across, but they stood in fairly deep water at the moment. Dani wondered if low tide would ultimately grant her passage over the sunken causeway, realizing that only time would provide the answer, but meanwhile, nature's symphony raged on.

A powerful wind joined the rain to raise the stakes of waiting. Dani turned her back to it, glad she'd put on her rain pants that morning before she'd started walking. The west coast of Ireland almost always offered rain and wind, bursting on, then off, several times a day. But this storm was the strongest she'd endured thus far in her journey, and its bitter chill was steadily seeping into her.

Dani was now facing a small car park, presumably there for people who wanted to walk onto the island when the tide went out.

Only one car sat in the lot. She couldn't see clearly into the windows due to the blasting rain, but while she was trying to ascertain if someone was in the car, the driver's side window came down a few inches, and a hand reached out. The fingers of the hand were long and slender, and with a flick of the wrist it waved her toward the car, then disappeared inside.

As Dani approached, a woman's voice emerged.

"Go round the other side and get in!" the voice commanded, in a strong Irish accent. The window rose and sealed shut, tempting Dani to follow the woman's order and join her in the warm, dry automobile.

Dani believed from experience that if the woman was Irish, she could be trusted. And there was also something about her voice, something familiar, that made Dani feel safe. She ran around to the left side of the car, urgently removed her pack, yanked open the door, and jumped into the front passenger's seat. She shoved the soaking, wet pack onto the floor in front of her, then quickly shut the door. The thump of the door closing muffled the sound of the storm. The car's warmth enveloped her, and her rapid breathing added to the fog on the windshield. She turned to the woman, who had a welcoming smile on her pretty, freckled face and whose gray-blue eyes peered back with energy and intensity. A depth of emotion in the woman's gaze was a little unsettling to Dani, but she was happy to be there nonetheless.

"Thank you for inviting me in," she said. "That's a strong storm! I'm sorry I'm getting your car wet."

"Wet's a way of life in Ireland," said the woman. "No trouble a'tall."

"I'm Danielle Peterson," she said, extending her right hand to shake. "But most people call me Dani."

"Eye-deen," said the woman, shaking Dani's hand. Her grip was firm, and her hand was a bit rough, as if she worked in a trade.

"What a beautiful name!" exclaimed Dani. "How do you spell that?"

"A-i-d-e-e-n."

"I've never known anyone with that name."

"Means 'little fire.' Last name's O'Brien, which means 'noble.' So, I'm a noble little fire. But I can be managed if you work at it!" Aideen's smile widened, and Dani sensed joy in the woman that didn't seem commensurate with the circumstances. Aideen looked out across the water. "So, you're waitin' for the tide to go out, are ya'?" she asked. "Goin' for a walk round our little island there?"

"Yes, I hope to," said Dani. "If the tide really does go out."

"Oh, it does. Twice per day. About two hours before low tide, the water in the channel will be gone, and people can go across then, 'til around two hours before high tide. So once the water's down, ya' can go back and forth for quite a stretch of time. Won't be long now."

"And why are you here waiting?" asked Dani, wondering if she was being too forward. Aideen paused for just an extra second, then responded.

"I've been away for a bit, but I live out there," she said. "I'm the only permanent resident of Omey Island, since Pascal Whelan passed, back in '17."

"I see," said Dani, hoping Aideen O'Brien might be the special find her research had so far been lacking. Perhaps her luck was turning. "I didn't realize there were no permanent residents out there," she said.

"One," corrected Aideen.

"Yes, of course," said Dani. "I hate to be forward, but I'm writing my dissertation on the Wild Atlantic Way, and meeting you seems like, well, maybe you could help me by telling me about it from your perspective."

Aideen stayed quiet, seemingly pondering how to respond.

Then she opened up.

"How much time do ya' have?" she asked.

"I have a lot of time," said Dani. "My dissertation is all I have left to do before getting my PhD in cultural anthropology."

"Well then," said Aideen. "You'll be a guest at my home. As soon as the feckin' tide goes out!"

Chapter 2

"Are you telling me you can drive across this channel?" asked Dani.

The rain had stopped soon after Dani entered the car, and not long after that the water level in the channel had begun to drop precipitously. Now only small, narrow rivulets of water remained in the sand of the causeway.

"Indeed, you can," said Aideen. "Hard as a rock, that sand."

Aideen drove out of the car park and eased down the ramp into the channel. Dani felt her eyebrows raise, and she sat back in her seat, waiting to sink into the wet causeway. But they didn't sink. Aideen got the car going about 30 kilometers per hour and didn't look back, but Dani *did*. She could see tracks in the sand from the car's tires, but they weren't deep, barely denting the hard surface of the channel bottom. In only a minute or so, they were across. Aideen curled left onto an old road that was mostly sand, with a little gravel mixed in and tufts of grass running down the center, traversing the easterly edge of the island. Every now and then, Dani saw a home set back from the road.

"What are those houses?" she asked.

"Vacation homes and rentals," said Aideen. "Only a few of

them though. And rarely occupied. People want more action than you can find out here. There's not a single shop or pub on the island. Nothin' but peace and quiet. Seems no one's lookin' for that anymore."

"But you *are?*" asked Dani.

"It's what I know," Aideen replied, ending the conversation.

Aideen turned left down a narrow sand and gravel driveway that led to a small rectangular cottage, nestled at the bottom of a gentle hill and not far from the edge of the channel they'd just crossed. The front of the cottage was beige stucco, but the sides were made of stone. The roof was gray slate. Two windows flanked the sides of the wooden front door, which was painted in a soothing light blue.

It was three in the afternoon in mid-March, so the air was brisk, around 50 degrees Fahrenheit, but the sun was now shining. The breeze felt good on Dani's face when she and Aideen got out of the car. Aideen went to the back and pulled a small suitcase from the hatchback, where two bags of groceries also sat. Dani put on her pack and grabbed them, closed the hatch, and followed Aideen toward the front of the cottage. Aideen used a key from her key chain to open the door.

"Come on in then," she said. "And thanks for carryin' the groceries. I only bought for one, but if you stay a while, we can go back to town for some more. The kitchen's just back there. And you can put your things in the spare bedroom over there. There's only one bathroom, so we'll have to share the jacks."

"The what?"

"The toilet. Have you not yet heard the term 'the jacks' on your travels? It's the common name for a public toilet in Ireland."

"Well, I have now," said Dani. "Can you explain it to me, please?"

"Jack Power, from Thurles down in County Tipperary, invented the multi-cubicle toilet in 1806. Man had 38 children, and they needed to use the toilet quite a lot, often at the same time. So, he built a big outhouse with a bunch of toilets in it. Made him quite famous, and rich, and the Irish people have been calling the toilet *The Jacks*, to this day. But I don't think Jack Power appreciated that at 'tall. I'm told he actually changed his name after that phrase took hold."

"Now that's what I'm talking about!" said Dani. "Gems like that could end up in my dissertation, more than likely. But no worries about only one *jacks*. "I'm just so grateful you invited me here that I'd go outside if I had to."

"Wasn't so long ago, that's just what we did!" said Aideen.

Dani put the grocery bags on the counter and went to put her backpack in the spare bedroom. She noticed a large bookshelf in the living room, full of books of all sizes. She saw several she'd read before—by Hemingway, Dostoyevsky, Karl Marx—and this was encouraging. So far on her journey, she hadn't met anyone she'd thought of as having an advanced education.

When Dani returned to the kitchen, she got a good look at Aideen while she unpacked the groceries. Her wavy, red hair flowed down to the middle of her back and was just beginning to show signs of gray, and there were crackles of wrinkles at the corners of her beautiful gray-blue eyes. Her complexion was pale but with a rosy hue, and she had freckles, but it was difficult to guess her age. She wore jeans that held firm legs and a green, flannel shirt, which combined with the jeans to display a woman with a shapely physique who didn't seem to care if people saw that or not. She stood straight and tall and moved about the kitchen with the fluidity of someone in good health and familiar in her surroundings. Dani finally decided that Aideen was in her late forties, or at most, early fifties.

"So, you're walkin' the Wild Atlantic Way, are ya'?" asked

Aideen.

"As much of it as I can," said Dani. "With the help of taxis on long stretches of highway. But 2,500 kilometers is a long way, no matter how you travel."

"It 'tis," said Aideen. "And you started up in Inishowen, did ya'?"

"Yes. I've been on the road for 15 days so far."

"Averagin' a bit over 20K a day then," said Aideen.

"Yes. I know I could do more, but I tend to linger, hoping to meet someone interesting, like you! So, you know how far it is to Inishowen?"

"Of course! I've done a lot of walkin' along the Wild Atlantic Way, all the way from up north, near Inishowen, to way down south near Cork."

"Wow! That's awesome! What a coincidence!"

"Maybe," said Aideen, and this confused Dani.

"What do you mean?" she asked.

"I don't really believe in coincidences, Dani."

"Oh? So, *fate* brought us together?"

"More'n likely. We'll see."

"How will we know?" asked Dani.

"We'll figure it out," said Aideen, casting her gaze downward so Dani couldn't get a direct look at her face. Dani once again felt the emotion in Aideen but had no idea what the source of it was.

"Would you like a glass of wine, Dani?"

Chapter 3

"**W**here in America are you from?" asked Aideen. They were sitting out back on the pea gravel patio, drinking an excellent French Pinot Noir that Aideen had pulled from a cupboard.

"I'm from the Chicago area," said Dani. "The northern suburbs. Have you ever been to the US?"

"Certainly have," said Aideen.

"Have you been to a lot of other places in the world?" asked Dani, wondering if by chance she'd stumbled upon a woman who not only possessed local knowledge, but also the perspective that traveling internationally can bestow.

Aideen put the glass to her lips and drank a long, slow pull of wine before replying.

"You could say that," she said. "And you wouldn't be wrong."

Aideen's response frustrated Dani. She wasn't sure if Aideen's tendency to gloss over details was part of her personality, or if she was being purposely evasive. It was a little irritating, and Dani wasn't a patient person by nature, which might suggest a short future as an anthropologist. Nevertheless, she followed her gut and pushed harder.

"What do you mean by 'you could say that'?" she asked.

Aideen didn't seem at all put off by Dani's pushiness.

"I travel a fair amount," she said.

"For business or pleasure?" asked Dani.

"A bit of both," said Aideen.

"What business are you in?"

"We'll get to that," said Aideen, suddenly switching the subject. "Why do you keep your hair so short, Dani?"

Aideen's resistance to her questions was annoying, but Dani decided it was best to let it go, hoping that at some point Aideen would open up with her.

"Actually, my hair *was* much longer, before I came on this trip," she said. "I thought the buzz cut might help me attract less attention from aggressive Irish men, or more to the point, men in general."

"So, you don't like men? Is that it?"

"No, I like them fine," said Dani. "But not when I'm traveling alone in a foreign country. I'm not here to find a boyfriend."

"Of course, that makes sense," Aideen responded. "Point of fact is the men up in this corner of Ireland *do* have the more *traditional* values. They like their ladies with long hair. But even with it short like that, I can still imagine it would grow out wavy and shimmering, soft as a black cat's coat. And you can't hide the rest of you. You're tall and strong, and with the bone structure of your face and those wide, green eyes, it's hard for you to hide your beauty."

"Thank you," said Dani, lowering her eyes and blushing, embarrassed more by the passion in Aideen's voice than her complimentary words. She took a sip of the wine, marveling at how delicious it was compared to what she'd had at the pubs along the way.

"Have you had any problems on your walk, so far?" asked Aideen.

"Not too many. It's the off-season for walking, so I haven't seen a lot of tourists, which is by design. I waited until Ireland lifted all Covid restrictions before I came, but by coming in March, I thought I'd improve my chances of meeting locals who can help me with my research. My goal is to meet people like you. But my options for that have been limited so far. The pubs are primarily occupied by local men, the vast majority of whom speak Irish, which I can't speak, and most of them, well frankly, I wouldn't want to talk with anyway."

"Yes, the proverbial traditionalists I mentioned, yeah?"

"For sure. I *did* meet a few helpful women who work in the B&Bs and pubs, but you're the first highly educated local I've met, so I have high hopes for you!"

"What leads you ta' believe I'm highly educated?" asked Aideen.

"The books on your shelves inside," said Dani.

"Ah yes, those."

"You've read most of them, right?" asked Dani.

"All of them, yes. Most more than once."

"Several of them are required reading in university programs. Did you go to college?"

"No, I didn't," replied Aideen. "I just like to read."

"I see," said Dani, a little surprised. "Regardless, if you've read those books, you're a highly educated person, at least in my mind."

"You may be right," said Aideen. "But that's a rather progressive view of education, isn't it? What's your dissertation about, Dani, if you don't mind me askin'?"

"It's called *Remnants of the Wild Atlantic Way.* What makes it *anthropological,* as opposed to *archeological,* is that the 'remnants' I'm looking for are stories that local people have handed down for generations. And I think I might have found a good source here on Omey Island. Am I right?" Dani smiled as she made this inquiry, trying to lighten the weight of the question.

"You may have," said Aideen, failing to elaborate and then

adroitly switching subjects.

"Why don't we make a plan then," she said.

"About what?" asked Dani.

"About the next few days. I propose we have a quick meal tonight and get to bed early. We'll do a full walk round the island in the mornin'. Then we'll catch the low tide tomorrow afternoon and go shoppin' for some food in Clifden. And we'll make a feast meant for queens tomorrow evenin'! What say you?"

"I say, sounds great!" said Dani, genuinely excited and still hopeful that Aideen might be just the kind of person she had in mind when she'd selected the topic of her dissertation. But there was something else, something between them that she didn't understand, and if she was honest with herself, she was more intrigued by that mystery than by Aideen's potential as a subject for her research.

Chapter 4

Dani woke to the sound of rain tapping on the slate roof and the smell of freshly brewed coffee in the air. She got up, dressed quickly, and left the bedroom, passing through the living room and into the kitchen. Aideen was at the kitchen table, sipping coffee and reading a book.

"Good morning," said Dani. "What are you reading?"

Aideen looked up from her book, a welcoming smile on her face.

"Mornin', Dani. This book's called *The Last Watch*. It's by an American woman named J.S. Dewes. Science fiction. Quite clever, actually."

"Maybe when you finish it, I can read it," suggested Dani.

"Have it now," said Aideen, placing the book on the table in front of her and pushing it toward Dani. "I've read it before. I read so fast that sometimes I can't get to the bookstore quick enough for a new book. So, I read the ones that I have over and over again. I was looking back at a passage I favor in that one."

"Thank you," said Dani. "I read some sci-fi, so if *you* like it, I should try it."

"As you wish," said Aideen. "Please sit down and join me.

Coffee?"

"Yes, please," said Dani, taking a seat and reaching for the book, perusing the front and back covers.

Aideen got up and poured a cup of coffee, then brought it to Dani.

"You take it black, right?" she said.

"Why yes, I do," said Dani. "How'd you know?"

"Just a guess," she said, winking.

Dani wondered what that was all about, or if it was simply a guess on Aideen's part, as she had said. But then Aideen once again changed the subject, reaching into a cupboard, withdrawing a package of granola cereal.

"I was thinkin' you must be tired of the Full Irish Breakfast, are ya' not?"

"Quite tired of that, yes," said Dani. "It can give you a lot of energy throughout the day, but it's a little rough on the stomach during the first hour or two after eating it."

"Indeed it 'tis. So, we'll have some cereal and fresh fruit, a little yogurt if you like, then we'll be on our way."

After breakfast, they put on their rain gear and set off. It was 10 in the morning. The rain had tapered off and soon came to a stop, so they pulled down their hoods. They walked south along the old road they'd come in on. Aideen pointed out a section of the channel where dolphins congregated, but they didn't see any. They passed a deserted beach that Aideen said was called South Beach, then turned west along the road. After a while, another deserted beach came into view ahead of them, and Aideen told her it was called Omey Beach. Dani also noticed an inland body of water off to the right.

"That's Fahy Lough," said Aideen, pronouncing the words as *Fah-hee Lock*. "It's a freshwater lake. Lots of wildlife there. Mostly birds, but a few otters as well, and some tasty brown trout."

They turned north, skirting between the Atlantic on their left and the Fahy Lough on their right. The waves from the Atlantic crashed onto the rocks while ducks and swans paddled along peacefully on Fahy Lough. Dani pulled out her iPhone and took a short video of the chaos on the left contrasting with the peacefulness on the right.

The road ended and became a narrow trail. They eventually came to the northwest corner of the island and sat down on the rocks facing the sea, gazing out at a few barrier islands and nothing but endless miles of ocean beyond. Aideen reached into her daypack and pulled out two energy bars, handing one to Dani. Dani thanked her, and as she bit into the bar, she realized they had not seen a single person during their walk thus far.

"Do you think we're the only ones on the island?" she asked.

"Very likely," said Aideen. "There's no one renting this time a year, and no one camped here last night, so we won't be seeing anyone until the tide goes out, around two this afternoon."

"How do you know no one camped here last night?" asked Dani. "Is camping prohibited?"

"No, it's permitted."

"So, how do you know no one's here?"

Aideen paused, seemingly contemplating an answer, then responded.

"This is my home, Dani. The whole island is my home. I make it my business to know if someone's in my home."

"Uh, yeah, sure," said Dani. "But how …"

Aideen stood up.

"Shall we continya' on?" she asked, slinging her pack on and walking east. Dani caught up and joined her, forcing herself not to pursue her question any further. She wanted Aideen to tell her more about the old ways of this area, and upsetting her wouldn't help the cause.

They headed east, toward the channel between the island and the mainland, following a path that led them to the remains of an old stone building. The outlines of the four walls were there, with a gable and doorway on one side intact, but there was no roof. Just the stones of the walls.

"This is what's left of Saint Feichin's Church. Saint Feichin was a seventh-century man of the cloth who had quite a big monastic settlement here, but this is all they've found intact. But that's still quite a lot, considering it was built nearly 1,500 years ago."

"I should say," said Dani. "Impressive."

Not far from the church, Aideen took Dani down a steep, short path to the water's edge. They followed the path, paralleling a small, sandy beach. The hill on their left became a cliff, about 15 feet high. Aideen stopped at some kind of structure that was embedded in the side of the cliff. There was nearly 10 feet of solid ground above the structure, which was made of rocks, arranged in an organized way in the side of the cliff.

"What's that?" asked Dani.

"An ancient tomb," said Aideen.

"How ancient?"

"The archeologists removed the bones and carbon dated them. They said the bones were over 5,000 years old."

"Wow, that's old! This is really an ancient island."

"All of Ireland is ancient," said Aideen, turning back toward the road.

After rejoining the main road, they continued on in an easterly direction and passed an old graveyard.

"This cemetery has around 500 graves in it, dating back to the time of Saint Feichin," said Aideen. "Pascal Whelan rests here, too. He was a good man."

Dani didn't respond, feeling a little intimidated by the old graves and by Aideen's references to the mysterious Pascal Whelan, whom she apparently had known. She would save her questions for later. They resumed their walk and turned south, and before long they were passing the channel causeway area, although the water was still too high to cross.

"Let's get home and have some lunch," said Aideen. "Then we can go into Clifden and get some proper groceries. The causeway crossing will be ready for us by the time we're done with lunch."

"Sounds great," said Dani, a little relieved to be getting off the island, at least for a while.

They enjoyed ham and butter sandwiches for lunch and washed them down with carbonated iced tea. While they were cleaning up, Aideen made an abrupt statement.

"If you're not comfortable here, Dani, I can drop you off wherever you like when we cross over to the mainland."

Dani was drying dishes, but she paused to look up at Aideen, who was staring back at her with those stunning gray-blue eyes. Dani thought she saw sadness there, but also hope.

"Where did that come from?" asked Dani. "Have I done something to make you think I'm uncomfortable?"

"It's not what *you've* done," explained Aideen. "It's what *I've* done. Haven't done, actually. I've not properly answered some of your questions, and I regret that."

It was true that Aideen had been somewhat less than forthcoming with information on several occasions, like when they were talking about Aideen's travels and her education, or lack thereof, and just today when Dani had asked how she knew no one was on the island. And if Dani was honest, she had to admit that her reaction to these situations had bordered on uncomfortable, but as she thought it through, she realized that what she really wanted was to know more about Aideen. So, she responded honestly.

"I'd just like to get to know you better," she said. "That's all."

"I'd like that," said Aideen, relaxing somewhat. "And if you stay, let's promise each other that first, we'll have a great dinner with some good wine, and then we'll open up more as the evening goes on. Can we promise that to each other?"

"I promise," said Dani, anticipation in her voice.

"The tide is out," said Aideen. "Let's go shopping!"

Chapter 5

After crossing over the channel at around 2:30 pm, Aideen and Dani drove for 20 minutes until they reached the outskirts of the village of Clifden. They stopped first at the Aldi on the N59, where they picked up most of their provisions, then drove toward the village center. While they were driving, Aideen asked Dani a question.

"Do you eat red meat?" she asked.

"I don't eat a lot of red meat back home," said Dani. "Mostly fish, chicken, and a lot of veggies. On the road over here, I've eaten a lot of salmon and fresh fish and chips, but I've had some Irish Stew along the way, too. If red meat is what you like, then I'm fine with it."

"I like all kinds of food," said Aideen. "Living on the coast, of course there's always fresh fish to be had, but I sometimes get tired of that and want a nice steak. And it so happens, we have the best butcher shop in all of County Galway, right here in Clifden!"

"Steak it is, then!" said Dani.

They parked along the main street in the village and bought some fabulous-looking steaks at the Des O'Brien Family Butcher, a bustling little shop that seemed quite popular with the locals.

Dani had offered to pay at the Aldi *and* at the butcher, but Aideen had waved her off both times. She didn't appear to be troubled by money, but Dani had yet to find out what Aideen did for a living. After a quick stop for some more wine, paid for again by Aideen, they drove back to Omey Island, crossed over the channel, and took the sandy road back to the cozy, little cottage.

After they unpacked the groceries, Aideen chopped up a green onion, minced some garlic and put it in a bowl, then added some thyme, rosemary, and ground pepper. She poured in a healthy portion of olive oil, some soy sauce, and added several ounces of Irish whiskey. She mixed it up and poured it into a rectangular glass baking dish, then laid the steaks into the dish, making sure to poke them with a fork to allow the marinade to enter the meat.

"We'll let that soak for an hour or so and maybe have some wine while we prepare the vegetables," she said.

"Is that an old family recipe?" asked Dani.

"Not a'tall," said Aideen. "Just Irish Whiskey Flat Iron Steak is all it 'tis. Quite common, actually."

"I'm glad we bought some more of that Pinot Noir!" said Dani. "Should go well with the steak. I'll open a bottle right now if it's okay with you."

"That would be grand!" said Aideen.

Dani went to the drawer where she'd seen Aideen pull out a corkscrew the night before and opened the bottle. "Should I let it breathe?" she asked.

"Why wait?" said Aideen, smiling.

"I couldn't agree more," said Dani, reaching for two glasses and pouring the wine.

They grilled the steaks out back on the patio but ate inside. The temperature was less than 50 degrees Fahrenheit and would go lower as the sun set. Before dinner ended, they were into their second bottle and having a great conversation, with lots of stories and laughing, but Dani still felt she wasn't getting to know much about Aideen's past. She decided to open things up by revealing something about herself that few people knew.

"You seem like a wise person, Aideen, so I'd like to share something with you about myself that I generally keep secret."

"As you wish," said Aideen, pulling her intense gray-blue eyes into direct contact with Dani's.

"I'm adopted," said Dani.

Aideen paused, then responded simply.

"And?" she asked.

"And what?" asked Dani.

"Well, I'm no psychologist, but 'how does that make you feel?' seems about right in this case."

Now it was Dani's turn to pause. She hadn't thought about how it felt to be adopted in quite some time. But it was a feeling she'd never forget.

"I feel like I was abandoned," she confessed, and a small weight was lifted from her.

"Do you know who your biological parents are?" asked Aideen.

"Yes."

"Do you have contact with them?"

"A little. But it's not fun for me. They have other children who they *kept*."

"Why didn't they keep you?" asked Aideen.

Aideen's probing and unexpected questions nudged Dani toward memories she preferred to avoid, but it was her own doing, so she let it happen. She remembered the first time she'd been introduced to her birth parents. She was eight and had known for some time that she was adopted, having been gradually introduced to the concept by her adoptive parents beginning when she was three, and then told definitively when she was five. Dani hadn't struggled much with being adopted, after all, her adoptive parents were the only parents she'd ever known. But then one day her birth parents came to visit her at her home. Her mom and dad had asked her if it would be okay for them to come, and she'd said it was fine. Dani didn't think much about it, but when they were all gathered together in the living room of her home, she felt awkward, and she wasn't completely okay with it anymore. *There* was the woman who had given birth to her, sitting in a chair on the other side of the coffee table, a tall woman with dark hair, who looked very sad. And her birth father, sitting in the chair next to his wife, a strong looking man with big hands, she remembered, with a frightened expression on his face. Dani had always been a direct person, so she'd asked the most important question first. And her birth parents had answered truthfully.

"They said they were too young to take proper care of me," said Dani. "They had me when they were both 16, and they didn't have other kids until they were in their late twenties. When they came to see me that first time, they were only 24 and hadn't had the other children yet. But they eventually did, and I found out about it."

"I see," said Aideen. "That *does* seem like a difficult situation. They gave you up because they weren't ready for children, but by the time they *were* ready, you'd been with your new family for a long time. Is that about right?"

"Yes, basically. And I love my adoptive parents. They're great people, and they've always treated me like I'm *their* child. Which I am."

"Do your adoptive parents have any other children?"

"No, just me. They couldn't have children of their own and didn't feel the need to adopt more kids. They gave their all for me, and I'm very grateful."

"I can see though, how you would feel abandoned by your biological parents. I understand the logic of their situation, but that *still* has to hurt deeply. I'm sorry you have to bear that burden."

Aideen reached out and took Dani's hand, squeezing it tightly, but released it quickly. Dani felt something new from that brief physical contact between them, as if a barrier had been breached.

"Thanks, Aideen. I appreciate your understanding." Dani was surprised and pleased at Aideen's sensitivity, which had been completely absent until now. She'd begun to think of Aideen as a very hard person, having lived out here on this lonely, harsh island for her entire life. But she'd been wrong. Aideen was more than that, and Dani took the opportunity to begin to probe more deeply. "What about you?" she asked. "Do you have children?"

"Ah, so now we arrive at the quid pro quo, eh?" said Aideen.

"We promised to open up to each other, remember?"

"We did," said Aideen. "But in my case, it's complicated. Hopefully before the night is over, you'll understand more about why that is so. But in answer to your question, no, I don't have any children."

"What about love interests?" asked Dani. "You're a beautiful woman. I'm sure the opportunities have been plentiful."

"Not so easy as you might think, with me livin' out here all alone. But I'm just returning from a long visit with a man I've known for quite some time. His name is Charles Burke, and he lives in Dublin. He's a professor at Trinity College."

Dani took a long draft of wine, relieved that it no longer felt like pulling teeth to get information from Aideen, so she continued with her questions.

"What does he teach?" she asked.

"Anthropology," said Aideen, raising her eyebrows.

Dani narrowed her eyes, perplexed by this new revelation. First, Aideen said she'd walked most of the Wild Atlantic Way, which is what Dani was attempting to do, and now Aideen appeared to be dating a professor of anthropology, which was the degree Dani was pursuing.

"Quite a coincidence, eh?" said a grinning Aideen, raising her glass for a toast. Dani raised her glass. "To coincidences then!" said Aideen, clinking her glass against Dani's and taking a healthy sip.

Dani decided to look on the bright side. She was the guest of a native of the Connemara region along the Wild Atlantic Way, who could turn out to be a substantial source of information for her dissertation. The cottage was warm and dry, and the wine was superb.

"I guess we'll figure it out!" she said, raising her glass, then guzzling some more of the delicious bouquet. Yet something still bothered Dani. Aideen had a secret and was doing her best to hide it from her.

Chapter 6

The two women talked and drank and laughed until well after midnight. Although there was no Wi-Fi in the cottage, the cellphone reception was strong, so Dani was able to do some internet searches during the evening. Before leaving on her trip, she'd signed up for a program with her phone carrier that allowed her to utilize her unlimited data plan overseas, for a fee of $10 per day, so she wasn't worried about data charges from her searches.

Dani was interested in learning more about Aideen's professor, Charles Burke. She searched on her phone and found the Trinity College website, looking for his name in the faculty section. She didn't find it, and this caused a small alarm to go off in her head. She decided to approach the subject as delicately as she could, which based on her current state of inebriation, was more like a bull delicately walking through a China shop.

"So, Professor Burke?" she asked, casually. "Is he currently on the faculty at Trinity?"

Aideen raised her eyebrows again.

"Not currently," she said.

"But he *was*, at some point, right?"

"At some point, yes," said Aideen.

Again, the evasiveness. Dani didn't like it, and her patience had run out.

"Aideen, why are you dodging my questions?" she asked.

Aideen didn't answer immediately, and Dani gave her time to think, but she never expected what came next.

"We've met before, Dani. I know you very well, actually."

Dani was stunned by Aideen's outrageous claims, but she attempted to remain calm, hoping Aideen was simply mistaken. "I have no memory of that," she said. "Where do you think we met?"

"It's not the where as much as the when that's goin' to throw you?"

"How so?"

"Because we met in 1978," said Aideen.

Dani shook her head, frustrated. "You must realize, Aideen, that I wasn't born yet, in 1978. That happened about twenty years later."

"I do realize that, Dani. But it's a fact that we were together in 1978. I've been waiting a long time to see you again."

Aideen's certainty confused Dani, but it also piqued her curiosity. "How is that possible, Aideen?"

"I can show you, if you want."

"When?" she asked, unsure what else to say.

Aideen looked at her watch. "Well, it's a quarter to one," she said. "Low tide tonight is at 19 past two, so I can show you right now. Grab your jacket and let's go!"

"Where are we going?" asked Dani, startled.

"For a little walk."

Aideen got up, found her jacket and her daypack, and put a few provisions and a water bottle in it.

"Bring your passport," she said to Dani.

"Why?" asked Dani, somewhat dumbfounded by this request. "Are we leaving the country?"

"Just get it. You're goin' to like where we're goin'. I promise."

Aideen headed for the door. On the way out, she snatched a small flashlight from a shelf. Dani jumped up, ran to the spare bedroom, pulled her passport out of her pack, stuffed it in her jeans pocket, then grabbed her coat and ran after Aideen.

It was pitch black outside. The temperature was around 40 degrees Fahrenheit, but it wasn't raining. They walked north along the road and came to the channel causeway area. Dani could hear the waves from the Atlantic crashing into the coastline further to the north. Other than that, all she could hear was their footsteps. The tide was out. Aideen stepped into the channel.

"Where are we going?" asked Dani, perplexed and a little frightened.

"I'm showin' ya' how we met, remember?"

"Well, yes, but I don't understand how this will provide the answer, is all I'm saying."

"Follow me and you'll have your answer," said Aideen. "Trust me, Dani. I would never put you in danger."

They walked into the channel toward the mainland for about 300 meters. Aideen came to a stop near one of the round signs with an arrow on it that pointed to the mainland. She turned right and began walking in a direction parallel to the shoreline, toward the south. She stopped after about 200 meters, shined her light on a large rock that was off to the right, slowly swept the light to the left, across the sand, and brought it to a stop at a spot that was directly in front of them. She put the flashlight in her pocket, then kneeled down on the sand and began digging where the light had been shining. She uncovered a metal handle.

"No one has any reason to come this far off the causeway crossing going to and from the mainland," said Aideen. "This spot is rarely seen by human eyes, except *mine* that is!"

Aideen leaned down and started scraping away the sand around the handle with her free hand. A round hatch appeared. She pulled the hatch open and climbed into it. Before she was below ground level, she turned to Dani, peering directly into her eyes.

"Trust me, Dani. You don't want'a miss this. I'm not exaggeratin' when I say the journey of a lifetime, of a hundred lifetimes, is just below us!"

And then she disappeared down the hatch.

Dani was confused and uncertain. But she believed in her heart that Aideen would not harm her. There was something Dani couldn't quite remember that made her feel safe with Aideen. She leaned down and stepped into the opening. Her feet made contact with the rung of a ladder. She glanced down and saw Aideen shining the light for her from a spot about 10 feet below her.

"Close the hatch," said Aideen.

Dani complied, then continued her descent. Her feet gained purchase on a hard surface that was covered by a few inches of water, repelled successfully by her hiking boots. Dani turned on the flashlight of her iPhone to get a better look at the chamber. It was made of ancient, stone blocks, except for one wall that was as smooth and black as obsidian, but it reflected no light when her phone pointed in its direction. The wall was solid and did not appear to be constructed of block. Something about it, some presence, hinted that it was more than mere stone, but no words came into her mind to adequately describe what made her feel that way.

"What is this place?" she asked.

"It's an ancient burial crypt," said Aideen. "The remains have been removed, as has the original wall that was once where the black stone wall is now. But we won't be staying here. When the tide comes in, this chamber will fill with water."

Aideen pointed her flashlight at the side of the chamber that looked like smooth black stone and walked toward it. She pressed her palm against the black wall, and an opening the size and shape of an arched doorway materialized. Aideen entered the opening.

"Follow me," she said.

Dani followed. She turned her head and pointed her light back toward the black stone wall and saw that the opening from the chamber had already sealed up. She increased her pace to catch up with Aideen, and as she moved ahead, she noticed that the tunnel, which was made of the same black material as the wall, was sloped downward. Dani was stunned and confused as to how someone could build this structure, under the channel itself, and apparently in secret. Her mind was sluggish from all the wine, but she was still very aware that she was involved in something beyond strange at the moment.

The tunnel ended at a wall, also smooth, black stone. Aideen placed her palm on the center of the wall, and another doorway opened, allowing them to pass through. They entered another chamber, made entirely from the same smooth, black material as the tunnel. The doorway opening disappeared, replaced once again by solid black.

The room was circular. The ceiling was perhaps 20 feet off the floor, and it looked as if something up there was providing illumination. Dani inspected the rest of the room. In the center of the floor of the chamber was a circular platform, about four feet in diameter and a foot and a half high. There were also two structures, one to the left of the platform and the other to the right. Each structure was made of the smooth, black stone and looked something like a bed, although much narrower. They stood about three feet off the ground and were about the same width as a cot, but concave, like the inward curve of a hammock. Aideen handed her daypack to Dani.

"Take the pack," said Aideen.

"Why?" asked Dani, confused. "Aren't you coming with me?"

"I will be with you," said Aideen. "Just take the pack and put it on. And take off your jacket. You don't need it."

Dani complied.

"Now give me your cellphone," said Aideen.

"Why?"

"You won't be needin' it for a while. It won't work where you're goin' anyway."

"But you're going with me, right?"

"I'll be there with you! Now please, give me the phone."

"But what if I want to take pictures?" asked Dani.

"It will become obvious why I'm taking the phone in very short order. Please, just give it to me!"

Dani handed the phone to Aideen, and she put it in the pocket of her jeans. Aideen then approached the black stone bed on the right side of the circular platform and got onto it, reclining as if she were lying down to take a nap. She reached out with her right hand and pointed at the platform.

"Now step onto the circular platform and take my hand, all right Dani?"

Dani stepped up onto the platform and reached over to take Aideen's hand.

"Aideen, what are we doing?" asked Dani, beginning to get scared.

"Keep holding my hand," said Aideen. "All will be well. I promise you."

Dani noticed Aideen squeeze some kind of control mounted to the far side of the bed with her left hand. Then the light from above began to increase in intensity, but there was no sound. The powerful light grew and grew, engulfing her and blocking any view of the black walls of the chamber. All Dani could see was the bright light, but for some reason the light didn't hurt her eyes. On the contrary, the light gave her a feeling of comfort and relaxed her, causing her mind to wander aimlessly. She still felt the strong grip of Aideen's hand against hers, but she was losing contact with everything else in the room. After about 10 seconds in the light, Dani's eyes closed, and her mind went blank.

Chapter 7

Dani's awareness returned, and she heard the sound of loud rock 'n roll music. She didn't recognize the band, but that was the least of her concerns. Her eyes remained closed, but she felt Aideen's hand in hers. Aideen increased her grip, and she felt lips against her ear.

"Open your eyes, sleepyhead," came Aideen's voice.

Dani opened her eyes. She was in some kind of rickety, over-sized cabana. The place was full of young people dancing to the blaring music. She looked behind her and saw mostly darkness, but she could make out the whitecaps of waves breaking gently onto a beach of sand. It was warm, much warmer than it should be, perhaps 75 degrees Fahrenheit.

Dani turned to ask Aideen where they were, but when she looked at her, she saw a woman who appeared to be in her early twenties. Dani's eyes traced the tanned, bare arm of the young woman down to the hand that was holding hers. She looked back up and saw the freckles on the woman's face, the wavy red hair, and the stunning gray-blue eyes.

"Aideen?" she asked.

The young woman leaned forward and once again pressed her lips against Dani's ear.

"Let's move away for a moment, Dani," she said. "It's too loud to speak in here."

She pulled on Dani's hand, and they walked out from under the cabana in the direction of the sea. When they were well away from the noise, the young woman stopped.

"In answer to your question, yes, I'm Aideen."

"But you're young!"

"Younger, yes. I'm the same age as you now, actually. Twenty-four."

"What's going on, Aideen? This is crazy!"

"I told you I was goin' to show you how we met, Dani. Well, this is how."

Dani's heart rate increased. She began to hyperventilate, knowing but not believing what had just happened.

"So, you're saying we traveled back in time?" she asked.

"One of us did," said Aideen. "But it wasn't me. I come here to Pelekas every summer for a long holiday."

What's Pelekas?" asked Dani.

"It's a beach on the island of Corfu in Greece."

"What year is this?" asked Dani.

"1978," said Aideen.

Dani collapsed onto the sand. Aideen sat down beside her and put her arms around her.

"It's a lot to take in," said Aideen. "But I'm here and I will take care of ya', Dani."

Aideen's words and calm demeanor helped Dani settle down, but she still had many questions.

"So, if you're 24 right now, and this is 1978, but I'm from 2022, that makes you 68 years old back in Ireland?"

"That's right," said Aideen. "But let's not worry about that right now."

"But back in Ireland, you didn't look *nearly* that old! At most, early fifties, but not 68!"

"It must be the fresh sea air, then! But hey, we'll talk more. We've got plenty of time, Dani. I'll tell ya' all I know soon, but right now let's enjoy the party. And by the way, the music is Patti Smith. There's a guy from Scotland who comes to live here every summer, and he brings this amazin' sound system and a lot of albums. Right now, he's playing Patti Smith. But he loves the Rolling Stones, so don't be surprised if we hear a lot of that tonight."

"So, we're staying?" asked Dani.

"I thought we might," said Aideen.

"Where will we sleep?"

"I have a hut I made from bamboo down the beach a bit. There's no road access to Pelekas, at least in 1978 there isn't, so the people who come here are mostly young. You have to walk down the mountain, through the olive groves to get here. I'll show you that tomorrow."

"Okay, but I'm really confused right now, Aideen. And a little scared. Is everything going to be okay?"

"I promise you with all my heart, Dani. This is the beginning of something you'll never forget. And yes, you're safe. As long as you're with me, you're completely safe. And I also promise that tomorrow I'll explain how it all works. Let's go back in and have a good time, all right?"

"But what about the people in there?" asked Dani. "Didn't they just see me pop in from nowhere?"

"No, that's not the way it works," said Aideen. "At the instant of your appearance, time stops for a microsecond, which is all it takes for a person to stabilize into the new time. So, when you appeared, all the people in our immediate surroundings were frozen in time."

"But what if someone had been looking at you just before I appeared? One second you were alone, and the next second I'm here, holding your hand."

"The time stop throws off people's thought processes, too. When time starts back up, they have to reorient themselves into their environment and are a bit hazy about what was happenin' just before you arrived. So, we're fine, Dani. You are welcome here in this time. Trust me. Please."

Dani thought for a moment, remembering she had trusted Aideen to get her this far, so why stop now? She was alive, and it appeared she was safe, and she had to admit that she always felt safe when she was with Aideen. She had from the beginning.

"Okay," she said, a tentative smile on her face.

"First, we've got to get you out of those hiking boots and that flannel shirt. Take off your daypack, okay?

Dani took off the pack and laid it on the sand.

"What do you have on under that shirt?" asked Aideen.

"A bra and a T-shirt," said Dani.

"Good. So, you can take off the flannel shirt and put it in the daypack. Then take off your hiking boots and socks. The socks will fit in the daypack, and we can carry the boots and put them aside when we get back in. Okay?"

"If you say so," said Dani.

When Dani had finished shedding her clothing, Aideen grabbed her hand and pulled her back toward the cabana. As they approached, Dani could see that the structure was just some rippled roofing applied to a haphazardly constructed wooden frame. It didn't look sturdy. They came closer, and Dani spotted the Scottish man off to the left. He had a full beard and was dressed in a kilt, but he wasn't wearing a shirt, displaying a tanned chest and torso that were nearly as hairy as his face. He was holding a round, black disk, about 12 inches in diameter, getting ready to replace the Patti Smith album. Dani had seen pictures of records before, but she never imagined she'd actually see them being used in real life. If this *was* real life.

They entered the structure, and Dani got a chance to observe the people who had gathered there. They ranged in age from around 18 to late twenties, and virtually all of them were barefoot and scantily clad. Most of the women wore T-shirts and nothing underneath. Some of the men were shirtless. The music stopped while the Scot changed the album.

"We call this the Disco," said Aideen.

"Makes sense," said Dani. "But isn't there at least some kind of dress code?"

"Not that kind of place," said Aideen. "People just gather here. It's not an official club or anything."

"Where do they get their drinks?" asked Dani.

"People go to town during the day to buy food and drink. And if you don't have any of your own, those Greek guys over there at the makeshift bar will sell you a beer or some booze. In fact, why don't we go get some!"

The music started up again, and Dani recognized the Stones. Mick Jagger belted out "Brown Sugar" from the huge speakers. They approached the bar, which was just a piece of plywood set onto two stacks of cinder blocks. Aideen pointed at a bottle on the bar and held up two fingers. A young Greek man poured a clear liquid into two plastic cups. Aideen reached into her pocket and pulled out some kind of currency that Dani didn't recognize.

"What kind of money is that?" Dani yelled.

"Drachma," Aideen yelled back. "No Euro in '78."

"And what is that drink?" asked Dani, wondering why she had no feeling of drowsiness or hangover from the wine they'd been drinking back in Ireland.

"Ouzo."

Aideen handed a glass to Dani, then slugged hers down in one gulp. She tipped her empty glass in the air to indicate Dani should do the same. Dani chugged the drink, which tasted like alcohol-infused licorice.

"Let's dance!" said Aideen. She helped Dani remove the daypack and dropped it on the sand, along with her hiking boots, then snatched Dani's hand and tugged her out into the center of the room.

Aideen began to dance, and Dani tentatively joined in, still trying to figure things out. For the first time, she noticed Aideen's clothes. She wore a simple, white, sleeveless blouse, with just three or four of the lower buttons clasped and nothing under it. She had on a ragged pair of cutoff jean shorts and no shoes. She danced freely and rhythmically, her hands above her head at times and then bending low at others. Dani tried to follow, but there was no pattern. It was just free expression.

A man in his early twenties approached and started dancing with them. Another man joined, then a woman. Soon there were what seemed like dozens of people weaving in and out and around as Jagger's voice exploded from the speakers. Dani started to move more freely, wishing she'd had more than one drink to loosen her up, but she was getting the hang of it. As she got into the rhythm of the music and merged with the free-flowing motions of the people around her, a feeling of belonging enveloped her. She was enjoying herself, here on some beach named Pelekas, on an island named Corfu, in the country of Greece, in 1978! She moved over to Aideen and yelled in her ear.

"Can I have some Drachma?"

Aideen reached into the pocket of her jean shorts and handed some wrinkled bills to her. Dani left the dance floor, went back over to the bar, and ordered two more Ouzo. She chugged hers down, then Aideen joined her, grabbed the second glass of Ouzo, and downed it. This was going to be a fun night.

Chapter 8

Daylight streamed in through the roof and walls of the flimsy bamboo hut and woke Dani from a deep sleep. She was covered by a sleeping bag, but she felt a warm, smooth body pressing up against her and saw that it was Aideen. Neither of them had on any clothes. She looked around the inside of the hut and saw their clothes piled in a heap, and in another corner was a large backpack, obviously Aideen's. Dani had a headache, and her mouth felt very dry. She didn't remember much from the night before, except that the Ouzo had been flowing pretty heavily, and the music and companionship had been awesome.

Aideen's eyes opened, and she smiled at Dani.

"I'd kiss ya', but I'm sure both our mouths are horrid," she said.

Dani's heart skipped a beat, and she wondered what had transpired between her and Aideen the night before.

"Were we, uh, together last night? You know, like, together?"

"Not really," replied Aideen. "Just some kissin' and playin' around, as I remember, then we both passed out."

"I've never been with a woman before, like that," said Dani.

Aideen smiled.

"Ah well, your loss," she said. "But no matter, because you still haven't, not really. Maybe another time."

Dani felt her face flush and quickly changed the subject.

"Speaking of time," said Dani, "how do we get back to 2022?"

"We'll get you there, any time you like."

"What about you?"

"I'm already there. But I'll explain at breakfast. Right now, we need to clean up a bit."

Aideen threw the sleeping bag cover aside and got up. She stood up straight and stretched, and Dani saw a woman gifted with natural beauty, not yet tainted by the passage of time. She wasn't as pale as the older Aideen, probably because she was spending time in the sun on a beach in Greece, and she was in great shape, similar to her older self but without any flaw of age. Aideen reached down, grabbed a two-liter bottle of water and drank from it, then tossed it over to Dani. As Dani watched Aideen move about the hut, it became clear that she had no tan lines. Dani began to realize why when Aideen ducked down and went outside through the doorway of the hut.

"What are you doing!" yelled Dani. "There might be people out there!"

Aideen leaned down and peered in, a grin on her face.

"I suppose I forgot to tell you, Dani, that Pelekas is basically a nude beach. The only time most of us put on clothes is when we're at the Disco or going to get supplies or food."

With that, Aideen spun away and started walking toward the water. Dani turned onto her stomach and used her elbows to help her shimmy over toward the door, poking her head out. She saw Aideen in the distance, going into the water. As she advanced, she waved at several people, both men and women. Most of them were naked, although a few of the women had on bikini bottoms and some of the men had on tight, tiny swimsuits. But Aideen and most of the others wore nothing at all. Dani didn't consider herself a shy person, and she wasn't ashamed of her body either, so after taking a long swig of water and telling herself, *When in Rome…*, she got up and walked down to the water to join Aideen.

The waves were calm and broke gently onto the beach. Dani entered the warm water and waded out past the waves, into water that was about three feet deep. She looked down as she walked and could see her feet kicking up puffs of sand. She joined Aideen, who had gone all the way underwater to get herself completely wet, and now stood, washing herself. Her hands flowed all over her body, under her arms, across her chest, then disappeared underwater, washing everywhere that needed cleaning, just as one would in the shower. Dani stooped and went under the water, then duplicated the washing movements of Aideen. She saw other people in the water, and on the beach, sitting on sleeping bags. It seemed Aideen was one of the few who actually had a shelter. Most others were simply sleeping on the beach.

"There's fresh water over there," said Aideen, "if the saltwater feels too sticky on you." She pointed at a pipe coming out of an embankment at the top of the beach. "But there's nothin' like the ocean to heal a hangover, wouldn't you agree?"

"Agreed," said Dani, feeling better for certain.

"Let's go back and get some clothes so we can go for breakfast," said Aideen.

"Where do you eat around here?" asked Dani.

"Most people either pack food in or go to town, but I've made other arrangements, since I stay here for the entire summer nearly every year. Follow me."

The two made a pit stop at the hut to get some clothes. Aideen threw a pair of shorts and a T-shirt at Dani, aware that Dani had arrived dressed for Ireland in March, not a Greek island in August. Aideen put on the same clothes she'd worn the previous night, grabbed the water bottle, and walked toward the hill behind the beach. Dani followed her onto the hill, which was covered with olive trees. They walked onto a path that seemed to wind up the hill, presumably the pathway to and from town. Suddenly, a terrible stench hit Dani's nasal passages.

"What the heck is that?" she asked, frowning and nearly vomiting.

"Aideen pointed to a pile of human feces about 10 feet off the path.

"Most people are more considerate and go further into the trees," she said. "But there's always a few arses, literally, who don't think about what they're doin'. Just keep movin'."

They left the smell behind and continued up the trail. About halfway up, Dani saw a small house to the side of the path. Aideen turned off and approached the house. A Greek man of around 50 years of age came out, waving at Aideen and speaking Greek to her. Aideen surprised Dani by addressing the man in his own language, and not just a word or two. They were having a full-blown conversation. Aideen turned to Dani and introduced her to the man.

"This is Georgios," said Aideen.

"Yiasoo," said Georgios, extending his hand. Georgios was black-haired and had a lot of hair on his arms. Even though he was clean-shaven, his face showed the dark of his beard below his swarthy skin.

Dani shook the man's hand and attempted to repeat the greeting back to him.

"Yia-soo," she said.

"Good," said Aideen. "You're learning Greek already!"

They all laughed together and made their way over to a small table on a stone patio off to the side of the tiny home. Aideen and Dani sat at the table while Georgios slipped inside.

"Georgios is an olive farmer," said Aideen. "He farms this

side of the mountain for the owner of the grove. He lives here by himself. I help him with his chores from time to time, and even though he says I don't need to pay him for fixin' me meals, I do anyway. My guess is he needs as much money as he can get. I don't think the landowner pays him much, but he *does* get to live here for free, and that's something."

"So, we're going to eat here?" asked Dani.

"Yes," said Aideen, sipping from the water bottle and handing it to Dani. Dani drank fully from the bottle and placed it on the table. Georgios rushed out of the home, carrying two steaming cups of what appeared to be coffee, placing one in front of Aideen and the other in front of Dani. Dani noticed foam on top of the coffee.

"So, is this coffee?" she asked. "I normally take it black." The thought crossed her mind that maybe this was the way older Aideen had known she took her coffee black.

"That foam isn't milk," said Aideen. "It's from the coffee itself. You'll see. Greek coffee is really strong, but it can also be sweet. And don't drink it all the way to the bottom because the grinds are down there." Aideen put the cup to her lips and drank, letting out a soft sigh of pleasure as the coffee went down her throat.

Dani picked up the coffee and took a sip, and as the delicious brew ran into her body, she felt herself healing from the hangover before the coffee even reached her stomach.

"Wow, that's good!" she said.

"It 'tis," said Aideen. "Georgios makes it with a lot of sugar, but I don't mind that, and it seems you don't either. Anyway, you have questions."

Dani laughed.

"So many I don't know where to begin," she said.

"Then let me begin for ya'. You've been through a mind-blowin' event over the past 12 hours or so, and for somethin' like that to happen, you must understand that some of the explanation might be just as shockin' as the event itself. You can understand that, right?"

"Of course," said Dani, getting a little nervous even as she feigned confidence.

"First, I'm the same Aideen you met in Ireland in 2022, just younger. You've already got that. But the older version of me is still in Ireland, in 2022, in that chamber under the channel that sent you back to 1978. By the way, that place is called the Time Station."

"Okay," said Dani. "But what about me?"

"You're in a different situation," said Aideen. "Right now, you're in 1978. And you're not in 2022. The role I play is to establish the connections, with the help of the Station, between the two times. So, older Aideen and younger Aideen's minds were connected when the Station went on, and a portal was then opened for you to travel back to here."

"But why here? Why now?"

"*I* decided that. The older version of me, that is. The Station knows me and can pick up where and when I want the Traveler, you in this case, to go. I wanted you to have a great experience during your first trip. So, I sent you here."

"And what are you doing right now, back in Ireland in 2022?" asked Dani.

"Absolutely nothin'," said Aideen. "Older Aiden is in a deep sleep, and the dream she's havin' is what you and I are doing right now! And trust me, she's livin' it just as we are, and lovin' every second of it. The other interestin' thing about older Aideen right now is that during the time you're here, she won't age. Remember last night when you said that older Aideen looked to be in her early fifties, at most, but then you calculated her true age at 68?"

"Yes, I remember," said Dani.

"The difference is the sum total of all the time that older Aideen has spent sending Travelers to various places and times over the years. She doesn't age while those trips are transpirin'.'"

"That's a lot of years!" said Dani. "So, she does this a lot then."

"Yes, we do," said younger Aideen.

"So, you do it, too?"

"Oh yes. Because as I told you, Aideen and I are the same person. I'm only distinguishing between older and younger Aideen to make it easier for you to understand what I'm tryin' to explain to you. So, by default, yes, I do it. My mother is a Time Link as well."

"Time Link," mused Dani. "What does that mean, Aideen? What's the purpose of a Time Link?"

"First of all, don't worry about callin' me a Time Link. It's just a name we've been given to describe our role. And yes, we *do* have a purpose, and it's important, and eventually, I'll tell it to ya'. But not now. Of most immediate concern to you, Dani, is to *know* that we Time Links make sure no one on these pleasure trips misbehaves while they're outside of their natural time. For example, right now, I'm kind of your chaperon here in 1978. I'll make sure you do nothin' to upset the balance of time."

"Like what could I do?" asked Dani.

"You could blow up a building in downtown Athens, for example. The people who die in that explosion, and all others involved in it, would leave a ripple through time that might be disastrous for the future."

"I see," said Dani. "But what if I got away from you and did some mischief?"

"You won't get away from me," said Aideen. "In fact, if you get *too* far away from me, you'll end up back where you started this journey, in the Time Station in 2022."

Dani took in this information, processed it, and continued with her questions.

"Okay, so what if I did something while we were together?"

"I wouldn't let ya'."

"But what if I tried?"

"You have to stay close to me in order to stay in this time, so by default, I'll always be around to stop you from gettin' into trouble. Or you could run from me, and then after you got around 300 meters away, you'd pop back to 2022."

"Why does that happen?"

"No idea," said Aideen. "The Travelers tell me it's a restriction they put on us when we use the Time Station for pleasure trips like this. It doesn't seem to happen to them unless they want it to."

"Who are these Travelers?" asked Dani.

"I can't tell you that, yet," said Aideen.

Chapter 9

Georgios brought the women fried eggs and toast, which they dipped in bowls of olive oil. Literally all of it was fresh. The chickens that provided the eggs were scurrying around the area, pecking for food, the olive oil came from the olives on the trees in the grove, and Georgios made the bread himself. After they finished, Aideen discreetly left some Drachma on the table. When they stood to leave, Georgios came out of the house. Aideen took both of Georgios's hands in hers, then kissed him on both cheeks. Dani shook hands with Georgios, and they departed. The two friends headed back down to the beach, refreshed and ready for the day.

"We have some choices for what we do today," said Aideen.

"Like what?" asked Dani.

"We can lie around and do nothin', or we can go fishin'."

"What kind of fishing?"

"A kind you've never done before and will likely never do again."

"Then I'm all in on the fishing!" said Dani.

"Let's stop at the hut, to change and also get my toothbrush."

They went to the hut, and Aideen stripped off all her clothes and fished two bikinis from her pack. She threw one of them over to Dani and started to put hers on.

"We're close to the same height, so that should work," she said. "Now hurry up, or we're goin' to be late."

Dani took off her clothes and put on the bikini. Both the bottom and top were a little tight because she was more muscular than Aideen, due very likely to her many years as a competitive swimmer. She put her T-shirt back on and followed Aideen out of the hut. They brushed their teeth at the freshwater pipe, and after they returned the toothbrushes to the hut, Aideen led Dani toward the far end of the beach. Dani thought the walk might be a good time to ask a few more questions.

"You seem to know a lot of the same things that older Aideen knows, things about me, about yourself even, that haven't happened yet," she said. "How does that work?"

"That's simple," said Aideen. "When the Station makes the connection between older and younger Aideen, our minds merge in order to form the portal between the two times. During that merging, everything that's in older Aideen's mind automatically becomes part of my mind."

"Okay, I understand that, but how does the Station make the connection itself?"

"The science of the Station is not the area of expertise of Time Links. We *have* been told that the Station somehow harnesses a large amount of the right kind of energy to make the connection and to sustain it."

"So, you know who put the Time Station there then, right?"

"Well, that's another big secret. But I *do* know the answer. Fact is, I've met the folks many times. We work together, actually. But it's too much, too soon, Dani."

"So, you're not going to tell me?"

"I *intend* to tell you. But we have to take things one step at a time, okay?"

"I don't like it, but I guess I'll have to live with it. But can I ask another question?"

"Of course."

"How many of these Stations are there?"

"Just the one at Omey Island is what we've been led to believe," said Aideen.

"One more question," said Dani. "Why did you send me back in time? And why aren't you telling me everything?"

"That's two questions," said Aideen, smiling. "But the answer to both is the same. I want you to become my apprentice. When you agree to that, I'll tell ya' everythin'."

Chapter 10

Not far after the beach ended, Aideen and Dani crossed over a smooth, rocky section of terrain and made their way to a small, single-story home, made from cinderblocks. Dani saw two boys around 10 years old playing outside of the house. As they approached, a man in his mid-thirties came out and waved at them. Aideen and Dani both waved back. When they reached the house, Aideen stepped forward, extending both her hands to the man. The man clasped his hands to hers, and they performed the same double kiss that Aideen had done with Georgios. Aideen turned to Dani.

"This is Dimitrios," she said.

Dani approached the man and shook his hand.

"I'm Dani. Yiasoo."

"Yiasoo," replied Dimitrios, smiling.

Aideen and Dimitrios then spoke together in Greek and turned and walked toward an inlet not far from the house. Dani followed them and saw a boat tied up against a small wooden dock. The boat was around 20 feet long and had an outboard motor on the back. Another man was moving netting from one side of the boat to the other. He looked up as they approached and waved, a smile on his face.

"That's Yannis," said Aideen, jumping onto the boat and shaking his hand.

Dani followed, while Dimitrios removed the ropes that secured the boat to the dock and threw them on board.

"Dani," she said, shaking hands with Yannis. "Yiasoo."

"Yiasoo," he responded, then returned to his work.

Dimitrios got on and went to the back of the boat, then pulled a cord to start the motor. He sat down with his hand on the handle of the motor and guided the boat away from the dock and out of the inlet. Dani was struck by the haphazard nature of this fishing adventure. The dock had been nearly falling down, and the boat was small and old and didn't even have a steering wheel. She told herself to trust Aideen, who had shocked her several times, in both deeds and words, over the past day, but who had so far kept her safe.

The boat went out into the deeper water. Dani marveled that even when the depth reached 20 or more feet, she could still see the bottom. She saw a school of fish swimming nearby and noticed that Dimitrios had suddenly shut off the outboard motor. She swung her attention to Yannis and was stunned when she saw him remove a stick of dynamite from a sack. He lit the dynamite, waited a few seconds while the fuse burned down, then tossed the stick into the water near the school of fish. The dynamite went into the water, and a muffled explosion thrust a fountain of water and fish into the air. The resulting waves pushed the boat back. Dani heard the motor start up again.

Dimitrios maneuvered the boat closer to where the explosion had occurred, and Dani saw dozens of fish floating on the water. The blast had obviously either stunned or killed them. Yannis swung the net above his head and hurled it out into the water, then pulled on a cord and the net compressed, encircling many of the fish. He hauled the net back in, then emptied it onto the deck of the boat, a bevy of unmoving fish spilling out. Yannis then gathered the net and threw it back out, capturing more fish. Eventually, there were only a handful of fish floating randomly on the surface of the water.

"Okay, our turn," said Aideen, pulling her T-shirt over her head and throwing it onto the bench they'd been sitting on. She gingerly stepped onto the side of the boat and dove in. When she came back up, she yelled to Dani, "Come on! We have work to do." Aideen swam over to a fish, grabbed it, brought it over to the side of the boat, and heaved it in.

Dani now understood what the job was and followed Aideen into the water. After about 10 minutes of gathering, the two women returned to the boat. Yannis pulled them in, Dimitrios started up the boat, and they motored back to the inlet. After the boat was docked and the fish were unloaded into baskets, the four of them carried the day's catch back toward the house.

"What will they do with the fish?" asked Dani.

"They'll eat some of them, of course, and sell the rest," said Aideen. "Dimitrios lives here and will keep what he wants for his family. Yannis, his brother, lives in town and will take what he needs for his family and sell the rest at the fish market. The two will split the money and use it to buy other things."

"Well, you were certainly right about that being a kind of fishing I've never done before," said Dani. "I mean, dynamite? Is that legal?"

"I'm not sure," said Aideen. "But if it *is* legal, it won't be for long. Right now, this area is completely undeveloped, but the developers will come soon, and Pelekas will become just like every other beach in the world, full of hotels and obnoxious tourists."

"And you know that to be fact, right? Since you know everything that older Aideen knows."

"That's right," said Aideen. "So, I try to enjoy things while I can.

Anyway, let me introduce you to Dimitrios's family, and then we'll eat."

They entered the cinderblock home, which was just one room. There were beds off at one end, a kitchen area in the middle, and a dining area on the other end. The dining table was a piece of plywood sitting on cinderblocks. A woman was scurrying around the kitchen, yelling at the boys while she worked. The boys grabbed some plates and brought them to the table. The woman carried over a bowl full of what looked like squid in one hand and a bowl of potatoes in the other. She was short and stocky with medium length dark hair, and she wore a colorful blouse and a long skirt. She placed the bowls on the table and then smiled at Aideen, came over, and shared two kisses with her.

"Dani, this is Sophia," said Aideen. "And the boys are named Dimitrios and Christos."

Sophia and the boys smiled and tilted their heads forward in greeting. Dani duplicated their gesture. The boys ran and sat down at the table and started grabbing the food. Dimitrios senior sat at the head of the table, and Yannis sat at the foot. Aideen took a seat in one of the white, plastic chairs and motioned for Dani to sit next to her. Dani sat. Sophia sat in the chair that was closest to the kitchen. Everyone served themselves and poured olive oil generously on all the food. Aideen took the opportunity to warn Dani.

"Sophia will notice if you don't use enough olive oil and will try to drench your food with it, but it's okay to tell her you don't want it. She already knows I don't like it in the same amounts they do."

"As if on cue, Sophia cried out and grabbed the bottle of olive oil, rushing to pour it on Dani's food. Dani raised her hand, palm up, smiled, and said, "No, thank you."

Aideen said something in Greek, and everyone laughed.

"What did you say?" asked Dani.

"Stupid American," said Aideen.

"Oh well, I guess it worked," said Dani, digging into the food.

The squid was fabulous, and the potatoes did their job of filling up their bellies.

"I guess if you're willing to do a little work, you can get fed pretty easily around here," said Dani.

"Yes and no," said Aideen.

"What do you mean?"

"Yes, if you're a friend of the people who have the food. No, if you aren't, which is 99 percent of the people on this beach."

"I understand," said Dani, thinking that Aideen would make a good anthropologist, befriending the locals but adapting to their way of life, rather than trying to change it.

After lunch, Aideen and Dani said goodbye to the fishing family and walked back to the beach. It was around 3 pm, and the beach was still quite full and active. Aideen explained that people from different countries tended to congregate together. She pointed at their hut and said it was in the English-speaking area. People whose first language was English gathered there, including the English themselves, Scots, Irish, Australians, Americans, and Canadians.

Scandinavians had an area of their own, as did Italians, Greeks, and Spaniards. The French most definitely had their own area, and Germans, Austrians, and the Dutch gathered together, along with German-speaking people from Belgium and Switzerland. All of the people on the beach had one thing in common. The vast majority of them had no clothes on during the day.

"Let's go for a swim, then maybe take a nap," said Aideen, removing her clothes as they approached the hut and throwing them in through the door and running down to the water. Dani undressed and followed her. The two had a nice swim, then returned to the hut for a peaceful sleep.

They had a chicken dinner at Georgios's house up in the olive grove that evening. He had some delicious red wine that Aideen had asked him to pick up for her in town. They brought a bottle with them to the Disco and drank all of it, then switched to beer. Dani chose not to have Ouzo on her second night at Pelekas. She wanted to have her wits about her that evening. She enjoyed the music and the dancing, and she was surprised that she'd felt a flare of jealousy when she saw Aideen kiss another woman during a dance.

The evening came to a close, and the two women walked hand-in-hand back to the hut, the waves breaking gently on the beach, the stars out above, and a buzz in their heads from the wine and beer. *As close to paradise as I could ever imagine,* thought Dani. When they got to the hut, Aideen made a comment.

"You're more sober than you were last night," she said, a sly smile on her face. "So, I'm assumin' we'll just be goin' to sleep tonight."

Dani surprised herself again, moving up to Aideen and kissing her. Aideen responded, and the kiss lasted a long time.

"Suddenly, I don't feel very tired," said Dani, eager to live fully in each moment of this incredible adventure.

They entered the hut and reclined together onto the sleeping bag.

Chapter 11

They spent the next three weeks on Pelekas. The days and nights were the same as they'd been since Dani arrived, in short: wonderful. Dani felt she had so much in common with younger Aideen that she was certain the feelings blossoming inside her were also growing in Aideen. They both loved the outdoors, and doing adventurous and exciting new things. They liked the same books and the same music, and they loved being together. Dani didn't want this dream to end, and she could tell that Aideen didn't either.

But when August passed into September, most people went back to their lives or moved on. The Disco closed down when the Scot went home, and the beach was nearly empty by the second week of September. The days were still sunny and beautiful, except for the occasional rainstorm. One day, as they sat on the beach looking out at the beautiful water, dark clouds rolled in and blotted the sky, and the wind began blowing ferociously. They heard a man yelling behind them and saw Dimitrios, the fisherman, waving them to come toward him.

"Must be a bad storm comin' in," said Aideen. "Come on. Let's go!"

They got up, ran to Dimitrios, and followed him to his home.

They rushed inside and gathered with his family to ride out the storm. The wind picked up further, and gusts of rain pelted the side of the home. A cataclysm ensued, blocking visibility to the ocean, but the sturdy cinderblock home held up. When the storm was over, they thanked Dimitrios, Sophia, and the boys. Aideen gave them long hugs, as if this was a permanent goodbye of sorts, and they made their way back to their hut. The hut had been completely flattened by the storm, and their belongings were soaked and covered haphazardly with sticks of bamboo.

"What should we do?" asked Dani.

"I think we should go to Egypt," said Aideen.

"Why on Earth do we need to go to Egypt?" asked Dani, exasperated.

"I think you'd enjoy it, that's all. Quite an *anthropological* place, Egypt is!"

"But how will we get there?"

"It's quite simple, actually. All we do is take a ferry and a train to Athens, buy a plane ticket to Cairo, and go. It's just a one-hour flight across the Mediterranean."

"I brought my passport because you asked me to, but that won't help since I haven't been born yet!"

"It'll be fine. Border Security in 1978 is a very different animal than in 2022."

The sun came out, so they dried their wet clothes as best they could by laying them on rocks at the top of the beach. They packed, then began the long walk up the path through the olive grove, stopping to say goodbye to Georgios, then continued on to the top of the hill and caught the bus to the port where the ferry departed. They took the ferry across the water to the mainland of Greece and boarded a train to Athens. When they got to Athens, they took a taxi to a travel agency that Aideen knew of and bought two round-trip plane tickets from Athens to Cairo. After a quick stop at the Acropolis, where they played tourist, then went to the airport.

They landed at Cairo International Airport in the late afternoon. Before they reached immigration, Aideen spoke to Dani.

"Give me your passport, please," she said.

Dani handed over her passport. Aideen reached into her pack, pulled out her wallet, and removed a fresh $100 bill. She folded the bill in half, opened Dani's passport to the identification page, inserted the bill, and closed the passport. She handed it back to Dani.

"Give this to the man at immigration and say nothing, okay?"

"Okay," said Dani.

When they reached immigration and it was Dani's turn to go through, she stepped up to the booth and handed the man inside her passport. He opened it and discreetly removed and pocketed the $100 bill. He went through the motions of looking at the picture on the passport and looking up at Dani, and then he put the passport down, stamped it, and handed it back to her. Dani moved ahead and joined Aideen, who had already passed through.

"Well, that was easy," said Dani.

"Told you so," said Aideen, smiling.

"Why US dollars instead of the Egyptian currency?"

"They prefer US dollars. Much more stable than the Egyptian pound. He'll wait until the pound weakens and then convert the $100 to pounds and make a big profit."

"If you say so," said Dani. "All I know is that it worked!"

When they departed the shabby terminal, Dani was blasted by the heat. It was like stepping into a sauna. She saw that they were truly in the desert now, surrounded on all sides by endless sand, with the sun blazing down relentlessly on everything. In the distance, she spotted a bus coming toward them. As the bus slowed, she saw people chasing after it and struggling to climb in the windows.

"What are they doing?" she asked.

"They don't want to pay," said Aideen. "They *can't* pay, really.

People in Egypt are typically very poor."

"And the driver doesn't care?" asked Dani.

"He accepts the reality of the situation, very likely. What can he do? Fight the people? No, he cannot. So, he just drives on to where the bus is supposed to go."

The bus stopped, and they boarded. Aideen paid their fare. The bus was nearly full and smelled of sweat and bad hygiene. The people were dressed in long robes, both men and women. The women had long scarves over their heads. Most of the men wore flowing head cloths with a headband over them to hold them in place, but some of the men wore turbans. The younger children weren't wearing anything on their heads.

Eventually, the bus came into downtown Cairo. Aideen seemed to know where to get off, and they departed the bus. The streets were busy with people and honking cars and very dirty. Dani remembered thinking how filthy Athens was during their brief stop there, but now Athens seemed like a much cleaner place when she compared it to Cairo. But the grime didn't seem to keep people off the streets. They were everywhere, bustling about, going into shops, stopping to get something to eat. Street vendors were selling all kind of wares, including food and drink. Dani was hungry.

"What should we eat?" she asked.

"Nothing from the street vendors," said Aideen. "You won't like what that does to you. Guaranteed parasite. There's a restaurant in the hotel we're goin' to that'll be fine."

They weaved their way through the nasty streets, followed from time to time by groups of children who cheered them and begged for money. The children could spot Westerners a mile away. At one point, a child with no legs and only one arm rolled up to them on a board on wheels, begging for money. Dani was sickened by the sight. Aideen threw some coins onto the boy's cart, then pulled Dani forward, and they left the child behind.

They soon arrived at a section of town that seemed cleaner than where they'd started. Aideen turned and went up some steps to a building that had two bronze lions on the sides of the entryway. They entered the foyer of the hotel, and Dani saw that the floors were made of marble and very clean. Aideen approached the desk and registered them for a room. Dani noted that the woman behind the registration desk spoke good English. Aideen reached into her daypack and handed the woman two US $100 bills.

"They take dollars here?" asked Dani.

"No, she's going to change the money into Egyptian pounds, after deducting the fee for our room."

"How much is the room?"

"Around $50 US a night," said Aideen. "That's about twice the amount you'd pay for a hotel room near the bus stop where we disembarked. But it's worth it."

"How many nights will we be staying?" asked Dani.

"Two nights should be enough. Let's get to our room and then have some food."

After they showered to wash away the grime from a long day of traveling in two filthy cities, the two friends went to dinner. When they arrived at the restaurant, Aideen informed Dani that the beef they served here was imported from the US. It was very expensive, but worth it.

"I don't want you ta' think I'm a beef aficionado," said Aideen. "But when you're in a city where 99 percent of the food can make ya' sick, my advice is to take the sure bet."

"As always, I'm following your lead," said Dani. "Beef sounds great!"

So, they treated themselves to steak and potatoes with steamed vegetables, and both of them ate everything on their plates. They were served French wine and had Crème Brulee for dessert. Having had a very long day, they went to bed and slept soundly. When they woke up the next morning, Dani had something to say.

"I want to become your apprentice," she said.

"Good," said Aideen. "Now I can tell you all that I know."

Chapter 12

At breakfast, Aideen told Dani to eat as much as she could hold. It was a buffet, so that was easily accomplished. The women also packed away some bread and bananas in their daypacks, to be eaten later. They purchased bottled water at the hotel store and then left the hotel. They walked to a nearby bus stop and got the next bus. Dani noticed the destination sign on the front of the bus above the windshield said "Giza."

"Are we going to the pyramids?" asked Dani, intrigued.

"Indeed, we are," said Aideen.

"That sounds cool," said Dani.

"And tonight, there'll be a special surprise at the pyramids."

"What's that?"

"You'll see."

The bus trip didn't take long since the town of Giza was only eight miles from the center of downtown Cairo. They got off the bus at a stop right beside the pyramids and made their way over to the massive structures. A sea of tourists and locals merged into a mass of humanity bustling around the site. Camel rides were obviously a popular activity. Dani also noticed that a large stage had been constructed in front of the Great Pyramid, Cheops. Huge speakers were set up on the sides of the stage as if a band was going to perform.

"What's that?" Dani asked.

"That's the surprise!" said Aideen. "You've heard of the Grateful Dead, I hope?"

"Of course, everybody knows about them," said Dani. "Are you telling me they're playing here tonight?"

"Yes, they *are*! It's their final night of a three-night show. I guess we were lucky to get hit by that storm after all."

"Yes and no," said Dani. "I didn't want Pelekas to end," she said, dropping her head.

Aideen took one of Dani's hands in hers and placed the fingers of her other hand under Dani's chin, lifting Dani's head up, peering directly into her eyes.

"Neither did I," she said. "But we can have some more adventures together before you go back!"

"How much longer can I spend in this time?" asked Dani.

"There is a *definite* limit," said Aideen.

"What's the limit?"

"Normally, it's 30 days. But for this trip, I received approval for 60 days."

"Do these Travelers you work with have a time limit on how long they can stay?"

"Not that I'm aware of."

"That doesn't seem fair," said Dani.

"If you think about it, Dani, it's really *very* fair. Knowin' what you already know about how our actions can potentially change the future, I think it's quite reasonable. And the reality is that trips like this are quite rare for us because of the secrecy of the whole operation. The only reason you're here is because I'm recruiting you to be a Time Link."

"But I don't want to go back," said Dani.

"I don't want you to either," said Aideen. "But the reality is that you're needed in 2022."

"For what?" asked Dani.

"The Time Chain needs you. We need there to be two Time Links in every Time Level, and right now, there's just me in 2022. The Time Masters are growing impatient with me to add a second Time Link."

"Who the heck are the Time Masters?" asked Dani.

"They're the people who built the Time Station," said Aideen. "Charles Burke is one of them. And by the way, they don't call themselves the Time Masters. They just call themselves Travelers, and they would be offended to be called Time Masters. It's just a name we made up to remind us that we should follow the rules, or we'll have to answer to the Great and Powerful Time Masters."

"And where did they come from, these Time Masters? The ancient past?"

"The opposite, actually," said Aideen. "They come from the future. They built the Time Chain, which is a word they *do* use, so they can travel back and forth, looking for things they might want to change so things get better in the future."

"I thought you said we're not allowed to disrupt time," said Dani.

"Time Links are not allowed to. That's exclusively for the Time Masters."

"And why is changing their history so important to them?"

"Apparently, things got very bad at some point in the future, and most of the Earth's population died. A group of scientists working on time travel were isolated in a protected spot, and they eventually came up with the Time Station."

"Was the protected spot Omey Island?"

"Yes. Omey Island and virtually all of northwest Ireland was apparently completely deserted at that point, so their work could be carried out in secrecy there. We don't know what happened because they're not inclined to tell us much a'tall about their time."

"So, you haven't traveled forward in time to find out?"

"Time Links rarely travel. We facilitate the travel of others. I've never been forward in time, and I only go backward every now and then, for fun. It's not encouraged. And we're not permitted to work with Time Links from different eras to send anyone up or down the chain beyond our own lifetimes, except the Travelers themselves. That's against the rules."

"But what if you want to break the rules?" asked Dani.

"Then we would be replaced, and none of us wants to find out what that means."

"So, do you work for these people under threat of death, or what?"

"There's never been any threats, Dani. Just logical arguments of why it would be harmful to the people of the future for us to break the rules. All Time Links sincerely want to help save the future, Dani. If that's not how you're feeling, then it's not too late to back out. But before you do, please consider the fringe benefits, like this adventure we're on together!"

"First," said Dani, "I'm all about helping the people of the future. That's why I chose anthropology as a field of study. We learn from the past and present, the good and the bad, and we try to apply it to the future. And the fringe benefits of being a Time Link *do* seem quite good!" Dani smiled and took Aideen's hand in hers.

"You don't know the half of it," said Aideen, pulling Dani forward toward the Great Pyramid. "Hey, let's go for a climb!"

As they approached Cheops, they were confronted by a variety of Egyptian locals claiming they were official guides to the top of the Great Pyramid. Aideen ignored them, and they eventually came to the base of Cheops. The blocks that composed the base were about four feet high, but Dani could see that the stones higher up were much shorter than that. Dani was shocked to see children scaling up and down the sloped walls of Cheops.

"Isn't the climbing bad for preservation of the artifact?" she asked.

"I would think so," said Aideen. "And it's actually been illegal to climb them since 1951. But enforcement is lax. I know from older Aideen's memories that it wasn't until the late '80s that enforcement picked up, after a British man fell to his death after falling asleep up top. After that, the law was more strictly enforced, but even in *your* time, people will bribe the security people to be allowed to climb up."

As Aideen was explaining the realities of pyramid climbing to Dani, an Egyptian man rushed up to them.

"Hello, ladies!" yelled the man. "I am official guide of the pyramids! I will take you to the top of the Great Pyramid, Cheops!"

Dani looked at Aideen, who was smiling.

"No, thank you, sir," said Aideen.

"Veddy dangerous to climb by yourself," he said. "And illegal! *Only* with *me* can you be sure not to be hurt or put in jail!"

"No, thank you!" said Aideen, in a louder voice, frowning and waving the man away.

The man shrugged and left.

"Shall we?" asked Aideen, approaching the first block and hoisting herself up onto it. Dani followed, and the climb began. After they got past the first several rows of tall blocks, the climbing became easier. In around 10 minutes, they were at the top—a flat surface, about 12 feet square. It was packed with at least a dozen Egyptian boys, ranging in age from around 8 to 10 years old. One of the boys approached Dani.

"Are you Amedican?" he asked.

"Yes," she said.

"I love Amedica!" screamed the boy, and the others began to

gather around the two women.

"We love Jimmy Carter!" screamed another boy, and then a cheer erupted from the shabby group, now jumping up and down.

Aideen leaned in close to Dani so she could hear her over the screaming of the boys.

"The Camp David peace accords are being concluded as we speak. The Egyptian President, Anwar Sadat, is there with the Israeli Prime Minister, Menachem Begin, and the American President, Jimmy Carter. The peace treaty between the two countries will be signed tomorrow, September 17, 1978. Everyone in Egypt knows it's coming, even though it's supposed to be secret. It's a big deal to these people."

"Please take me to Amedica!" said the first boy. "I love Amedica!"

"What should I do?" asked Dani.

"Just smile, wave them off, and turn away," said Aideen.

Dani did that, and the boys quieted down. She looked out and saw the endless sand of the Sahara Desert to the west. Aideen was beside her and had more to say.

"Take a look at the two other large pyramids, Khafre and Menkaure," she said. "Do you see the smooth surface at the top of Menkaure?"

"Yes," said Dani.

"All the pyramids used to be completely covered with that smooth stone. It's white limestone. Unfortunately, greedy developers took away most of it to make buildings in Cairo. But during the time of the pharaohs, the white limestone was polished regularly and would gleam like a mirror in the sun."

"Can you use the Time Station to get back to that time?" asked Dani.

"No, right now, the Time Chain only goes back to around 1850."

"Why?" asked Dani.

"I'm not really sure. As I said, the Time Masters are very

secretive about their work."

"Have you ever gone back to 1850?" asked Dani.

"As I said, that's not the role of the Time Links," said Aideen. "The Time Masters do that work. We just help to get them there."

"What do they do when they go back in time?"

"We assume they're looking for opportunities to change things that they think can ripple through time to improve the future. But we don't know for sure."

"Isn't that dangerous?" asked Dani. "What if they make a mistake?"

"It 'tis dangerous," said Aideen. "That's why the Time Masters have to be well trained and very careful. Charles Burke, the anthropologist I mentioned, seems to be in charge of all the Time Masters. He'll go back in time looking for ways to make very subtle changes. For example, he might identify an individual who did something important during their time, then he'll follow the impact of that event forward in time, lookin' for how it might have gone wrong and how it might have contributed to what went wrong in their time. It's a long process. At this point, they're still studyin' the situation. I don't think they've tried to change anythin' yet."

"What *did* go wrong?" asked Dani. "Was it global warming?"

"No, I know it wasn't global warming," said Aideen. "That issue was brought under control during *my* lifetime."

"How?" asked Dani.

"Two things will happen that bring it under control," said Aideen. "First, the industrialized countries will make some good progress in reducing greenhouse gas emissions. But that progress won't be enough to stem the tide of global warming in time to prevent catastrophic results. Luckily, the Americans will develop a way to make the clouds whiter, and that will increase the reflectivity of the atmosphere and reduce the amount of light and heat that gets through. And this will slow the rise in temperature until further progress can be made. My understandin' is that with continued advancements in greenhouse gas reductions, as time moved forward, the cloud shields became less critical, and global warmin' abated."

"Amazing," said Dani. "Do you think it was nuclear war? Someone like Putin went crazy and pushed the button?"

"Well, it definitely wasn't Putin. He ruined his country with the war he's waging in Ukraine during your time, but luckily, he didn't push the button. And some years later, he will finally be removed from power."

"So, we just don't know, then, is that right?" asked Dani.

"The Time Masters have yet to tell us. But with someone like you joining our ranks, someone who's going to be an anthropologist, just like Charles Burke, they might become more comfortable in telling us more."

"How far in the future are we talking?" asked Dani.

"The Time Masters come from the 23rd century."

"So around 200 years in the future."

"231 years, to be exact," said Aideen.

"It seems like they have a lot of restrictions on what Time Links can and can't do."

"It's true that we can't travel outside of the framework of our own lifetimes, and they do set time limits on our personal travels, but other than that, I find them quite flexible, actually."

"Like when they let you bring me back in time, for example?" asked Dani.

"They know I'm seeking an apprentice, and they understand that I need to provide proof of what we're talking about in order for a person to agree to become an apprentice. So, it was in their best interests to let that happen. But in general, the Time Masters don't micromanage us. They let us travel every now and then within our boundaries, as long as we follow the safety protocols when we move about in time and don't interfere with their work. They normally give us a few months advance notice before they make a trip along the Time Chain, so I wouldn't have sent you back unless I knew they had nothin' planned for a few months."

"I suppose it would have been easier if you had a son or daughter to pass the responsibility on to," said Dani. "I hope I'm not stepping out of bounds here, but are you not able to have children?"

"I can have children. Even older Aideen still can, because she's spent so much time in suspended animation. But I choose not to have them."

"Why?"

"Because I want to spend as much of my life as I can with you, Dani."

Chapter 13

After they scaled back down from the top of Cheops, Aideen led Dani over to see the Sphinx and some of the smaller pyramids, as well as the two cemeteries that housed lesser nobles than the pyramids themselves. After that, they walked a good distance away from the pyramids to an area that contained tents of various sizes. Inside the tents were merchants selling all sorts of trinkets and memorabilia and food. Aideen located one tent in particular and entered. Dani followed, looking at her watch and noticing it was around four in the afternoon. The sun was already beginning to dive down toward the western sand of the Sahara. She remembered that yesterday it had become dark by 6 pm.

Inside the tent were two Egyptian men. One appeared to be in his twenties, and the other was middle-aged. Aideen walked up and offered her hand to be shaken, first by the older man, then by the younger one. The implication was of a long-standing friendship, but the greeting was not nearly so intimate as the double kisses between Aideen and her Greek friends.

"This is Dani," she said to the men. To Dani, she said, "This is Asim," extending her arm to point out the older man. "And this is his son, Sadiki."

Both men gave slight bows. Dani got the impression there would be no handshakes between these men and a woman they didn't know, so she simply gave a slight bow of respect.

"I met Asim and Sadiki on one of my previous visits," said Aideen. "I enjoy coming to the pyramids. It gives me a good reminder of how much humans can accomplish. Even ancient humans."

The tent was a square, about 20 feet on each side. In the center was a large hookah for smoking, with six hoses extending from it. Six chairs surrounded the hookah, which sat on a large metal plate, presumably to keep it level. Asim gestured for the two women to have a seat. Aideen sat in one of the chairs surrounding the hookah, and Dani sat beside her.

"Would you like some food?" asked Sadiki.

"No, thank you," said Aideen. "We brought some with us."

Aideen reached into her daypack and drew out the bread and bananas. She offered the food to the men, and each of them shook their heads and said no, thank you. She handed a few slices of bread and a banana to Dani. The women began to eat. The men sat in the chairs and waited for them to finish. When they were finished, they drank water from Aideen's bottle, and Asim leaned forward.

"Would you like to smoke?" he asked.

"Yes, thank you," said Aideen.

"Tobacco or hashish?"

"Hashish for me," said Aideen. "Dani?"

"Hashish is fine," said Dani, hoping the hash wouldn't make her fall asleep.

Sadiki got up from his chair and went to a table at the side of the tent. He returned with a large block of hash that was about one inch square. He placed it in the receptacle at the top of the hookah and applied a lighter to it. While he did this, Asim drew a large breath through the mouthpiece of his hose, and the hash began to glow. Asim sat back, holding in the smoke, while Sadiki sat down and repeated the process with his hose to ensure that the hash was well lit. Both men exhaled large plumes of smoke. Aideen took up her hose and drew heartily from the mouthpiece, but she didn't hold the smoke in nearly as long as the men had, coughing slightly when she exhaled. Dani followed, and almost as soon as the smoke hit her lungs, she began coughing mightily. Aideen and the men smiled.

"It takes some getting used to," said Asim. "So, Miss Aideen, what are your plans?"

"We'd like to attend the Grateful Dead concert this evening," said Aideen. "I was hoping we could stay in your tent for a few hours until then."

"Of course," said Asim. "I'm sure you realize, however, that business will be brisk due to the concert."

"I understand," said Aideen.

"What business are they referring to?" asked Dani.

"They sell hashish," said Aideen.

"Isn't it illegal?" asked Dani.

"Very much so," said Aideen. "But so is scaling the pyramids!"

The men laughed along with them. Soon after that, young people started coming into the tent, buying hash, and sometimes sitting down to smoke it from the hookah. Aideen and Dani moved to some more comfortable chairs off to the side of the tent where they could rest and speak privately.

"How do Time Links make money?" asked Dani. "Do you have other, normal jobs?"

"Time Links are very wealthy people," said Aideen.

"But where does the money come from?" asked Dani.

"Think about it," said Aideen. "We *know* the future. At least, enough of it to make some good investments."

Dani thought about this, and some ideas leapt into her head.

"So, you could invest in companies you know are going to be successful, for example."

"Exactly," said Aideen. "Like Apple. On December 12, 1980, I will buy Apple shares during its first public offering. By 2022, the stock will have split five times. An investment of $10,000 in 1980 will be worth over $7 million by 2022. I will put in $25,000 at the initial offering, and that will be worth more than $18 million in 2022. That's more money than I'll ever need, just from one investment."

"So, how rich are you?"

Aideen laughed.

"As I said, I have more than I need. The Time Masters grant us our indulgences, but they can't allow us to upset the proper functioning of the free market by betting large sums of money on sure things. And frankly, we don't pay a lot of attention to the money aspect of knowing the future. It's just not important to us. Our role in the Time Chain is what drives us, along with our own little adventures, like this one."

There were no customers in the tent at the moment, so Aideen asked the men if they could have another smoke. They moved back over to the hookah and joined the men. The four shared a smoke and had a conversation that fascinated Dani, centering primarily on the Camp David Peace accords. Around 7:30 pm, they heard music coming from the direction of the pyramids. The concert had begun, and it was time to go.

As they were leaving, Aideen shook hands with the men and whispered something to them, which led to a short conversation in hushed tones. Dani wondered what they had discussed. The entire encounter with Asim and Sadiki took on a new light in her eyes. She wondered how Aideen had gotten to know the men so well. There was something under the surface, something unsaid, about the relationship. But whatever it was, Aideen obviously wanted to keep it private, so Dani didn't push her on it. She simply bowed to the men, thanked them, and departed with Aideen for the show.

Chapter 14

On the way to the concert, Dani noticed she was being bit by mosquitos. The same thing was happening to Aideen. While Dani slapped at her arms and neck, Aideen came to a stop, put her daypack on the ground, and withdrew a small bottle of insect repellant.

"Forgot to apply this back in the tent," said Aideen. "Sorry."

They each squeezed the liquid from the bottle and applied it to their arms, legs, face, and neck. The onslaught of biting subsided, and they proceeded, the sound of the Grateful Dead becoming clearer. Dani didn't recognize the song, but the unmistakable sound of the band that no one had sounded like before or since was in the air. Dani's college roommate had been a fan of rock 'n roll from the '60s and '70s. Dani liked that era's music, and while she didn't know many of the Grateful Dead songs, she knew their sound, and this was it.

As they reached the concert grounds in front of the Great Pyramid, Dani was captivated by the magic of the entire scene. A full moon was rising, casting a gentle shine over the entire area. Spotlights shone on Cheops, the Sphinx, Khafre, and Menkaure, and a vast swarm of hundreds of bats swooped above the stage, devouring mosquitos as if they were protecting the legendary band from harm at this site of ancient power. The crowd of thousands swayed to the music, hypnotized, probably wondering how they'd gotten here almost as much as Dani was.

Around an hour into the concert, Aideen leaned over close to Dani's ear.

"Did ya' notice the moon?" she asked.

Dani looked up, but she couldn't locate the moon.

"Where did it go?" she asked.

"It's there," said Aideen, pointing at a spot in the sky. "It's a total lunar eclipse! The Earth is directly between the sun and moon, and the Earth's shadow is now covering the entirety of the moon."

Dani looked closely where Aideen was pointing and could see the very edge of one side of the moon beginning to reappear as it moved out of the Earth's shadow. She was overwhelmed.

"How do I *not* tell people I saw a full eclipse, while attending a Grateful Dead concert, at the pyramids, in 1978?" she asked.

"Sometimes it's not easy," said Aideen. "But in cases like this, if the subject comes up, and by no means should *you* bring it up, you simply tell people that you've read about it and heard that it was quite a show. Something like that. Avoid the details."

"I understand," said Dani, remembering how deftly older Aideen had handled her questions back in 2022. "I'm sure I'll get used to it. But what about family and friends? Will I still get to see them?"

"Absolutely," said Aideen. "As I mentioned, the Time Masters typically announce their trips several months in advance. So, you'll be able to see your family and friends as often as you want to."

"What about my dissertation? Am I going to have to abandon that?"

"Not at all. Older Aideen will help you with it, actually, by sending you to some times when the real storytellers still roamed the countryside of Ireland."

"Really?" asked Dani. "That sounds exciting."

"It will be," said Aideen. "For both of us. Don't forget that I'll always be at the other end of any trip back in time that older Aideen decides to send you on!"

Dani's heart swelled at the thought of being able to see younger Aideen again. So much had been happening that she had yet to think fully about the implications of leaving younger Aideen back in 1978 and returning to older Aideen. She liked older Aideen, but it was hard to think of her as the same person she'd gotten to know so well in 1978, in almost every way.

The Dead burst into a long rendition of "Truckin'," a song Dani recognized. Jerry Garcia belted out a protracted solo on lead guitar, supported by Bob Weir on rhythm guitar and Phil Lesh on bass, then Weir broke into the lyrics of the song, with Garcia and Lesh providing supporting vocals. The song went on for more than 10 minutes, every second of it amazing. The band played several more songs, and the women stayed for the entire performance.

When the concert finally ended, Aideen and Dani slowly moved away from the pyramids, in a bit of a nirvanic daze, and not at all frustrated as they plodded away, caught in a crowd of equally satisfied people. Eventually, they took a bus back to town and walked to their hotel, hand-in-hand, as happy to be together as two people could ever be.

Chapter 15

Aideen and Dani flew back to Athens, then rode a train to the coast and boarded a ferry that took them across the northern edge of the Ionian Sea, crossing into the Adriatic Sea and then landing at Brindisi, Italy. From there, they traveled by train to Florence, where they went to see the statue of *David*, a sight that affected Dani deeply. The statue was made from stone, but it seemed alive in a way she would never forget. The idea a human being could create something so close to life that you almost believed it *was* alive made her wonder how close to being gods the human race could actually become. And this reminded her of the Time Masters, the gods of time. But something had gone wrong along the way, or those gods would not be trying so desperately to fix things. She yearned to know more.

From Florence, they went by train to Marseilles, then on to Barcelona, indulging in seafood feasts the likes of which Dani had never experienced before. Then they traveled on to Bordeaux, France, where they drank glorious wine and ate succulent French food. Then to Paris, where their budding romance could not help but blossom further.

After a week in Paris, young Aideen and Dani had been together for nearly two months. Aideen told Dani they would have to part soon because both of them had work to do back in 2022. The Time Masters would be coming through on a mission shortly. They flew from Paris to London, spent one night on the town, carousing through the extraordinary music pubs of the late 70s, listening to the thriving punk rock scene and drinking plenty of beer and bitter. Then they went on to Dublin, next a bus to Galway, and a taxi the rest of the way to Claddaghduff, the town directly across the channel from Omey Island.

It was mid-afternoon when they arrived at the channel, and the tide was out. Dani's heart was breaking because she knew this was the end of the most amazing time of her life, in literally every way. The taxi let them off at the car park beside the channel, the place where Dani had first met older Aideen.

"You wait here, alright, Dani?" said Aideen, her voice somber.

"Where are you going?" asked Dani, beginning to tremble, even though it was a warm spring day.

"I'm goin' home, across the channel there," said Aideen.

"I want to go with you! It'll be my home, too, won't it?"

"It 'twill, Dani. But 44 years from now. In 2022."

"I want it to be my home now!" screamed Dani. "I want it to be *our* home, but not in the future. I want it now!"

"I know. I want that, too. But we've already gone over the approved amount of time for your visit. The Time Masters have been patient, but now you've work to do in *your* time."

"How long until I can come back to you?" asked Dani. "I know you *know*!"

"Soon," said Aideen. "After the Time Masters complete their next mission."

"How long will that take?" asked Dani.

"Just a few months, maybe less. No time at 'tall."

Dani could see in Aideen's face that her heart was breaking, too, and that made her sadder and angrier. "It's not fair!" she screamed.

"What we had can never be taken from us, Dani. Remember that. Let it carry you forward until we meet again, which will be soon. And please, try to remember that my older self is still me and loves you just as much as my younger self does."

Aideen stepped forward and hugged Dani tightly.

"I love you, Dani," she said.

"I love you, Aideen!" Dani squeezed back with all her strength, hoping that would convince Aideen to let her stay. "I want to stay with you!"

"Not in this time," Aideen reminded her gently.

And then Aideen pulled away, pivoted, and stepped into the empty channel. With each step Aideen took, Dani could feel her life in this time slipping away from her, just as the tide slipped away from the channel twice per day. When Aideen got halfway across, she turned back and waved to Dani. Dani waved meekly, tears flowing down her face. Aideen turned away again. At that instant, the sight of Aideen walking away into the channel was replaced by a black void.

Chapter 16

Dani regained her senses. She was holding Aideen's hand. Aideen was lying on the black stone bed. The chamber looked the same as it had when she'd left. She peered down at Aideen, whose eyes were just opening. Dani could see the slight wrinkles at the sides of her eyes and a few gray hairs mixed in with the red. Tears leaked from Aideen's eyes, and Dani realized that older Aideen had just experienced young Aideen's goodbye with her and was obviously saddened by it. Aideen looked up at her and smiled.

"Welcome back," she said. "How do ya' feel?"

"Confused. Sad."

"Yes, you've been cryin'."

"Because I miss you," said Dani.

"You got to know my younger self much better than you got to know me."

"Uh, *yeah*," said Dani. "Not to mention I fell in love with your younger self!"

"And I you," said Aideen. "But let's not talk about that right now, shall we. By the way, this thing I'm lying on is called a Time Cradle." Aideen rose from the Time Cradle and looked down at the digital watch on her wrist. "Well then, it's May 16, 2022," she said.

"So, you were gone for 61 days. I see your hair has grown out a bit. And you have quite a nice tan. I'm jealous."

"Young Aideen explained that *you* wouldn't age while you were in the, uh, cradle thing, until I got back. But she didn't say anything about me aging, or not aging. So, I'm a little confused about that." *But not nearly as confused as I am regarding how I feel about older Aideen,* she thought to herself.

"As for the Time Link," said Aideen, "in this case, me, it has to do with my connection to the Time Station during your time in the past. While I'm in the cradle, the Station takes over my mind and also my body. It puts my body into a state of suspended animation until the trip comes to an end. For you, the one who traveled through the portal the Station and I created, life went on, just in a different time. So, your body aged, but mine didn't."

"It's logical, sort of," said Dani. "Maybe we can ask the Time Masters more about it when they come here," said Dani. "We should try to learn more from them about everything."

"We certainly can try. I'm hoping that *very* thing happens because of you. Charles Burke seemed truly excited to have an anthropologist joining the team." Aideen looked down at her watch again. "Alright, it's a quarter past midnight, so if you'll hand me that daypack, I'll check the tide chart."

Dani handed Aideen the pack, and Aideen went through it, pulling out a small handbook that listed high and low tide for each day of 2022. She went through the book and found what she was looking for.

"Low tide's at 20 past 3, so we should wait around for an hour to make sure the channel is clear of water. Otherwise, we might drown."

"That gives us time for some questions then," said Dani. "Do you have enough strength to talk some?"

"I'll do my best. What can I tell you, Dani?"

Dani gathered her wits and began.

"The first time I saw you was in the car park on the mainland side of the channel, right?" she said.

"Yes, that's right, from your perspective," replied Aideen.

"But the first time you saw me was 44 years ago on Pelekas, right?"

"That's more complicated," said Aideen.

"What do you mean?"

"Look, I'm no scientist, but what the Time Masters have explained ta' me is that time has two dimensions, at least there's two they *know* of. They caution that there might be others, unknown even to them."

"Okay, so tell me about the two dimensions the Time Masters *do* know about."

"The first dimension is the one we all know. That's the chronological dimension, also known as linear time. In that dimension, time moves forward, and all things, both animate and inanimate, get older. The second dimension of time is called *static* time, and it's harder to understand. This dimension has been speculated upon for many years and is also known as the B-Theory of time. It says that the past, present, and future exist simultaneously. The existence of the Time Station proves that the B-Theory is true because the Station successfully moves people back and forth to different points in time. And because it *is* true that time is static, while at the same time being linear, then by definition, I met you at the same time, here and there."

"But you *knew* me when I walked over to your car, didn't you? I now understand that you were trying very hard to hide that from me, which is a whole other subject, but you knew me, which means you met me first in Pelekas."

"That's the dilemma," said Aideen. "We're human. We perceive the passage of time. So yes, as a human being, who thinks only about time in chronological terms, I met you first in Pelekas. Our emotional bond was formed in Pelekas. So, it's true that I already knew you when you walked over to my car in that car park. But because I'm a Time Link, Dani, and my younger self knows all that I know, I also already knew you when you first came to Pelekas. The truth is that there are no beginnin's and no ends in the static dimension of time. It's all happenin', all at once."

"Okay, I can accept that. But it will take some getting used to."

"I can say from experience that you *do* get used to it, most of it anyway," said Aideen.

"Why didn't you just tell me all about it when we first met?"

"That's easy. You wouldn't have believed me! You would have thought I was crazy and walked away. And then all that we had together in Pelekas, and in other places, would never have happened."

"So, it's true that I'm going to get to see younger Aideen again?" asked Dani.

"Quite true. Yes."

"Well, that's something," said Dani, catching herself too late and wondering if she'd offended older Aideen by what she had said. But Aideen seemed calm and gave a heartfelt response.

"It's still me, here, right in front of you," she said. "Yes, I'm older, but I still love you, and I know you love me."

"I *do*, Aideen. But it's simply too much for me right now. It's hard for me to think of you as the same person I just left. You can understand that, right?"

"Absolutely I can. And while I wish it didn't have to be that way, I understand what you're goin' through. I wasn't supposed to fall in love with my apprentice anyway."

"Really? So, that was an accident. That you fell in love with me."

"Nothin's an accident, Dani. It was meant to be."

"Fate again?"

"Call it what you want. It was meant to be."

Aideen changed her focus *and* the conversation, gazing over at the wall of the chamber.

"You see that message over there, do ya'?"

"No," said Dani. "I don't see anything except black stone."

"Of course you don't. But there *is* something there that I *can* see."

"What?"

"It's a Time Mission plan that says we've got 72 hours before they come."

"Who?"

"The Time Masters, Dani."

"Do I have to do anything official? Or are you going to introduce me to them?"

"No, you'll be workin' same as me, as a Time Link."

"But I don't know how to do anything! How can they expect me to be a Time Link with no training?"

"I'll teach ya'. There's plenty of time. Let's go get some food and talk."

Chapter 17

Aideen and Dani made it back to the cottage at 3 am. They cooked some pasta, and while they were eating, Dani had more questions.

"How long have you been handling the Station by yourself?" she asked.

"Not long. Just since my mother passed about four months ago."

"How old was she?"

"She was 138 years old when she passed."

"What? That's not possible! No one has ever lived that long."

"Think about it, Dani. You know we don't age when we're sendin' out Travelers. And that causes our biology to last longer than normal, in all ways. The younger version of myself told you I'm still able to bear children, even though I'm 68 years old. But in my mother's case, both her old age and her extended fertility were mostly due to some kind of medicine the Time Masters gave her. They recruited her when she was 69 years old, in 1953, and they encouraged her to have a child who could join her when she reached adulthood. They gave her a pill that restored her youth and revitalized her ability to bear children. She was 70 years old when she had me."

"How did she get pregnant?"

"The old-fashioned way," said Aideen. "Went to a pub and got picked up."

"Are you serious?"

"No, just kiddin," said Aideen. "She was artificially inseminated. It was expensive back in the 1950s, but the Time Masters gave her money until she had time to get rich on her own. She could also afford a live-in nanny to take care of me while she was working."

"Why didn't the Time Masters make *you* have a child when your mom was getting really old?"

"I told them I had a better idea, that's why."

"And that was me?"

"Indeed, it was. I told them I was going to provide them with a real-life anthropologist. And as I've already mentioned, they liked that idea. Charles Burke is looking forward to meeting you. This whole thing could open up some new opportunities for us, Dani!"

"Like what?"

"Like them tellin' us what the feck is going on in the future, for one thing!"

"I think I need a drink," said Dani.

"Me, too." Aideen got up, opened a bottle of Pinot Noir, and poured two glasses. She returned to the kitchen table and changed the subject.

"Dani, when this mission is over, I think it's important that you finish your dissertation."

"So do I," she said. "But how can I do that while I'm apprenticing with you?"

"I have some ideas. But now that I know you *want* to finish it, we don't have to discuss it any further at the moment, because we've got to get ready for the arrival of the Time Masters. They're going to expect you to play your part."

"Which is what?"

"Your role will be just like any other Time Link. I'll give you a summary right now, and over the comin' days, I'll elaborate. So, for this mission, the Time Masters have selected Charles Burke to travel.

He's their head man and has been on most of the missions since the beginning."

"How long has this been going on?" asked Dani.

"For nearly 70 years," said Aideen. "My mother was one of the first recruits. And when I turned 18, I also became a Time Link. So, I'm a veteran now. Been doin' this for 50 years."

"Well, you certainly don't look it!" said Dani. "But what about Professor Burke? He must be very, very old if he's been doing this from the beginning."

"He *is* very old," said Aideen. "Over 100, at least. But he doesn't look it."

"Why? Did he take the same medicine he gave your mother?"

"I believe he did," said Aideen.

"So, why didn't you take it?" asked Dani.

Aideen paused, obviously uncomfortable.

"It's complicated, Dani."

Dani could tell that Aideen was reluctant to speak about the medicine from the future that made people younger, so she let it go. "Anyway," she said. "Please continue. I'm sorry we got off track."

"Very well," said Aideen. "Now, Charles Burke is the Traveler for this mission. He'll ride the Time Chain back until he gets to a time that contains an older version of yourself. Then, your older self will transport him back to this time."

"But I don't know how to do *that*!" Dani exclaimed.

"We've got 72 hours. I'll teach ya' what you need to know."

"That's the shortest apprenticeship I've ever heard of!"

"We *did* cut it a bit close, I admit, but I wanted all the time together in '78 we could squeeze out of it. And I know you did, too."

"I *did*. But I'm still very nervous."

"I'll give you a crash course then. First thing we have to do is take a walk around the island."

"But it's nearly four in the morning!"

"It 'tis. And we're both tired, but it's part of the job. Whenever, a Time Event is about to unfold, we have to know if anyone's on the island, and if so, where they are. We can't risk being seen going down into the Time Station."

"So, *that's* why you knew no one was on the island before we went on our 1978 adventure!"

"Yes, I walked the island while you slept. But no sleeping for you tonight. Three days from now, you'll graduate and become a full-fledged Time Link."

"I'll believe that when I see it," said Dani, shaking her head.

The women walked the island and spotted a tent on the northern side of Fahy Lough. Aideen told Dani they'd keep an eye on them over the next couple of days, but she was not at all alarmed by their presence. She also explained that most of their work during the coming days would be done at night, so it was convenient that dawn had nearly arrived. They would sleep as much as they could during the daytime, so they would have their wits about them at night.

When they arrived back at the cottage, they were both desperate for sleep, and the moment Dani had been dreading had arrived. She steeled herself and dove in.

"Aideen, I'm thinking that for now …"

"Yes, you should stay in the spare room," said Aideen, but Dani could see the pain in her eyes. "You've gone through a lot," she continued, "and I understand you have some feelin's to sort out in regards to me. Take the time you need. Sleep well, Dani. I love you."

"I … love you, too," said Dani, feeling guilty, but not at all inclined to change her mind about where she would be sleeping that night.

Aideen retired to her bedroom, and as she walked away, Dani noticed she didn't stand as tall and proud as she normally did. Dani wandered into the spare room, torn by the separation from Aideen, conflicted because she was still trying to get used to the idea that older Aideen was the same person who she'd fallen in love with in 1978. She wondered if she could ever accept that fact in her heart.

Chapter 18

Both Dani and Aideen slept until past noon, and when they woke, they enjoyed a cup of coffee on the patio out back. Dani could see the channel was already empty, allowing visitors to the island to cross. She saw a few walkers coming over, but no vehicles as of yet. After the coffee, they showered, separately, and drove to Clifden for lunch and to replenish their provisions. Dani bought a postcard, scribbled a few words on it, and mailed it to her parents in Chicago. She explained to Aideen that her parents had no expectation of hearing from her regularly while she was on this trip but that letting them know she was okay every few months was the least she could do.

When they returned to the cottage, they napped for a while, knowing it would be a long night. Then before the sun set, they walked the island to see if anyone was there. The campers from the night before had moved on, and they saw no one else on the island. The tide would be coming in soon, so unless someone had a reason to cross over in the middle of the night, their access to the Time Station would be unimpeded.

Their conversation was light, steering clear of their relationship. Aideen shared some of her ideas regarding Dani's dissertation, and when Dani asked questions about the responsibilities of a Time Link, Aideen brushed her off.

"We have time, Dani. It's a much simpler job than you might think. And to make it as easy to understand as possible, it would be best to start by going over the mission chart."

"Okay, let's do it!" said Dani, excited. "Have you got the chart?"

"I have it in my head. Because of my connection to the Station, I've been informed. After you're connected, you'll start receiving that kind of information as well, telepathically."

"How will I become connected to the Station?"

"It's simple. We'll do that tonight as soon as we get there."

"So, what's the mission? Is it going to be exciting? Dangerous?"

"It's hard for me to know," said Aideen. "I've never encountered a mission like this. No one has, I'm certain."

"What are we going to have to do?"

"Wait," said Aideen.

"But I don't want to wait!" exclaimed Dani. "Just tell me!"

"I just did tell ya'!" said Aideen. "That's what our mission instructions are. To wait."

The evening labored forward. Dani passed the time by picking up the book Aideen had given her, *The Last Watch*. It was an action-packed saga of a future-based group of people known as the Sentinels, located at the Divide, which was the edge of the universe. In the book, when the universe began to collapse, all hell broke loose, and the Sentinels had to use alien technology to hold the edge of the universe in place. The proximity to the Divide led to all kinds of deviations in the natural flow of time. The protagonist's lover, who traveled along the Divide as part of his responsibilities, didn't age while he was doing that. So, even though he started out much older than her, as his mission time increased, the gap was narrowing. Dani came to a passage that was highlighted in the book, in which the protagonist was calculating the amount of mission time her lover needed to experience before she would be older than him. It seemed she was wondering if he would feel the same about her when she grew older, while he remained the same.

Dani considered why Aideen might highlight that particular passage in the book. Was Aideen concerned that being so much older than Dani was a problem? If so, she was wrong, because Dani knew that wasn't the core of her problem. She simply had been unable to reconcile the stark contrast between her experiences with younger Aideen compared to those with older Aideen. But why did it matter? Dani was suddenly overwhelmed by a surge of guilt, followed by frustration. She was angry with herself for her confusion and uncertainty. She hoped she could eventually embrace the concept that older Aideen and younger Aideen were the same person, and the barrier that had come between them would disappear.

Chapter 19

At around 1 am, Dani and Aideen arrived at the Time Station. Aideen provided her first instruction.

"The hatch to the station is exactly 5 meters from the edge of that large stone over there. If you ever have trouble findin' it, a tape measure can help. But locatin' the station becomes second nature very quickly, I assure you."

Aideen located the hatch, uncovered it, and went down into the first chamber. When Dani caught up with her, she provided a new instruction.

"Come over to the black wall with me. We're goin' to get you connected to the station."

Dani moved over and stood next to Aideen.

"Now listen," said Aideen. "When we do this and you're connected to the station, it's like a marriage vow that you can't break. You'll be connected to the station for as long as you both shall live."

"So, the Time Station is alive?" asked Dani.

"Like I've said before, I'm no scientist, but I'm told by the Time Masters that the Time Station is composed of some kind of biomaterial, meaning it has properties of a livin' organism combined with inert materials. I really have no clue if it's alive or not, but I can tell you, I feel its presence in my life 24/7."

"Is it annoying? Bothersome?"

"Not at 'tall, Dani. It actually gives me a feelin' of power. So, are ya' in, or are ya' out?"

"Let's do it!"

"All right. Now, all you have to do is place your hand on the smooth black surface at the same time as me. So, hold your right hand up beside mine, and come near to the wall with it, but don't touch the wall until I tell ya.'"

Both women raised their hands and brought them close together, holding them palms out about six inches away from the wall.

"Now I'll count to three, and we'll press our hands against the wall, together. One, two, three."

They pressed their hands against the wall. As Dani's hand contacted the wall, she was surprised that it was warm. She had expected it to be cold because it looked like stone and they were down in a chamber that never saw the sun and was normally filled with the water of the icy North Atlantic. Instead, there was warmth and also a feeling of great vitality within the stone, if stone is what it really was. The longer Dani's hand remained pressed against it, the more its energy seemed to sink into her. She felt invigorated, her mind clear and sharp, yet she wondered why the doorway opening did not appear as it had before.

"What's the matter?" asked Dani.

"Nothin," said Aideen. "The station material is just gettin' to know you a bit better is all. Just keep your hand pressed against the black stone, Dani. It's almost done."

Suddenly, the door opening appeared. The two women entered, and as they traveled down the tunnel toward the heart of the station, an image entered Dani's mind. It was a chart. At the top of the chart was a heading. Dani pictured the words in her mind—Time

Mission: 187—and understood that this must be the information about the upcoming mission that Aideen had mentioned. They arrived at the end of the tunnel, and Aideen spoke.

"This time, press your hand, by yourself, against the wall, right about there."

Aideen pointed to a spot that was about chest height and in the center of the wall. Dani pressed the palm of her hand against the wall. The door opening appeared.

"You are now officially connected to the Time Station," said Aideen. "Shall we go in?"

Chapter 20

The two women entered the circular chamber, and Dani immediately saw the mission chart she had seen in her mind, up on a video screen that was embedded in the wall.

The heading at the top of the chart read "Time Mission: 187" and indicated that Charles Burke would be the sole Traveler on this mission. And then it clearly showed how Charles would make his way from 2253 back to 2022, using Time Links from each era to form a Time Chain, which was etched delicately into the chart to make the path of the entire trip quite obvious. Dani was surprised at how easily she could understand it, but she felt a little unnerved by the pattern of a chain on the chart. She wasn't sure why, but the idea briefly flickered through her mind that perhaps the Time Links were not only the facilitators of the Time Chain, but its captives as well. And then the thought was gone from her mind.

"So, this is the mission plan?" she asked. "And you could see this when we were here last time, when I arrived back from '78?"

"I could see it even *before* you went to '78," said Aideen. "I told you the Time Masters give us several months' notice when they're planning a trip."

"Okay, and now because I'm connected to the Time Station, I

can see it, too. But it looks pretty basic. Am I missing something?"

"Probably not," said Aideen. "It's actually so simple you don't even need the chart to know what the mission plan is. You can see that Charles is going to travel from 2253 to 2022. There's a Time Link with him in 2253 named Leah, and she must be very old, because she's going to send him back 98 years to her younger self, in the year 2155. In the station with younger Leah, in 2155, will be an older woman named Sophie, who will send Charles further back in time, to her younger self in 2074. That's where you come in. Your older self will be there in the station in 2074, and you will send Charles here to your younger self in 2022. But as you can see from the chart, you are directed to be in the cottage in 2022, as am I. Charles is obviously planning on spending some time with us in the cottage before moving on because he's got all of the Time Links in our past on standby."

TIME MISSION: 187

TRAVELER(S): CHARLES BURKE

TIME LEVEL	ARRIVAL YEAR	JUMP DISTANCE	TIME CHAIN TIME LINK 1	TIME LINK 2	ARRIVAL DATE
1	2253	0	Leah/Station		PRESENT
2	2155	98	Sophie/Station	Leah/Station	19-MAY
3	2074	81	Dani/Station	Sophie/Station	19-MAY
4	2022	52	Aideen/Cottage	Dani/Cottage	19-MAY
5	1972	NA	Aoife/Standby	Aideen/Standby	19-MAY
6	1902	NA	Roisin/Standby	Aoife/Standby	19-MAY
7	1850	NA	Ciara/Standby	Roisin/Standby	19-MAY

"Does the number 187 mean that this is the 187th Time Mission the Time Masters have conducted?" asked Dani.

"Yes. They do two or three trips a year, and as I mentioned, they've been doing this for about 70 years, so that's a lot of missions. And by the way, please remember not to call them the Time Masters to their faces. That's a nickname we've given them. It reminds us they're in charge and to behave ourselves."

"I'll remember."

"Any other questions, Dani?"

"Yes. The plural, 'Traveler(s),' suggests that sometimes more than one of them comes. Is that right?"

"Yes, that's correct. But nine times out of 10, it's just Charles. There've been a few others, but I hardly even remember their names."

"Was it just him last time?" asked Dani.

"It 'twas. That's the norm."

"Where did he have you meet him last time?"

"Copenhagen."

"But you implied you were in Dublin."

"Actually, I said *Charles* is a professor at Trinity College in Dublin, which is what he's told me, but I have no way to verify whether or not that's true because he lives in the year 2253. I don't even know if Trinity College still exists in 2253."

"What was he doing in Denmark on his last trip?"

"I've no idea. He left me as soon as he arrived, and I haven't seen him since. But I made a holiday of it. Denmark has very few Covid restrictions, and everythin' is open and runnin'. Copenhagen's a nice city. But let's stay with the Time Mission chart, all right, Dani? What else does it tell ya'?"

"The basic rule of thumb is that in any given time level, Time Link 1 is the older person and Time Link 2 is the younger person, right?" asked Dani.

"Right."

"So, on Level 5, in the year 1972, you're the younger member, right?"

"Yes."

"Who's the older member?"

"My mother, of course. Her name is Aoife. But as you can see from the chart, it's not pronounced the way it's spelled. It's pronounced Ee-fa."

"What's it like seeing your mother when she's younger? Especially..." Dani trailed off, embarrassed.

"Especially since she's just died in 2022?" asked Aideen.

"I'm sorry, Aideen. I wasn't thinking."

"It's not a problem. And remember, it's my younger self back there in '72. Older Aideen will be right here in the Time Cradle."

"But you told me back in Pelekas that when you're in the Time Cradle, connected to your younger self, you experience the past just like you did when you lived it."

"That's right," said Aideen. "And truth be told, I don't know how I'll feel because I haven't sent a Traveler back to a location where my mother was since she passed. I'm a little nervous about it, but on the other hand, it's a luxury most people don't have: to spend time with a loved one who's passed away."

"That's a good way of looking at it," said Dani. "I think you'll be fine. How old is your mother in 1972?"

"She's 88 years old in 1972," said Aideen. "Why do you ask?"

"I was just wondering what she looks like back then."

"She looks a lot like I do right now. She's not as tall as me, but we look very much alike."

"So, she looks to be around 50 years old?" asked Dani.

"She does," said Aideen.

"Is that because she took the medicine the Travelers gave her? The pill that made her younger?"

"Yes, it 'tis," said Aideen. "To my knowledge, she's the only Time Link who's taken that pill, except probably the ones on Level 1."

"Why is that?" asked Dani. "Why didn't you take it, for example?"

"They don't pass it out like candy, Dani," said Aideen, stiffening slightly.

Dani silently cursed herself for touching on a subject that she knew was sensitive for Aideen. She felt guilty for bringing it up, but Aideen didn't give her time to dwell on it.

"What about the Arrival Dates?" asked Aideen. "Do you have any questions or comments on those?"

Dani looked at that column on the chart.

"Yes, I have a question on that," she said. "Is it necessary for the Travelers to arrive on the same day of the year at each time level?"

"Not at 'tall," said Aideen. "In fact, I've never seen it happen like that before. It's as if they have one thing, and only one thing, in mind."

"Seeing you and I," said Dani.

"Yes," said Aideen. "But it's the *why* that has me bothered."

Chapter 21

"What do you think Professor Burke does when he goes to places like Denmark?" asked Dani.

The two were nestled back in the cottage after a long night in the Station. Aideen had made them breakfast, and they were getting ready to go to bed. But Dani still had questions, and Aideen was doing her best to answer them.

"He's said all along that he's lookin' for keys to reversing whatever nastiness is happenin' in his time. But for all I know, he's just partyin' and havin' a good time. The only reason I'm there at 'tall is to save him the trouble of travelin' from Omey Island to wherever he wants to be. He doesn't ever include me in anythin'."

"Have the Travelers initiated any changes yet? To try to fix things in the future?"

"Not that I know of. Charles is always sayin' he needs to be comfortable with what he wants to change, and *how* he wants to change it before he does it."

"So, you have no idea what the problem in the future is, or what the Travelers want to change," said Dani.

"No idea on both counts," said Aideen. "But this upcomin' mission leads me to believe they're goin' to try somethin'. And I also believe they're focusin' on 2022!"

"What leads you to think that, Aideen?"

"The nature of the mission itself. Charles always goes somewhere important. He's visited me in the cottage a few times on his way further back in time, but he's never designated the cottage as his final destination."

"But he *did* put the Time Links in our past on standby," said Dani. "So, he probably won't be staying here long."

"But why stay here at 'tall? What does he want from us? My suspicion is he wants our help in makin' some changes to the future."

"That's a bit frightening," said Dani. "I'd hate to be involved in something that might go wrong. If the time ripples aren't what the Travelers expect, that might even affect *our* future."

"Yes, it's a concern," said Aideen. "And speaking of frightenin', there's one thing you'll experience when Charles arrives that I need to warn you about."

"What? Is he a pervert or something?"

"No, Dani. It has nothin' to do with him. And you ought to wipe that smile off your face because it will be without question the most mind blowin' moment of your life."

Dani's eyebrows went up, and her smile disappeared. Aideen's tone was deadly serious.

"This will be your first connection with your older self. This is the moment when your mind will flood with all the memories you will have gained during the time between now and then. Just look at the Jump Distance from level 3 to level 4 on the Time Mission chart. 52 years. So, 76-year-old-Dani's mind will merge with that of 24-year-old Dani, in order for the time portal to be opened up by the Station. I can't emphasize enough that you need to be prepared for this."

Dani accessed the Time Mission chart in her mind and quickly confirmed the numbers Aideen had conveyed to her. That was a lot of years of memories to be data-dumped into her head, or however it was going to get there.

"What will I experience? What kind of emotions will I feel?"

"The whole gamut," said Aideen. "Deep sadness, extreme exhilaration, anger, denial, you name it."

"So, how do I cope with all of that? I don't want to make a fool of myself in front of Professor Burke."

"It doesn't matter if you do. He's aware that your younger self will be experiencin' all of this for the first time. Your older self will be a veteran, of course, and some of that comfort level and confidence in the process will come through in the mind merge. But the knowledge about all that has taken place in your life can be overwhelmin'."

"That doesn't sound good," said Dani, genuinely concerned.

"And here's the tricky part," said Aideen. "Not all of the information you'll be receiving is hard, cold facts. Big things *will* be, like the deaths of people you loved. But many things will be just the memories of a 76-year-old woman. Even as younger people, our perceptions of what happened in our past is not necessarily exactly what happened. And many things we simply forget. Forgotten memories may be in the subconscious and resurface at some point, but most of them will simply remain forgotten. What this means is that while you *will* have to cope with knowin' major events before they happen, most of the details of your upcomin' life will remain unknown to you. Sometimes you'll have a déjà vu experience when somethin' occurs, and that will probably be attributable to a memory from your future that's buried in your subconscious."

"So, how do I know what's real and what's not?" asked Dani.

"You don't," said Aideen. "The best way to handle things goin' forward is *not* to think about the future at 'tall."

"Why?"

"Because you simply *cannot* try to change anythin' that you don't want to happen, Dani. This one thing can't be emphasized enough. This is *the* cardinal rule that all Time Links must live by because if one of us changes somethin', we can't know the consequences for the future. Time ripples are unpredictable, so something you think would have no effect whatsoever on the course of future history might end up killin' thousands of people, or worse."

"I understand," said Dani. "But that has to be profoundly burdensome."

"It helps if you learn to think of time as havin' no beginning or ending," said Aideen. "But what helps even more is to cherish every moment of your life, both the good and the bad, even when you know what's comin'. I'll help you with that. I promise."

"What was it like for you, the first time?" asked Dani.

"For me, I got over the emotions quickly, because my mother had *some* knowledge of my future, and she conveyed a lot of events to me in advance."

"Can you do the same for me?" asked Dani.

"I don't want to, Dani."

"Why?"

"Because my knowledge of your future is very likely going to be obsolete after this visit from Charles Burke."

"Why?"

"Because if he's goin' to change the future during this visit, then the future I know will no longer be accurate. *Your* knowledge of the future, however, from the moment he arrives, *will* be the truth."

"How?"

"Because *you* are the one bringing him back to us, through your connection with your older self. At that moment, you'll know the next 52 years of the future, includin' whatever actions Charles takes when he visits us on May 19th."

Chapter 22

May 19 arrived. As instructed on the mission plan, Aideen and Dani waited in the cottage. Both of them were nervous, Dani because she was worried about the pending flood of knowledge that awaited her, and Aideen because she was convinced that the future she knew would be changed. While they were waiting, Dani tried to get some insight into what kind of person Charles Burke was.

"So, what should I expect from Professor Burke?" she asked. "What kind of a person is he?"

Aideen thought on that for a moment.

"There are pluses and minuses to Charles Burke," she said.

"How so?" asked Dani.

"The positive is that he's allowin' us to be part of something most people would never imagine. We get rich along the way, and we get to go on adventures of our own making, like Pelekas."

"And the minuses?" asked Dani.

"The negative is that he won't tell me anythin'!" exclaimed Aideen. "I've been workin' with the man for 50 years and know virtually nothin' about what he's doin'. It's frustratin' beyond belief."

"But you think my status as an anthropologist, or a soon-to-be anthropologist, might help us to learn more, right?"

"That 'tis my hope," said Aideen. "We'll see what happens."

Around 8 in the evening, while the two sat in the living room chatting, Dani felt something click in her mind.

"I think this is it!" she fretted.

"Stay calm," said Aideen. "I'll be here with ya' the whole way."

The click became an internal roar, like the sound of an out-of-control surge of water bursting through a dam and coursing over the peaceful countryside below. The flood began, and the download of data from older Dani poured in. She saw so much at once it was hard to separate one thought from another, but the emotional highlights stood out.

In Dani's memories from the future, she saw Charles Burke, a surprisingly young man of around 30 years of age, with long dark hair; a clean-shaven, angular face; and a sharp nose, arriving to reveal his plan for changing the future. She saw herself and Aideen, spending a long, happy life together, and this made her joyful. She saw the deaths of her parents, in a car accident in 2023, and overwhelming shock and sadness cascaded through her. She did *not* see Aideen's death, which apparently would take place more than 52 years in the future, and this gave her a feeling of relief. She also saw herself traveling back in time as part of Charles's mission to change the future. There she met a young girl of 12 who she came to love, but instead of the deep, warm feeling of happiness that comes with love, she felt sadness, but she couldn't remember why. But then a hand squeezed hers, and Charles Burke popped into existence. This interrupted her survey of all the new knowledge she'd acquired in a microsecond. Dani had tears in her eyes, but she was pleasantly surprised that she'd survived the flood. Her emotions were stable, but she knew that sometime soon she would wrestle with some of it, again and again.

Charles Burke quickly released her hand, obviously requiring no emotional support or explanations about where he was, a veteran going through the motions of his job. Burke was dressed rather strangely, wearing a long, heavy coat over a linen shirt. His slacks were breeches, coming to just below the knees, under which were wool stockings, covering his calves and leading down to heavy, leather shoes. He was facing Aideen, so he greeted her first.

"Hello, Aideen," he said, his voice smooth and melodious, but his accent wasn't Irish. It was English.

"Welcome to our home, Charles," she responded. "May I introduce you to our new Time Link, Danielle Peterson."

"We've already met, of course, just a moment ago, 52 years in the future," said Charles, turning to Dani and extending his hand.

"Yes, I remember," said Dani, shaking Charles Burke's hand then wiping away her tears. "It's good to see you again, Dr. Burke, and I look forward to spending more time together than just a few moments."

"Oh, we will," said Charles, a pleasant smile on this face. "And let's dispense with the formalities of calling me *Doctor* or *Professor*, please. I am both, yes, and that is more rare in my time than you might believe, but please, Charles is what I prefer."

"Very well, Charles," she said.

"If I may, Aideen, can I ask for a place to change out of these ridiculous and greatly uncomfortable clothes? They wouldn't fit in the suitcase, and I don't need them right now, obviously."

"Certainly, Charles," said Aideen. "You can use my bedroom. Plannin' on going further back in time I take it?"

"Yes, I am," he said. "But we'll get to that later."

Dani noticed that Charles Burke had a suitcase in his hand, with rolling wheels on it and a retractable handle. It crossed her mind that a suitcase like this very likely wasn't being used by people 231 years in the future, and that it had been carefully chosen for him so as not to arouse suspicion as to his origin, should anyone see it in the year 2022. The clothing he was wearing was a different matter, clearly meant for some time a good distance in the past. Charles rolled his suitcase into the bedroom, and in a few moments, he returned wearing jeans and a flannel shirt, very much like the clothing both Aideen and Dani were wearing. He had brought the suitcase back out with him.

"Would you like somethin' to drink?" asked Aideen.

"Some of that gorgeous Pinot Noir of yours would be great," said Charles, making it obvious to Dani he'd spent time in the cottage before.

Aideen poured wine for the three of them, brought out some cheese and crackers, and placed them on the coffee table in the small living room. The three of them took seats, Aideen and Dani on the sofa, and Charles in one of the comfortable chairs across from them. After taking a long pull from his wine, obviously enjoying it, Charles set his glass down on the coffee table and began.

"As I'm sure you suspect, Aideen, and you *know* Dani … by the way, may I call you Dani?" he asked.

"Of course," she replied. "Virtually no one calls me Danielle."

"Very well," he said. "The point being: I am here to announce a change in direction to you."

Aideen seemed to feel it was important to confirm to Charles that she could interpret a mission plan as well as anyone, so she spoke up.

"You're correct in your assumption, Charles, that I suspected as much," she said.

"What you don't know yet, Aideen, are the details. Dani, of course, knows because she's been recently *informed* through the connection to her older self. But for the purpose of making this official, I will provide you both with a summary, primarily of the *why* in all of this. And in so doing, I will be revealing for the first time to anyone not from my time era the truth about what happens to the human race over the next 231 years."

Charles stood and reached for his suitcase, opened it, extracted some papers, then closed it, put it aside, and sat back down. He handed a one-page document to Aideen and a duplicate to Dani.

"Aideen, please read this, and then I'll answer questions," he said. "And Dani, you need to read it as well because even though you remember reading it from the memory dump you just experienced, you need to actually *do* the reading in order for the memory to remain viable. It's something you'll get used to as you gain more experience as a Time Link."

Dani understood exactly what Charles was referring to because she'd been briefed on this by Aideen before he arrived. She was well aware that even though she knew what the document said, she needed to read it now, for the first time, in order to retain the memory of its content. She noted that Aideen was already reading intently, her eyebrows raised and a blush coming to her face, most likely shock. Dani took up the document and read.

Chapter 23

A Synopsis of the Future of the Human Race

In 2022, television, smartphones, the internet, social media, traditional media, gaming, virtual reality, voice command technology, digital pornography, and robotics, among other things, are changing the way people spend their time. The abilities to work remotely and to have almost anything delivered cause people to leave their homes less. They are more and more engrossed in activities that require only their minds in order to partake.

In the near future from 2022, people don't even need to talk anymore because software has been developed that convert their thoughts into speech. Software programs allow people to have digital children and raise them as their own. Soon after that, computers have surpassed the intelligence and power of the human brain and can exactly duplicate anyone's mind and load it into their databases, including intelligence, memories, emotions, and even biological sensations such as pain and sexual gratification. Because people use their bodies less and less in day-to-day activities, an increasing number have decided they don't need or even want their bodies anymore. The prospect of immortality—with none of the pain and suffering from aging that is inherent in their biological selves—is appealing.

Companies whose sole function is uplo[ading] to computers have proliferated. During th[e] process, people are allowed to select features versions of themselves. As computers evolve, ... move the contents of people's minds from one generation of machine to the next and to back them up in the cloud.

The first companies to sell the service of uploading human minds begin operating in 2098. Initial demand is driven by wealthy, elderly individuals. But as economies of scale evolve, the price of the uploads comes down dramatically, and it ultimately reaches a price point where the masses can afford a mind upload. The demand curve shifts from the elderly to young adults, the heaviest users of the new technologies that require so little from the human body and are designed simply to engage and entertain the human mind. The next wave comes from an unexpected demographic— the poorest people from the poorest places on Earth. For them, uploading is akin to going to heaven, leaving the filth and poverty of their world behind forever. The upload companies take a small profit margin from these souls, but although the margin is small, the volume is great. This wave creates the largest population drain of all time.

By 2225, far more people are living in computers than in biological form, and the biological birth rate has slowed dramatically. The world's biological population is down to less than 500 million people and declining rapidly. By 2250, only 100 million people are left alive in biological form, which is equivalent to the world population in the year 2000 B.C. Humanity was not overwhelmed by alien invaders or artificial intelligence, as so many of the books and films of the second half of the 20th century and the first half of the 21st century depicted. The irony is that the human race *willingly* chose to give up its humanity.

ᴛional governments no longer exist because all of the people ᴜ might have served have gone into the machines. The people who remain biological entities subsist in local enclaves much like our ancient ancestors, but unlike those fiefdoms, we don't make war on one another. We remain human because we value what it *is* to be human, and our shared values cause us to be peaceful. With so few biological humans remaining, the bounty of the Earth is more than enough to sustain us. There is no global warming threat because there are not enough people left to produce undesirable quantities of greenhouse gases through driving, flying, manufacturing, and raising crops and livestock that once plagued our world. The computers build themselves, and their power sources are overwhelmingly renewable. We are not at war with AI. In fact, we continue to utilize AI to help us in our mission.

A small group of us have gathered on the island known as Ireland, and we have harnessed the ability to move back in time. We search for a way to turn the tide of abandonment of our bodies that will ultimately end our species, back in favor of those who value *all* of what being human truly is.

There are no easy answers. Stemming the tide of technology that rolled over our world in the 21st century comes with obvious risks. But we are convinced that it *is* the 21st century where our efforts must be focused, and all of our research thus far suggests that the year 2022 is where mankind must initiate its final stand.

After Dani finished reading, she saw that Aideen had already placed her document down on the coffee table and was looking in her direction, her expression unreadable, but her eyes were wide and lit with intensity. Dani put her synopsis on the table as well.

"So," said Charles. "Questions?"

Aideen didn't hesitate. "This is not what I expected, Charles," she said.

"How so?" he asked.

"First, I live out here in the countryside, as do many people. And while I've been with you to many of the most technologically advanced countries, I never could have predicted a result like what you've summarized in your synopsis."

"Yes, well," said Charles. "I think it's safe to say it caught most people by surprise as it transpired, especially the speed of the transition, once it got rolling."

"And the second thing, which is more important," said Aideen, "is how can we possibly fix this, Charles, without bringin' on even more undesirable future events? Technological advancement is so broad-based, so vast, at least it is in 2022. Wouldn't it make more sense to go back a bit further in time, when things were simpler, to make changes?"

"It's actually the opposite of that," said Charles. "A moment, please. It seems I'm a little hungry." Charles helped himself to some cheese and crackers, then sipped his wine and put it down.

"Would you like us to make you some dinner, Charles?" asked Aideen.

"Perhaps, yes, thank you. But let me explain my thoughts here first."

Dani knew what his answer was going to be, and she wanted him to get on with it so they could move forward. She realized now that it was going to be a challenge to know the future but still *live* in the present. She marveled at how good Aideen was at it, and she hoped that one day she could control her emotions as well as Aideen did. Also not lost on Dani was that with the arrival of Charles, and the corresponding arrival of her memories of the next 52 years, an immediate shift had occurred in her relationship with Aideen. It was no longer Aideen who possessed the most up-to-date knowledge of what was going to happen next. It was Dani. Her reflections were brought to a halt, however, by Charles, who was proceeding to answer Aideen's question.

"The further we go back in time, the more important individual inventions become and the more profound the effects of delaying or changing them," he said. "Can you imagine if we were able to defer the harnessing of electricity in the 1800s for 50 or 100 years? It's impossible to say what that would lead to, but we know that you and I would very likely not even be here speaking if we tampered with that. One or more of us quite possibly wouldn't exist at all. And let's move forward 100 years to the invention of the microprocessor in the late 1960s and the introduction of the first commercial microprocessor in 1971 by Intel. Suppose we stop or delay that? What happens to the three of us?"

"I think I would be here," said Aideen, smiling. "The advantages of living in the country!"

"But you understand my point, don't you?" asked Charles.

"Indeed, I do," said Aideen. "So, what's the plan, Charles?"

Chapter 24

"The plan is two-fold," explained Charles, speaking while he finished the spaghetti that Aideen and Dani had prepared for him. "One, Hearts and Minds. Two, Sabotage."

"Please explain further," said Aideen.

"Of course. Let's start with Hearts and Minds. Dani can help me with this. Dani, what is the most precise definition of anthropology you can come up with?"

"Anthropology is the science of human beings," she said.

"Well done," said Charles. "Emphasis on *human beings*. The Hearts and Minds campaign must begin now, nearly 80 years before the first viable mind upload companies appear. We must remind people what being human really means."

"And how will we do that?" asked Aideen.

"Some time ago, you reported the title of Dani's dissertation to me," said Charles.

"*Remnants of the Wild Atlantic Way*," said Aideen, her eyebrows arching with curiosity.

"Yes," he said. "And you know that I am an anthropologist and that Dani is training to become one."

"Yes," said Aideen, anticipation in her eyes.

"I propose that we make Dani the most famous anthropologist of all time, based on her soon-to-be renowned dissertation, *Remnants of the Wild Atlantic Way*."

"And how we will do *that*?" asked Aideen.

"As part of Dani's research for her dissertation, she will travel back in time to an older Ireland," said Charles. "And then we tell the world that the basis of her research was time travel."

"I see," said Aideen, frowning.

"But let's not forget the definition of anthropology, emphasis on *human beings*!" said Charles, excited. "The essence of Dani's writing will be to remind people of the essence of humanity, and her work will be read far and wide due to her fame because of the time travel revelation."

"I can see how that might help some," said Aideen, "without necessarily eliminating any of us that are doing the work, by the sweep of random ripples of time."

Dani agreed with the logic of what Aideen was saying, but her memories from the future provided no evidence to support it.

"At this point, I can see forward only 52 years," she said. "And what's odd is that I don't see *any* effect from the Hearts and Minds campaign. In fact, I'm not sure the program ever even got off the ground."

"That's interesting," said Charles. "Maybe it never does. But this is new ground we are pioneering here, so maybe when we contemplate changing the course of history, we have to actually *make* the changes before anyone's future *actually* changes. So, we'll need to proceed with this mission."

"Can you explain the Sabotage part also, Charles?" asked Aideen.

"Of course," he said. "In the year 2098, the first mind upload company will be launched. We will need Dani to send someone to the future to prevent that from happening."

"And of course, that person will be me," said Aideen. "That way, the secret stays with the three of us and your colleagues in 2253. Am I right?"

"Right indeed," said Charles. "But our first priority should be Hearts and Minds. I'm wondering, however, if we can all agree that we're tired, so I'm thinking we should pick this all up again in the morning when we're fresh. Can we do that?"

"Certainly, Charles," said Aideen. "That will be fine."

They all finished their wine, making small talk, and then it was time to retire. That was when the issue of there being only two bedrooms in the cottage presented itself. But Dani quickly removed any doubt as to the appropriate solution.

"You can use *my* bedroom," she said to Charles. "I can stay in Aideen's room."

After they'd gotten in bed, Aideen asked Dani a question.

"What caused you to suddenly be okay with being in the same bed with the infamous *older* Aideen?" she asked.

"That's easy," she said. "I love you. And now I know that our love is timeless, and that *you* will always be the one and only person I fell in love with."

And with that, Dani pulled off her nightshirt and leaned down, kissing the love of her life with all the built-up passion her abstinence had engendered.

Chapter 25

"I will be frank with you," said Charles. "It's going to be challenging to extend the Time Chain further back than 1850."

The three were gathered in the tiny living room once again, having just finished a Full Irish Breakfast, which Aideen knew from experience that Charles favored. Dani was feeling better than she had since she'd returned from 1978, and this was attributable to her physical and emotional reunion with Aideen the prior evening. Aideen also appeared less burdened than previously, even though the task ahead would be perilous for both of them.

"You've never shared so much with us before," said Aideen. "In fact, you've shared virtually nothin'. So, it's unclear to me what kind of problems you might face goin' further back in time."

"It's very basic," said Charles. "The further back we go, the more frightened the people we're recruiting as Time Links become. Even the level 7 team back in 1850 is full of trepidation. It's a mother-and-daughter team, as most of them are, but they're so in awe of us that they actually call us the 'Time Masters!' Can you imagine that? As if we were gods from the future or something!"

Dani and Aideen broke out into smiles at the same time.

"What's the joke?" asked Charles. "Did I miss something?"

Dani looked to Aideen for guidance on what to disclose, but Aideen didn't hesitate.

"That's what we call ya', too," she said, the smile still on her face. "Behind your backs!"

"For heaven sakes, why?" asked Charles.

"It's not awe, I'll tell ya' that much," said Aideen. "Although it *is* quite marvelous what you've accomplished."

"What then?" he asked.

"It's a reminder to ourselves that we should pay strict attention to all the guidelines you've given us about how not to mess with time. Not to make up rules of our own. But after these past 12 hours, I'm thinking you folks from the future don't know much more than we do about the nuances of time."

"All understood," said Charles. "But suffice it to say that the further we move back, the more reluctance to participate we will encounter."

"But you'll carry on nonetheless, I take it," said Aideen.

"Indeed, we will. I've posted a revised mission 187 Time Chart, which both of you have undoubtedly seen. The chart ends at level 7, in 1850, because we have no idea what levels 8, 9, and beyond will look like, although our plan is to drill back in time as far as we need to."

Dani accessed the revised chart in her mind.

TIME MISSION: 187

TRAVELER(S): CHARLES BURKE, DANIELLE PETERSON

TIME LEVEL	ARRIVAL YEAR	JUMP DISTANCE	TIME CHAIN TIME LINK 1	TIME LINK 2	ARRIVAL DATE
1	2253	0	Leah/Station		PRESENT
2	2155	Complete	Sophie/Station		19-MAY
3	2074	Complete	Dani/Station		19-MAY
4	2022	Complete	Aideen/Cottage		21-MAY
5	1972	50	Aoife/Station	Aideen/Station	21-MAY
6	1902	70	Roisin/Station	Aoife/Station	21-MAY
7	1850	52	Ciara/Station	Roisin/Station	21-MAY

The first change she noticed was the addition of herself to the Travelers list. In addition to this, Charles had deactivated all the Time Link 2s from the future time levels, freeing them up to go on with their lives because their function for this mission had already been performed. But he'd activated all of the Time Links from levels 5, 6, and 7—the people in time eras of the past—and notified them to move to the station on May 21, which would arrive in 2022 tomorrow night at midnight. Charles was obviously planning on moving quickly to level 7—the year 1850—and then extending the

Time Chain further back in time.

"I'm going to initiate the recruitment process myself," said Charles. "Although frankly, I'm not as well trained in that area as some of our specialists. I should have brought a Recruiter with me, but my primary mission was to solicit the two of you to help us with our plan. I'm assuming you are both on board?"

"I'm in," said Dani.

"I'm not sure," said Aideen, a look of concern on her face.

"Is that because Dani will be coming with me on this trip?" asked Charles.

"I don't understand why it's necessary," said Aideen.

Dani stepped in to explain.

"The reasons I'm going back are because, number one, it's *my* dissertation. I want to be comfortable with my subjects. I want to make sure they have stories that will generate empathy for themselves and for the human condition. Number two, we want to be absolutely certain we go back far enough in time that the people I meet are so culturally different from today that when people from our time meet them, there will be absolutely no way the experts could view them as fakes."

"So, you're going to bring them back with you then!" yelled Aideen, stunned with the audacity of such a move.

"Just one," said Dani. "I'm sorry I implied it would be more than that."

"And just why are ya' doin' that?" asked Aideen.

"To prove that I actually *did* go back in time without showing people the Time Station. We can't let go of that secret. Ever."

Aideen paused before responding, thinking it through. "And ya' already know, from your older self, that you'll be alright, do ya'?" she asked, obviously accepting that this was going to happen.

"All will be well," said Dani. "I'm not saying the trip itself will be easy. A better description would be that it's a wild ride. But hey, would you expect me to shy away from a challenge?"

"I suppose not," said Aideen. "Just be careful, please!"

"We will," said Dani.

"How far back?" asked Aideen, a little anxiety still in her voice. She understood all the things that could go wrong when a Traveler was passed further and further back in time.

"I haven't figured that out yet," said Charles.

"Yes, but I already *know*," said Dani. "We end up back in the year 1751."

"Glad to hear it!" interjected Charles. "When I left 2253 for this trip, we had not yet been 'reoriented' to the new realities because we had not yet initiated this program. For the first time in history, humans are attempting to consciously change a future that has already happened. We are rewriting both linear *and* static time."

"Whatever," said Aideen. "Just bring Dani back safely, Charles. She's new at this, and I never expected she'd be traveling with you as part of her first mission."

"I'll protect her," said Charles, pride and confidence in his voice. "All right, let's begin our preparations!" He reached into his suitcase and removed some clothing. "You'll need these, Dani. Please try them on to make sure they fit reasonably well."

He handed Dani a thick, ankle-length skirt, a linen undergarment, a heavy blouse, a woolen shawl, a linen headscarf, and some heavy, leather shoes.

While Dani was in the bedroom changing, Charles had one more thing to say to Aideen.

"There's one more reason I'm taking Dani," said Charles.

"And what is that?" asked Aideen.

"She's a woman!"

Chapter 26

When Dani returned, dressed in her quaint new outfit, Charles elaborated on something Aideen had known for some time: The Travelers recruited *only* women to serve as Time Links. According to Charles, the rationale was three-fold. First, women were more appreciative of what being human really was, as evidenced by the fact that 80 percent of the world's biological population in the year 2253 were women. Charles explained that women had resisted giving up their biological selves more ardently than men, and this had led to the extreme skew in gender toward women. Second, women from the past were perceived by the people of the future to be more reliable than men to keep the existence of the Time Station secret and to follow the rules. And third, the further back in time one traveled, the more dependent on men women became. Recruiting women who had lost their husbands and had one child to take care of was a key tactic in the push to acquire Time Links. The Recruiters could offer financial security to those women, which they could not easily acquire themselves. Additionally, secrecy was more easily maintained when there were no husbands or other children. An only child could be counted on to join her mother as a Time Link in a very high percentage of cases.

The three decided that the planning for the Sabotage part of the plan could wait, especially because they had 76 years of linear time before that happened. There was also the possibility a successful Hearts and Minds campaign could at the very least delay the launch of the mind upload companies beyond 2098. Charles felt he would need to monitor for time ripples from Hearts and Minds for an undetermined amount of time. It was all new. The suspicion was that the effects from the campaign in future times would be felt immediately in the future, but there was no certainty in this. No one had ever attempted to change *known* future events before.

Before they left, Dani called her faculty advisor and formally requested an extension of time for the completion of her dissertation. The advisor said it would be no problem, but Dani might have to wait until the fall term to defend her dissertation in front of the faculty, depending on when she turned it in. Dani informed the advisor that she expected to complete the paper that summer. The advisor approved the extension, asking Dani to keep him updated on her progress.

Early in the morning of May 21, Aideen sent Charles and Dani back in time. They were both wearing the clothes that were supposed to help them blend in to the 1800s. Dani found the linen undergarment to be comfortable enough, but the shoes were killing her feet. She couldn't remember if they'd had to find other clothes as they went back even further in time, and she realized that not every detail of her adventures had come through with the memory dump. She assumed that *this* memory was somewhere in her subconscious, or perhaps it wasn't there at all. But Dani wasn't concerned. She knew it would all work out.

While both Dani and Charles clasped their hands to Aideen's right hand and wrist, Aideen squeezed the Station control with her left, gazing up at Dani from the Time Cradle with a stoic smile and a wink.

"See ya' in a second!" said Aideen.

The light went on and increased in intensity, and soon after that, Dani's mind went blank.

Chapter 27

Dani's awareness returned, and she looked around. They were still in the chamber, and both she and Charles were still holding Aideen's right hand and wrist, but it was a younger Aideen, and she was standing. There'd been no need for her to be lying in a Time Cradle in order to receive them in 1972. The Mission Plan had simply requested that she be in the Station at the appointed date, and there she was.

Aideen was 18 years old, and more beautiful than ever in Dani's eyes. Dani was aware that with the merging of Aideen's mind with that of her older self, in 2022, younger Aideen now knew all that older Aideen knew, not only about the plan, but also what Charles's synopsis had revealed about the future beyond 2022. Charles addressed that subject immediately.

"Best to keep what you've just learned from your mother," he said to Aideen.

Dani looked over at the Time Cradle on the other side of the chamber and saw a woman who appeared to be about 50 years old standing beside it in a relaxed pose, her hands gripping its side. She had the same red hair as Aideen, with a touch of gray, and the same fair skin and freckles. She wasn't as tall as Aideen, but she was trim and appeared to be in good health. And she was 88 years old in 1972, according to Aideen.

"You understand, Ma, don't ya'?" asked Aideen.

"I do," said Aideen's mother. "It was obvious from the Time Mission plan that somethin' was going on in 2022, and that it was different than a normal mission. I assumed this expansion of the mission has something to do with that."

"Indeed," said Charles. "And in the interest of time, it's best that we keep moving back."

Dani's heart rate ticked up. She wanted to spend more time with younger Aideen, who seemed to understand what she was feeling.

"I'll see you in six years," said Aideen, a broad smile on her face. "On Pelekas. But before ya' go, allow me to introduce you to my mother. Ma, this is Dani. I will spend quite a bit of time with her in the coming years."

Aideen's mother stood and walked over to Dani. Her eyes were the same sparkling gray-blue jewels as Aideen's. She extended her right hand.

"I'm Aoife," she said. "The spelling's a bit confusin' to those who aren't Irish."

"Yes, Aideen mentioned that me," said Dani, moving toward Aoife and shaking her hand.

"Did I tell you Ma's name means 'beautiful'?" asked Aideen. "And she *is*, is she not?"

"She is," said Dani, grasping Aoife's hand. "I'm so happy to meet you, Aoife," she said. "I hope one day we can spend more time together."

"Oh, we will," said Aoife. "Just not today."

Aoife pulled away and went to lie down on the Time Cradle. When she was in place, she spoke again.

"Come on, you two slowpokes!" she said. "Let's move ya' a bit further back in time."

Dani moved back to Aideen and kissed her on the cheek, squeezing her hand one more time. Aideen left the chamber smiling but with a hint of sorrow in her eyes. Dani stepped over to the Time Cradle where Aoife had positioned herself. Aoife extended her right hand over the edge of the cradle. Dani grasped it, and Charles took Aoife's wrist. The light went on and became very bright and soothing, and then Dani's mind went blank.

Chapter 28

Dani awoke holding the hand of another 18-year-old woman, who looked nearly identical to 18-year-old Aideen, except for the way she was dressed, and her being a few inches shorter. Aoife wore an ankle-length, cotton dress, pulled tightly at the waist and covering a full figure. Dani wondered how she fought off the suitors here in the year 1902.

"Hello, Dani, Charles," said Aoife, the knowledge of who Dani was arriving simultaneously with Dani herself. She already knew Charles from previous missions.

"Hello," said Charles, addressing younger Aoife.

"Over there is Time Link 1 of level 6, Roisin O'Brien, my mother," she responded. "She's got another one of those perplexin' Irish names that's spelled different than it sounds. R-o-i-s-i-n is pronounced Rosheen here in Ireland."

Dani and Charles pulled away from Aoife and approached Roisin, shaking hands and exchanging greetings. Roisin had red hair with pale skin and freckles, but the resemblance to Aoife and Aideen was limited to those features. She was short and stocky and had green eyes.

"I'm sorry to report, Dani, that Ma does nah speak English," said Aoife. "Only Irish. I've tried to teach her, but as you know, Charles, it's only in future years that the Irish hatred of the English dissipates a bit."

"Of course," said Charles. "But your mum and I get on just fine, especially since I speak Irish."

"Indeed, you do!" said Aoife. "Shall we proceed then?"

Aoife said a few words in Irish to her mother, and Roisin approached the Time Cradle on the right side of the chamber. The older woman got onto the bed and reclined into it. Dani and Charles took her hand and wrist.

"Until we meet again!" said Aoife.

The light increased in intensity, and off they went.

Dani woke holding the hand of a young Roisin in the year 1850. Charles was there as well, and he spoke in Irish to Roisin, then walked over to an older woman and shook her hand.

"Dani, meet Ciara," said Charles. "She's Roisin's mother. Her name is spelled C-i-a-r-a, but pronounced Kee-ra, in case you're interested. Another one of those tricky Irish names."

Dani moved over to the other side of the chamber and shook Ciara's hand. Dani noticed that both women were dressed in a similar way to herself. Ciara, was short and stocky, like Roisin, but her hair was black, not red. She supposed that Ciara had coupled with a man with red hair to produce Roisin, but she couldn't be sure. They were both quite gaunt with thin, bony faces and bulging eyes. As Dani pieced things together in her mind, she realized that 1850 was during the Great Potato Famine, which killed more than a million Irish people and caused over 2 million more to leave the country. Charles tapped her on the shoulder.

"It's time for us to go," he said. "This will be Ciara's first time sending someone back because we've never needed to go further than this. But Roisin has taught her what to do." Then Charles spoke in Irish to Ciara, and she got into the Time Cradle and reclined.

"This trip will be a little different than the others," Charles continued. "We can be very precise in our arrival time when our arrival place is the Time Station itself. That's because the Station controls the timing for those trips. It still needs an old and a young Time Link to be present in the Station at both ends of the time segment, but it doesn't need them to visualize the arrival time and place. But when our arrival is somewhere out in the world, it's up to the Time Link to visualize a moment they remember vividly. The Time Station picks up this memory and tries its best to put us there. It usually works out just fine."

"That doesn't sound very reassuring," said Dani.

"Well, as I said, it usually works. But this being Ciara's first time, we'll just have to hope she gets it right. I've told her to visualize a moment she remembers *extremely* well, back when she was around 16 years old. She's 65 right now, so that would put us only back to 1801, but it's a start."

"Do you have any idea what situation she's sending us to?" asked Dani, wondering why she didn't already know the answer to her own question. "Has she conveyed the memory to you, to give us a feel for where we're going?"

"Actually, she has not," said Charles. "She seems to be reluctant to do so."

"Isn't it important?" asked Dani. "And perhaps even more important is why don't either of us already know the answer?"

"For me, the explanation is simple," Charles answered. "I have no older Time Link feeding me the answers before they happen. I just go back in time and try to accomplish my objectives the best I can. But I *can* tell you this: You may be experiencing something all of us Travelers experience. We find that when we get well away from our natural time, around 100 years or more, we tend to lose some of the subtle details that we once remembered. We call it Time Fatigue. I myself carry a detailed written instruction sheet that describes my mission objectives in case I can't remember something as I go back in time. *Your* failure to remember the situation we're about to enter must mean that you are Time Fatigued, too."

"Well, *that* would have been good to know before we came," said Dani. "But anyway, what about Ciara, here. Isn't it important that she tells us the situation she's sending us to?"

"Look, Dani, can't you see she's terrified of me already? You might have better luck with her if you spoke her language, but you don't. And it's not critical anyway. You had no idea where you were going when you went to Pelekas in 1978, did you? And that all worked out." Charles raised his eyebrows, taunting her with his knowledge of her personal life with Aideen.

"How do you know that?" she asked.

"Time Links are required to provide full disclosure of any trips they initiate on their own that are not part of official mission plans."

"Oh, yes," said Dani. "Aideen mentioned that. But, getting back to Ciara, she's been briefed on the knowledge dump she'll experience, right?"

"Oh yes, she certainly has," said Charles, his tone impatient. "Well, can we get on with this, please?"

The two approached the Time Cradle and grasped Ciara's hand and wrist. Charles spoke to her in Irish, presumably reminding her to visualize her memory as accurately as possible, and when she was ready, to squeeze the control handle with her free hand. It didn't take long for Ciara to proceed. As the light increased in intensity, Dani noticed a look of sheer terror come onto Ciara's face. And that's when she knew: Something about where they were going was very wrong indeed.

Chapter 29

Dani regained consciousness and felt her hand still in Ciara's hand, but it was 16-year-old Ciara, circa 1801. The problem was that young Ciara was screaming. Dani opened her eyes and found herself on her back, lying on a large, uncomfortable bed. Directly beside her was Ciara, who was lying facedown on the bed, her skirts pulled up over her head. A man with red hair was on top of her, raping her with abandon. The man's trousers were pulled down to his ankles, but he still had all his clothes on, including his shoes. On the other side of the bed, she saw Charles, lying facedown with his arm caught between the furiously humping man and the backside of poor Ciara, his hand still grasping the girl's wrist.

Dani could smell the red-haired man. He stunk of sweat and whiskey and was in such a frenzied stupor that he didn't seem to realize he had two new bedmates. He continued pumping away for all he was worth, then gasped as he climaxed, while Ciara continued to scream. At that point, Charles released his grip on Ciara's wrist, yanked his arm free, rose up in the bed, and slammed his fist directly into the man's head. The force of the blow knocked the man into Dani, which threw her off the bed. She landed in a heap but rolled to her feet, uninjured.

Dani would never forget the next thing she witnessed. Charles pulled some kind of device from his pocket that looked like a metal cigar. He pointed the device toward the man's head, and the man immediately fell limp. Charles then rolled the man off the bed, the inert body hitting the floor with a thump, right in front of Dani. She didn't know if he was dead or not, but she would find out later, after she tended to Ciara. She stepped back up to the bed and helped the girl arrange her skirts and sit up in the bed. She sat down beside her and put her arms around her, then spoke to Charles, who had stepped off the bed and was standing idly by, no emotion whatsoever in his expression.

"Charles," said Dani. "Please tell Ciara that I will help her get through this."

Charles spoke to the girl in Irish. Ciara nodded meekly and leaned into Dani a little. Dani held onto her tightly, then glanced down at the man on the floor, who still hadn't moved.

"Is he dead?" she asked, horrified by the whole scene.

"As the proverbial doornail," said Charles, placing the cigar-shaped device back in his pocket.

"Was that necessary, Charles?" asked Dani, still in shock from all of the vulgarity and violence she'd just witnessed. "Doesn't that thing have a stun setting or something?"

"It does," said Charles, who seemed completely at ease, in spite of what had just happened and what he'd just done. "But I told you, I'm not trained in the fineries of recruiting Time Links."

"And you also said that everything would be fine!" yelled Dani. "But things are not fine, are they, Charles?"

"They could be better. I'll give you that."

Charles then began speaking to Ciara in Irish, but Dani cut him off.

"Charles, for goodness sake, give her a little time!" yelled Dani. "She was just raped."

"And by her father, no doubt," said Charles. "And she might also have lost her mother, who you see is lying over there near the hearth."

Dani glanced across the room and saw a woman lying facedown on the floor.

"Go and check the woman, Charles! Make yourself useful, please!"

Charles crossed the room and checked the woman's neck for a pulse. He looked up at Dani.

"Dead as a …"

"Don't say it!"

With that, Charles went silent. Dani sat there shaking her head, wondering just what kind of person Charles Burke really was, fearful now for her own safety. But she wasn't going to back down from him. He seemed to respond to her aggressive demeanor, so she continued on with it, issuing another order.

"Come over here and translate to young Ciara for me, please," she said, with authority.

Charles returned to the bedside, and Dani continued.

"Tell her everything will be okay," said Dani.

Charles spoke to the woman in Irish. After a moment, the girl responded. Charles translated to Dani.

"She says she knows that," said Charles. "She said she knows the future now, just like we told her older self she would."

"Good," said Dani. "Now ask her if that man you just killed was her father."

"I can tell you, Dani. He is."

"Just ask her!"

Charles spoke in Irish, the girl gave a quick nod, and the incest was confirmed.

"And the woman?" asked Dani. "Her mother?" Dani motioned her head toward the girl, indicating that Charles should ask the question, which he did. Another nod from the girl, who was still gasping for breath between sobs.

"What was that thing you used to kill that man, Charles?" she asked.

"It's a device that immediately stops all brain activity. It's the most painless way to die in the history of humankind."

"Congratulations," said Dani, shaking her head in disgust. "So, how are we going to handle this mess?"

"I was hoping you could tell me that," said Charles. "You have no memory of what we did to solve this problem?"

"None," said Dani. "I'm 221 years back from my natural time. I remember nothing other than the first 24 years of my natural life, and frankly, I'm struggling to remember that, too. What are we going to do?"

"First of all," said Charles. "This kind of thing was quite common in these times, as I'm sure you know from your studies. The problem is not the dead mother. It's the dead father. The authorities, if there *are* any, may very well place the blame on young Ciara, here."

"Ask her what happens," said Dani. "She's the only one of us who has any knowledge of the future at this moment."

Charles spoke in Irish to the young woman, who was now sitting up, having thrown her legs over the edge of the bed. The girl spoke and carried on for quite a moment.

"She says her father was the most hated man in town and that everyone will be happy he's dead. She says we should take her to her grandmother's cottage and request that her grandmother become a Time Link. She says her grandmother will do it, especially if they give her money, as they gave her older self."

"Is the grandfather still alive?" asked Dani.

Charles spoke Irish to the girl.

"She says he's alive, but he's a drunken fool and will be dead soon. She says he won't get in the way."

"Okay," said Dani. "Tell her to pack up her things, and we'll take her to her grandmother's cottage."

"Of course," said Charles. "You see. I told you things would be just fine."

"Except that you just murdered a man!" said Dani.

"I never said these things are smooth as silk, Dani. And the man was a scoundrel. Most hated man in town!"

"Okay, Charles, whatever you say. You have to live with it, not me."

Charles's demeanor suddenly changed from apologetic to defiant.

"Dani, I know for certain that Aideen warned you of how serious our purpose is," he said, his brown eyes boring into hers. "And from time to time, things like this *do* happen. But I make no apologies about my commitment to, and my belief in, human life. That's why I'm here."

Chapter 30

"**D**oes Ciara have any siblings?" Dani asked.

Charles asked Ciara the question, and she nodded, telling Charles something, then breaking into tears.

"She has three older brothers, but they've all left the village to go fight in the rebellion against England. I just remembered that 1801 was the year that Ireland was made an official part of the United Kingdom by the Acts of Union. They didn't regain their independence until 1922. Anyway, Ciara knows from the knowledge transfer from her older self that all three of her brothers were killed in the Second Irish Rebellion, in 1803, when they joined up with Robert Emmet to charge Dublin Castle."

"I'm sorry to hear that," said Dani. "Her life has been hard enough already."

"Not to be insensitive, but it *does* simplify things for us," said Charles.

"Yes," said Dani, sarcasm in her voice. "No father, no mother, no siblings. How wonderful."

They had gathered at Ciara's grandmother's cottage, not far from her parents' one-room hovel. The grandmother's name was Orla. She was short with gray hair, but a look in her eyes that said she was not to be trifled with, a look of a wise person with a sharp mind. The grandfather was nowhere to be found, although it was assumed he was drinking himself under the table at the local pub.

"I'm really very hungry, Charles," said Dani. "Aren't you? We've been moving fast, but it must have been at least 12 hours since we left, right?"

"Only six hours," said Charles. "But time travel is hard work. Tends to make one hungry."

Charles reached into his pocket, pulled out a tiny case, opened it, and handed Dani a pill.

"Swallow this," said Charles.

"What is it?" asked Dani.

"It's an immunity pill," he responded. "Will allow you to eat and drink whatever you want. And believe me, you'll need it. I don't think we'll be dining at the Ritz anytime soon."

"Does it have any side effects?" asked Dani. "And how long does it last?"

"No side effects," said Charles. "And it lasts for the rest of your life. It will make a permanent adjustment to your immune system that will be so strong and enduring that you could swallow poison and hardly feel it. It will also substantially extend your lifespan. And although you don't look like a person who will struggle with weight gain as you age, the pill has the added benefit of making a permanent adjustment to your metabolism. No matter what you eat, your body will metabolize it and dispose of it with no weight gain. In my time, there are very few obese people—only the ones who choose to be."

"Well, thank you, Charles. Can I have another one of those for Aideen?"

"Here," said Charles. "Take two. You never know when you might want to help someone out of a tough bind."

"Thank you, Dr. Magnanimous," said Dani.

Charles looked offended.

"Just kidding," she recanted. "I sincerely appreciate it."

After they had explained to Orla what had happened at Ciara's cottage, Orla went to the town constable and conveyed the information to him, lying about some of it. She claimed that Ciara had returned home to find both her parents dead and certain valuables missing from the home. The constable said he would arrange to have the bodies removed and prepared for burial. He made no comment about any kind of an investigation, so Orla had left and returned home, where Dani, Charles, and Ciara were waiting.

It had been dark the entire time they'd been in 1801, so they didn't know exactly where they were. Further inquiries indicated they were actually on the mainland side of the channel, in the village of Claddaghduff. Dani recognized the name because the car park where she'd met Aideen for the first time in 2022 was within the town limits of Claddaghduff.

Orla served them a meal of fish stew, bread, and ale. While they ate, Charles conveyed the responsibilities of Time Link 1 for Team 8, and Orla, though wide-eyed, nodded her head calmly at the two people from the future, most likely believing them to be the devil and his assistant. But Charles produced a sack of Irish coins from his coat pockets—which Dani was beginning to perceive as very large pockets indeed—and the money had the right dates on it and seemed to work the magic with Orla. She was all in. And with that, Charles saw no reason to wait around.

After midnight, the four of them walked down to the channel, staying as quiet as possible, with Charles lighting the way with a thumb-sized flashlight from 2253 that the two women must have considered to be serious magic. The tide was out far enough for them to walk into the channel and locate the Time Station. Along the way, Ciara spoke to Orla in Irish, apparently briefing her on all that was about to transpire. Charles was listening, and every now and then he would add something to the conversation. Even though Dani understood very little of what was being said, it was clear that Orla was receiving a crash course in time travel so that she and Charles could move on without delay.

It had been determined that Orla was 62 years old, which was about 20 years more than the average life expectancy in Ireland at the time, so the luck of this find was beyond doubt. Ciara had confirmed that her grandmother would live another three years, and while this would not be desirable to keep the Time Chain viable for long, it was enough for the purposes of Charles and Dani.

When they got into the Time Station, after giving Orla some time to settle down, Charles informed Dani that in order to make the longest jump possible, he was going to ask Orla to attempt to bring them back to the time when she was 12 years old. This would make it a 50-year jump and bring them to the year 1751. Dani insisted that Charles make clear to Orla that her memory from when she was 12, while distinct, should not be a tragic one. This caused the woman to fret, and she explained that she had no memory of any good times whatsoever from her entire life. Charles, seemingly unconcerned as to whether or not the memory was good or bad, encouraged the old woman to remember anything she could from the time when she was 12 years old that might have been of particular significance to her. Dani was surprised to see the old woman nod almost immediately after Charles made the suggestion.

"Ask her what it is she remembers," Dani demanded.

Charles spoke in Irish, and Orla responded.

"It was her father being hanged," said Charles. "That could be helpful! We won't have to worry about him getting in on our secret!"

"My God, Charles, you are an insensitive bastard," said Dani, shaking her head once again at the man's total lack of empathy.

"I'm sorry," said Charles, sounding sincere. "I *do* realize how it appears. I'm just so desperate to help the people of my time that sometimes I lose my bearings."

"All right, Charles," said Dani. "But remember, *these* are people, too. That's why we're doing this, right? To find the most human of humans. Someone who can evoke the empathy of people in my time."

"You're right, of course," said Charles. "Do you have any more questions to ask Ciara or Orla before we do this? I'll have to ask Ciara to leave the chamber before Orla initiates the jump."

"I suppose not," said Dani. "We'll find out more when we get there."

Chapter 31

Dani regained consciousness, holding 12-year-old Orla's hand in the year 1751. Charles was holding the girl's wrist but let go immediately. Dani held on. They were standing in a square in the middle of a crowd of several hundred people in front of a gallows. The gallows was constructed of wood with a stairway that led up to a platform. There was a trap door in the floor, which would be released when the time to hang the prisoner arrived. A noose hung from a structure constructed on top of the platform.

A man with his hands tied behind his back looked out at the crowd. He had dark hair, appeared to be in his thirties, and was very likely Orla's father. Another man stood beside him, presumably the man who would perform the hanging. The hangman wore no uniform, just the same type of breeches, stockings, and heavy coat that all the other men in the crowd were wearing, including Charles. Dani gazed out at the channel and saw Omey Island, concluding that they were still on the mainland, most likely in Claddaghduff.

The hangman yelled something out at the crowd, and all the people fell silent. The prisoner was being given the chance to make a speech. His last words. The prisoner stepped forward and addressed the crowd, speaking loudly and clearly, but not for long.

"What did he say?" Dani quietly asked Charles.

"Frankly, I'm having trouble understanding his Irish. Seems we're getting far enough back in time that modern Irish is no longer the norm. I'm not trained in early modern Irish."

"Then ask the girl!" Dani hissed.

Charles spoke quietly to Orla, and she whispered something back.

"Her father said he felt it unjust that a man should be hanged for the simple crime of theft, especially when he had returned the goods to their rightful owner."

"What did he steal?" asked Dani.

Charles spoke to the girl and got a quick response.

"A plow. She says he wasn't stealing it, only borrowing it."

"My god," said Dani. "This is … well, it's …"

"Primitive," said Charles. "People don't realize how awful a world it was not so very long ago. This is all part of what's known as the *Bloody Code*, a harsh set of laws out of England that were carried over to Ireland when the English conquered them. People are executed for all sorts of petty crimes during these times."

The crowd went silent again as the prisoner stepped onto the trap door. The hangman placed the noose around his neck and cinched it tight. He stepped back, and without hesitation he pulled a lever that released the trap door. The prisoner plunged down, his fall abruptly brought to an end by the noose around his neck. He now dangled below the platform. His eyes were bulging, but he clearly wasn't dead. He kicked his legs and squirmed in a futile effort to free himself. Charles leaned over toward Dani.

"Seems the neck was not properly broken," he said. "Happened more often than people know."

Dani slowly shook her head back and forth, clearly frustrated again at Charles's insensitive attitude. He was like a child watching a movie and didn't believe it was truly real. The thought crossed her mind that this very attitude was likely the prevailing cause of where his people ended up—in computers. They were no longer able to distinguish between what was real and what was not real, and this enabled them to choose to become data in a box rather than people in physical, living bodies.

Dani was still holding poor Orla's hand and felt the shakes of the girl's sobs. She squeezed the girl's hand tightly and led her away from the square, not wanting her to witness her father slowly strangling to death. Charles followed closely behind them, speaking to the girl, then reporting to Dani.

"Her home is not far from here," said Charles. "I told her to take us there."

"Ask her who lives there," said Dani. "We need to know what we're walking into."

Charles spoke to the girl and received a response.

"Just her mother," said Charles.

"Why didn't her mother come with her?" asked Dani.

"The woman very likely didn't have the intestinal fortitude of young Orla here. We'll find out more when we get there."

"No siblings?" asked Dani.

"She said she had a younger brother and sister who both died during the Irish Famine."

"You must be happy about that," said Dani, facetiously.

"I'm not happy about any of this, Dani!" Charles retorted. "Please, let's try to remain civil with each other as we go through this process. Can we do that?"

"I suppose we can," said Dani. "As long as you don't kill any more people!"

"I know it might sound odd, coming from me, but I can't predict the future, Dani, at least not from one moment to the next in this ancient time. You should remember that I'm 502 years back from my natural time. It's true that I've studied the history of these eras, but it's a different thing all together to actually *be* here."

"That's one thing we *can* agree on," said Dani. "Now let's go meet Orla's mother."

Chapter 32

Orla's mother was named Shauna. She was about 25 years old, short and stocky like her daughter, with dark hair, also like her daughter. The cottage was located around a half mile out of town, and the three had trudged through muddy streets to get there. There was no need to remove their dirty shoes upon entering because the floor of the one-room cottage was dirt as well. There was a small tract of land out back where a few vegetables seemed to be growing, but very few. The mother and daughter exchanged a few words, then both broke down into tears, hugging each other tightly. Charles decided that now was the time for a history lesson.

"The Irish Famine of the 1740s resulted from a decimated grain crop all across Ireland," he said. "The potato was not yet the staple of Irish food. That came later. The more famous Great Famine of 1845 to 1852 was due to the loss of the potato crop from a pathogen that affected the plant. But in the famine of the 1740s, the livestock suffered with no grain, so there was a milk shortage as well. Disease became rampant, and the Irish lost 20 percent of their population, a greater death toll percentage even than the more famous Great Famine of 100 years later."

"Are you done?" asked Dani, her eyes wide with anger.

Charles looked taken aback.

"I suppose so," he said, defensively. "Just trying to add some context is all I'm doing."

"Charles, I'm a PhD candidate, writing her dissertation on the old Irish of the Wild Atlantic Way. Don't you think I would know *all* of the history you feel so compelled to lecture me about?"

"Well, uh, yes, of course. Forgive me. I'll refrain from such extrapolations from this point forward."

"Good, thank you. Now, can we gather some details on Shauna?"

"The problem is, I'm not able to understand what she's saying, and very likely she can't understand me either."

"Then ask Orla to ask her the questions!" said Dani, frustrated at Charles's lack of common sense.

Charles spoke to Orla, then came back to Dani.

"She says she doesn't need to ask her mother any questions. She knows the whole story and will tell it to us."

"Okay, great," said Dani.

Orla began speaking. Before Charles translated, Dani listened to the tenor of the little girl's voice as she recited the trials and tribulations of her family, in Irish. The girl's voice was melodic, captivating actually, and Dani knew then that *this* was the little girl who would go with her to 2022.

Charles's translation of Orla's speech followed. Shauna thought she was 26 years old, but she wasn't certain because she couldn't count. She had married her husband, a man named John Kelly, when she was 14 and already pregnant with Orla. A year after Orla's birth, she bore a son, whom they named John, and two years after that, another daughter, whom they named Clodagh. When Orla was five years old, little John was four, and Clodagh two, the crops had long since failed, dying from some mysterious disease. The cow was also long gone, so there was no milk, and the family was starving. Her husband, John senior, could find no work, so he stole food at night from the few fields that were growing in the area and from anywhere else he could find it. But then little John caught an illness and died, and Clodagh lasted only a few weeks before succumbing to the same illness. Orla seemed impervious to the disease, and at the age of five, she began begging in the streets for food. Somehow Orla and her parents survived. When the famine was over, John tried to get his fields going again, but he was found to have stolen the plow he was using to till the fields.

After hearing this story, Dani was more convinced than ever that Orla should return with her to 2022, and she vowed to find a way to make that happen.

"Charles, is there a way for us to take young Orla forward with us?" she asked.

"Would be easier to take older Orla," he said.

"But older Orla doesn't bring the empathy of this sweet child," said Dani. "And yet, we have older Orla here as well, don't we, in the little girl's mind."

"We do," said Charles. "Let me think."

While Charles was thinking, Shauna asked Orla a question. The child then spoke to Charles.

"What is she asking?" asked Dani.

"The mother is asking for us to please remove the demon from her child's mind that is telling her the future."

Chapter 33

"I know how we're going to do this," said Charles.

Charles, Dani, Orla, and Shauna were sitting in uncomfortable wooden chairs around a rectangular wooden table, eating fish stew and bread that had been prepared by Shauna and Orla. Dani found the stew to be surprisingly good. The fish was obviously fresh, and the potatoes were tender. It wasn't clear what the stock was, but it definitely had a lot of salt in it and made her thirsty. Reluctantly, she drank the yellow water from the ceramic cup she'd been given.

Charles had lied to Shauna, assuring her that the demon in her child would be removed, even though Orla's knowledge of the future was never going away. Next Charles spoke to Dani in English because neither the girl nor her mother could understand it, although they wouldn't have understood the information he was conveying to Dani even if it was spoken in their language.

"The fact of the matter is, the plan is risky, no matter how well conceived it might be," he said.

"How so?" asked Dani.

"Because neither of us can be here to execute it."

"Why?"

"First, I've got to return to my time so I can announce the new mission to the Time Links who will be involved."

"You can't do that from here? You revised Mission 187 when we were in 2022, didn't you?"

"Actually, no, I didn't do it that way," said Charles. "The expanded scope of the mission had been prearranged. I told the staff in 2253 to broadcast the revised mission exactly 12 hours after my arrival. The assumption was that both you and Aideen would agree to the plan and move forward with us."

"A big assumption," said Dani.

"Not in my mind," said Charles. "Aideen has always been a loyal supporter of the cause. And she's an adventurous sort, but she's never traveled forward in time. No Time Link has, at least not through the Time Station. All of us move forward chronologically, but I'm talking about the leaps that the Time Station facilitates. We knew Aideen would be keen to be one of the first to actually see the future with her own eyes, rather than through the memories of her older self."

"Why have Time Links been restricted from jumping forward?" asked Dani. "Are you hiding something, Charles?"

"Not at all, Dani," Charles responded, curtly. "The missions have all been backward movements to date because we've been solely focused on research—research that has enabled us to formulate the plan. Now we are in the execution phase of the plan, and certain people will be authorized to move forward in time as part of future missions. Orla, for example. I am trying to convey that plan to you right now, if you would only let me get to it!"

Charles was obviously frustrated with Dani's questions about the restrictions, but she didn't care. She was beginning to suspect that he hadn't been completely honest about the situation in the future, and she no longer trusted him. A man who could murder outside of the constructs of both written and moral laws, with no emotion, was not to be trusted. But right now, she needed him.

She told herself two things. First, if she walked away at that very moment, literally walked away and tried to get back to 2022, Charles would hunt her down and kill her. She sincerely believed that. And second, she'd been sucked in by the promise of fame. She was disappointed in herself, but she knew it was true. She wanted to do this. So, she backed down and encouraged Charles to proceed.

"I'm sorry, Charles," she said. "I didn't mean to get off track."

"I was speaking of risk," he said. "The fact that neither of us can be present during the execution of the plan to bring Orla back to 2022."

Dani thought about this. She realized that Time Links would be needed to move Orla forward in time, and that right now, the most senior Time Links were all lying on the Time Cradles in suspended animation because they had sent both Charles and Dani back in time. In order to free them up, both Charles and Dani would have to abandon Mission 187 and return to their natural times.

"I figured it out," she said. "You and I need to get back to our natural times to free up the Time Links for Orla's forward jumps. But even knowing that, I still don't fully understand how we're going to pull this off."

"I'll explain," said Charles. "The first thing we have to do is recruit a Time Link here in 1751 who can send Orla forward—as far forward as possible. It doesn't have to be all the way to 1801, just somewhere in the vicinity. We would want to find a recruit here in 1751 who we know is going to live a long life."

"And we can try to find that out from Orla," said Dani. "She knows the future up until she's 62 years old, right?"

"That's correct," said Charles. "And before I put the details of the mission in place, we'll need to know who that person is and how long they live."

Chapter 34

Charles spent some time explaining to Orla what they needed to do. Orla was already a Time Link, so it wasn't difficult to get her to understand they needed another one. Charles told her they needed someone she'd known, or known *of*, her entire life: someone who was still alive in the early 1800s, as she was. Orla explained to Charles that in 1801, she was the oldest person in Claddaghduff. Charles asked if she knew of someone in a nearby village who had lived a long life like her. Orla thought about it, and nodded her head, then told Charles. Charles made his report to Dani.

"There's an old man living on Omey Island. She says that in 1801, he was reputed to be 66 years old."

"I thought you didn't use men as Time Links, Charles," said Dani.

"We don't, but this is a unique situation. We only need this person for this one assignment."

"True, but what about the knowledge he'll have about the project and the location of the Time Station?"

"We can get around telling him anything about the project. People this far back don't really understand what we're talking about anyway. To them, we're some kind of spirits, or the devil, or whatever, and while they don't like that, they *do* like the money we give them."

"But he'll know where the Station is, won't he?" asked Dani.

"He doesn't have to. We could blindfold him."

"So, take him by force?"

"Not necessarily," said Charles. "If he's four years older than Orla, that would make him 16 years old right now. And even though we're a long way back in time, I think we can depend on the fact that the young man's hormones are quite active, if you know what I mean."

Dani shook her head, disappointed, appalled actually, that Charles would stoop so low.

"Yes, I know what you mean, Charles," she said. "So, you want a 12-year-old girl to lure this young man to the Station with a promise of what? Sex?"

"Have you had a good look at young Orla?" asked Charles. "She's obviously gone through puberty, and she has a pretty face."

"Not happening. Let's move on. I refuse to participate in this charade."

"Very well then," said Charles. "Money it is. At least that's Plan A."

The next afternoon, Charles, Dani, and Orla crossed over the channel at low tide. The weather was brisk, and Dani wrapped her shawl tightly around herself. She was stunned by how many people were living on the island in 1751. She saw dozens and dozens of cottages along the water and on up the rise toward Fahy Lough. She estimated the population of the island to be at least 400 people.

A small area on the island had a few shops and a pub. Charles instructed Orla to begin asking around about the boy, whose name was Liam Murphy. A man outside the pub told her that Liam worked on a fishing boat that normally docked around four in the afternoon, after which the crew went to the pub. Orla asked the man what time it was, and the man extracted a watch from his pocket and told her it was half past three. Dani assumed the man was well off, from his clothing, which was more of a suit than it was anything else, which would explain why he owned a watch. She suspected he was either a local businessman, one of the town leaders, or both.

The three stood and waited by the pub, and soon after that, the area began to bustle as the fisherman came in to shore and went to town. The men were young and old, and they were not going to be delayed by speaking to a group of strangers when thirsting for their first ale of the day. Charles announced that they would have to go into the pub to find Liam. Dani reminded Charles that women were not allowed to enter pubs in Ireland until around 1920, so she and Orla would have to wait outside while Charles attempted to find and extract Liam. Charles said that his struggles with early modern Irish were going to limit him, but he had another sack of coins in his coat pocket that might help him get the job done. Charles went into the bar.

After what seemed like an interminable wait, Charles eventually came out of the bar, his arm around the shoulders of a strapping young man with dark hair and a muscular physique, presumably Liam Murphy. As they approached the two women, Charles pointed at Orla, who he'd asked to wear her Sunday best, even though it was a Wednesday. Charles spoke in Irish to Orla, who was now blushing, but managed to extend her hand to shake Liam's. A smile on his face, Liam pulled Orla's hand to his mouth and kissed it with reverence.

Dani began to wonder if Charles had been right all along. *I should have known*, she thought. After her own experiences in Irish pubs, she had to admit she wasn't surprised. She was also aware that until a law was passed in 1972, raising the legal age of marriage in Ireland to 16, girls could legally marry from the age of

12, and boys from 14. So, while hard to stomach, she was looking at a girl and a boy who were each of legal age to marry.

Within seconds, Orla and Liam ran out of things to say to one another, so Charles stepped in. He told Orla to suggest to Liam that he come to her home with them right now to have dinner and meet her mother. Dani gathered that the boy was not yet aware that Orla was the daughter of the man who'd been hanged yesterday in Claddaghduff because he readily accepted and seemed eager to move the courtship forward. If he'd known she was the daughter of a convicted thief, he very likely would have declined the invitation.

The four of them crossed back over the channel, the boy apparently unconcerned that if he stayed too long at dinner, the tide would come in and complicate his journey back to Omey Island. But if she knew Charles, Liam would very likely be accompanying them to the Time Station that evening, and not returning home for some time. Charles was a lot of things, but a dilly-dallier wasn't one of them.

When they arrived back at Orla's cottage, the sun was beginning to set. They entered to the smell of food cooking, and it didn't take long for Dani to ascertain that fish stew was on the menu once again. Introductions were made, and Shauna, who Charles had briefed through Orla about the possibility of this visit, seemed well prepared and relatively at ease.

They all sat down at the wooden table and ate. Dani found the fish stew to be less tasty than the night before, rather fishier, and she concluded that yesterday's fish stew was now today's fish stew, and the absence of refrigeration had taken its toll. Throughout the meal, Shauna continued to refill the boy's mug with ale she had purchased that day with money from Charles. Dani assumed this was also part of Charles's instructions to Shauna.

Charles wasted no time and began to weave the story, through Orla, of what they really wanted of him. Dani had no idea what was being said, but as she watched Liam's expressions, she could easily ascertain how Charles was handling this. When the boy raised his eyebrows, she knew he was being told something about the mission. When he turned toward Orla and smiled a sly smile, she could tell that Charles was making promises to the young man of rewards beyond mere money.

The night wore on, and the ale continued to flow. Liam was thoroughly drunk and seemed barely able to keep his eyes open. Dani felt she should check in with Charles as to what he had in mind as a next step. She got up from her seat and pulled Charles away from the table. She spoke to him quietly, but seriously.

"The boy is about to pass out," she said. "Is that part of the plan?"

"Well, perhaps we didn't time it perfectly because we still have around four hours remaining until the next tide allows us to access the Station. The good news is that we have the boy in our possession and simply need a way to get him from point A, this cottage, to point B, the Time Station, at the appropriate time. I'll give him something that will keep him out for a good 12 hours."

Charles reached in his pocket and extracted his pill case, took out a small pill, then stepped back over to the table and dropped it discretely into Liam's cup of ale. The boy didn't even notice. Charles returned to continue the conversation with Dani.

"What was that?" asked Dani.

"A pill to make him sleep," said Charles.

"As drunk as he is, he probably doesn't need it!"

"He very well may not," said Charles. "But better safe than sorry."

"But he's agreed to be a Time Link?" asked Dani.

"Well, uh, you see …"

"Charles, what have you done?"

"Now, Dani, we've only known each other for a few days, but it's obvious to me that you're a person of the highest moral standing. I, on the other hand, as I'm sure you've figured out … am not."

"You didn't tell him?!" she snapped.

"I've told him … some general things," said Charles.

"Such as?" asked Dani.

"Such as, he's going to be rich, and Orla is in love with him. Things like that."

"So, he actually knows nothing, then. Is that it?"

"Yes."

"How are we going to get him to the Station?" she asked. "We can't carry him! He's a massive young man."

"We'll have to improvise," said Charles.

Chapter 35

After another half hour and one more mug of ale, Liam passed out, his head and torso falling forward and coming to a rest on the wooden table. Charles then briefed Dani on the plan they would need to follow.

"Shauna says they own a cart that they once used to haul goods to and from the market. The only problem is they no longer own any livestock to pull the cart. That means the three of us will have to pull it out to the Time Station with Liam Murphy, the passenger."

"But there are four of us, including Shauna," said Dani.

"Shauna cannot know where the Time Station is. I've told her she must remain safely inside the cottage, or she'll risk being infected by the same demon that has infected her daughter."

"There's some truth in that," said Dani, laughing. "You being the demon, of course."

Charles frowned.

"Can we stay on task here, Dani? We must get this right."

"Fine," said Dani. "Well, it'll be the middle of the night, at least. But what about you and me? I thought we needed to be gone for this thing to work."

"We do," said Charles. "But if we can get Liam into the Station and secure him to a Time Cradle, we can leave at that time. Orla will know what to do after that. I'll only need a few minutes to post the new mission. And because *this* mission is still in process, all the Time Links we need are either in the Station already or nearby."

"Okay, so let's go over the Time Chain you'll be setting up," said Dani. "Just so I know who's doing what?"

"Very well," said Charles. "Liam will send Orla to the pub on Omey Island in the year 1801. Orla said that Liam was known far and wide to have never missed a night at the pub for his entire life. Even at the age of 66, he could be found there every night."

"But young Liam doesn't know he'll be in the pub 50 years from now!" said Dani, confused.

"Quite true," said Charles. "But there are things about the Station you don't know, Dani. I can access numerous controls embedded in the walls, and I believe I can manually program a time and a location as long as it's near the Station for young Liam to connect to older Liam."

"Have you ever done this before, Charles?"

"Well, uh, no. But I've been trained to do it in the event of an emergency."

"Okay, more risk. I hope for the sake of this poor girl that you get it right."

"As do I," said Charles. "Now, please, let's keep moving. We still have some things to go over. You wanted to know the details of the Time Chain. So, assuming Orla makes it to the pub on May 23, 1801, she will then run out of the pub, where she's not allowed to be anyway, make her way to the station, and waiting for her there will be young Ciara, her granddaughter. The Time Mission plan will direct older Orla, who also exists in 1801, to be somewhere other than the Station. It wouldn't ruin things if older Orla was there, but to avoid any unnecessary emotional complications, we'll just make sure older Orla isn't there at the time."

"Good move," said Dani.

"Young Ciara will send young Orla to older Ciara in 1850, who will be in the station and simply has to pass her over to young Roisin, who will send her to older Roisin in 1902. Older Roisin hands her over to young Aoife, who sends her to older Aoife in 1972. Older Aoife hands her over to young Aideen, who sends her to older Aideen in 2022."

"And where will I be in 2022?" asked Dani.

"In the Station, of course. Moments before Orla arrives, you will have returned to older Aideen yourself, in the Station, which is where you started. And it's the right place for you to be because older Aideen will need your help with the child."

"Of course, we'll care for the child for as long as necessary," said Dani.

"Yes," said Charles.

"And how long will that be?" asked Dani

"Until you finish your dissertation."

"And then what? How will she be sent back?"

"We'll want her on stage with you during the press conference when you announce what you have done. That's when her time in 2022 will come to an end. She will disappear in front of everyone's eyes."

Chapter 36

At 2 am, Charles, Dani, and Orla loaded the still-incapacitated Liam onto the old wooden cart. Shauna remained inside her home, terrified that the demon that had possessed her daughter would take hold of her if she set one foot outside. Charles and Dani each grabbed one of the two wooden struts at the front of the cart, which were intended to hold a horse in place, or in cases like this, when there was no horse, enabled *people* to drag the cart. Orla went to the rear of the cart and pushed, also keeping an eye out to make sure that the inert Liam didn't roll off during their transit.

Once they got the cart moving, the exertion required was reduced, unless they came upon a mud puddle in the road, of which there were several. All of them were covered in mud up to above the ankles, and Dani felt the goo sliding down into her uncomfortable, heavy shoes, making the trip even more miserable for her.

The village was quiet, with no lamps burning inside of the homes. Even the lamps in the local pub were out. The trio labored forward until they came to the sandy ramp that would take them to the floor of the channel. They made it down the gentle slope and headed in a diagonal direction toward the large rock a few hundred meters away that would help them find the Station. After several more laborious minutes, the exhausted haulers came to a stop around 10 meters from the large rock. They took a brief rest, then gathered around Liam, who was still asleep and snoring loudly.

Charles reached for the rope they'd brought with them, worked it around Liam's chest, then tied it securely. Then the three of them lifted the heavy body off the cart and dropped it as gently as they could onto the ground, laying Liam on his back. Charles and Dani each grabbed the young man under the shoulders and dragged him to the location where both of them knew the hatch was located. Charles turned to Orla and said something to her in Irish. Orla rushed over to the empty cart, snagged one of the handles, swiveled the cart around, then pulled it slowly away from their location toward the shore of Omey Island.

While Orla moved the cart away from the Station, Charles and Dani scraped away the sand to reveal the hatch. They opened it. Orla returned, panting from her exertions. Charles spoke to her in Irish, and she immediately entered the hatch and disappeared down the ladder. Dani and Charles then maneuvered Liam's body and placed his legs into the opening. They both stood and took hold of the rope, pulling it taut and raising Liam's upper half into a vertical position. Charles put one of his feet against Liam's back and pushed on it. The body began to slide into the hole.

Dani and Charles held the rope tightly, slowly lowering the body down into the first chamber. Orla had been instructed to keep any of Liam's extremities from becoming tangled on the rungs of the ladder, and while they couldn't see her, they assumed she was succeeding because the body went down and then came to a stop at the bottom, relieving the tension on the rope. Dani and Charles let go of the rope and went down the ladder one after the other.

Orla had managed to drag Liam's body away from the bottom

of the ladder to make it easier for the two of them to get down. Charles turned on his light so they could see, pointing it at the black stone wall they all knew so well. He gave the light to Orla and spoke to her in Irish, and she went to the wall and placed her hand on it, and the opening appeared. Dani and Charles got hold of Liam's shoulders again and dragged him down the tunnel, with Orla leading the way using Charles's light.

When Orla reached the wall at the end of the tunnel, she placed her hand on it, and the doorway appeared. She entered the chamber, which was already lit up. Charles and Dani dragged Liam into the room and over to one of the Time Cradles. Orla came over to them, and the three of them lifted Liam onto the cradle. Charles removed the rope from Liam and used it to secure him tightly to the cradle.

Chapter 37

"I've got to program the machine now," said Charles. "I'm going to try to get young Orla to the pub on Omey Island on May 23, 1801. She knows what to do if she gets that far."

"I hope she does, Charles," said Dani. "You don't want another dead body on your conscience."

Charles was not perturbed. "She'll be fine, Dani. Now please let me work!"

Charles turned to the wall of the chamber and pressed his hands against it, a foot or so below the large screen that showed the mission parameters. Suddenly, a small touchscreen appeared, displaying numbers and symbols that Dani could not decipher. Charles spent quite a bit of time tapping on the screen with his fingers, apparently inputting instructions. Dani noticed that the larger screen above, the one that displayed the current mission, did not change when Charles worked on the lower screen. Charles anticipated her question.

"Dani, the reason the mission screen isn't changing is because it's completely independent of the controls I'm operating now. As I said, the mission screen can only be changed from headquarters in 2253. This small touchscreen is for emergency use only, and it allows the initiation of a forced time jump. I've programmed it to connect young Liam's mind with the mind of older Liam in 1801. I believe it will work."

"Good, so now what?" she asked. "You're sure Orla can pull this off from here?"

"As sure as I *can* be," said Charles. "I've gone over it with her several times. Also, remember that she has the benefit of the experience of her older self, which is invaluable in a situation like this."

"Agreed," said Dani. "But I still haven't figured out how the two of us will get back to our natural times."

"Do you remember when Aideen left you standing in the car park and walked 300 meters into the channel and then you returned to 2022?"

"You saw that?" asked Dani, perturbed.

"We *planned* that," said Charles. "The Station also functions as a kind of worldwide radar. It can detect Time Links and Travelers wherever and whenever they are. A Time Link can be programmed, without knowing it, to lose their Time Hold on a Traveler based on proximity. We always program in 300 meters for pleasure trips like that, and we have AI monitoring all time eras 24/7 to see if any Time Links become active. If they do, the AI programs in the standard 300-meter proximity limit, unless other arrangements have been made in advance."

"Okay," said Dani. "So, how has this trip been programmed? You had no idea Orla was going to be our Time Link in 1751 before you left 2253. So how will we do this?"

"I'll simply go over here and program it in," said Charles. Charles took a few steps to his right and again placed his palm on the wall. Another touchscreen appeared. He then spoke in Irish to Orla, asking her to come over to where he was. Orla walked over to him, and Charles took her hand, touched it to the screen, then pulled it away. After that, he pressed a few keys on the touchscreen and stood. The screen disappeared into the wall.

"All right, that's done," said Charles. "The Station has been reprogramed to enable Orla's time hold on us to be rendered ineffective at 100 meters. I'll be the first of us to leave. After I leave the Station and walk 100 meters away, I'll be jumped back to my natural time. Wait here until the mission screen changes. When it does, you can leave the Station. When you are 100 meters away, you'll be jumped back to 2022. That will release all the Time Links that will be needed for Mission 188, which is the forward movement of Orla. Are you clear on this?"

"Clear, Sir," said Dani, saluting. "Why so formal, Charles?"

"I'm just doing my best, Dani. I'm sorry it doesn't meet your casual standards."

Dani wondered if she'd gone too far and made an effort to remedy that.

"My apologies, Charles," she said. "In all sincerity, I can't believe you're about to pull this off. We've had any number of unanticipated situations pop up, and you've gotten us through every one of them."

Dani wondered if Charles would buy her less than sincere speech, but he seemed to relax after that, a peaceful smile appearing on his face.

"You've done well, too, Dani. Take care of the child now, will you?" He extended his hand. "Until we meet again," he said.

"I hope we do," lied Dani, shaking Charles's hand.

He pulled away, went to the Station wall, and pressed his hand against it. The door opening appeared, and he departed. The opening sealed up, enclosing Dani, Orla, and Liam in the chamber of black stone.

Chapter 38

Dani went to Orla and took her hand, leading her to the circular pedestal that was between the two Time Cradles. They sat on the pedestal together, and Dani put her arm around the girl's shoulders. Orla's body relaxed, and she leaned heavily into Dani. The girl's emotions poured into Dani like water into a receptacle. Dani squeezed harder, trying to communicate with body language that she would protect Orla. *She's an innocent young girl, who's just lost her father, and she knows from her older self that she will lead a miserable life.* From that moment forward, Dani vowed to give the girl a better future than what fate had allotted to her.

After about 10 minutes, the mission screen changed. Charles had been quick. Dani reviewed the screen, checking to make sure everything was as she'd expected.

TIME MISSION: 188
FORWARD JUMP
TRAVELER(S): CONFIDENTIAL

TIME LEVEL	ARRIVAL YEAR	JUMP DISTANCE	TIME CHAIN TIME LINK 1	TIME LINK 2	ARRIVAL DATE
9	1751	0		NEW RECRUIT	PRESENT
8	1801	50	NEW RECRUIT	Ciara/Station	23-MAY
7	1850	49	Ciara/Station	Roisin/Station	23-MAY
6	1902	52	Roisin/Station	Aoife/Station	23-MAY
5	1972	70	Aoife/Station	Aideen/Station	23-MAY
4	2022	50	Aideen/Station	Dani/Station	23-MAY

Dani saw that Charles had not disclosed the identity of either the Traveler, Orla, or the new Time Link, Liam. She agreed that it was good to protect Orla's identity, and Liam would be a Time Link as a one-time service, so there was no need to list his name. He'd sleep until Orla returned, then she would hopefully untie his ropes and help him to get free. It was unclear to Dani what instructions Charles had given Orla as to how to handle Liam when she returned. She would ask Orla later.

Dani reviewed the mission plan one more time. Orla would travel to 2022 through Liam, Ciara, Roisin, Aoife, and Aideen. Dani was worried about how the jump through Liam would turn out, but Orla seemed more than willing to go. Considering what she'd just endured, it was understandable. Dani was now free to leave. She turned and hugged Orla, and Orla hugged back. A bond had been formed between the two, and Dani felt the weight of responsibility for the child's well-being.

"I know you can't understand me," said Dani. "But I will take care of you. I promise."

To her surprise, Orla responded.

"I know sume English," said Orla, her words a little garbled, but Dani could make them out. "I doan' trust Charles. But I due trust yue, Dani."

Dani was stunned, but deeply touched. She embraced Orla again, and as she left the chamber, she had one more thing to say.

"See you soon!" she said, waving to the brave little girl.

Young Orla waved back, and then the door to the chamber sealed up and became black stone.

Chapter 39

Dani came to her senses back in the chamber, holding Aideen's hand. By looking at Aideen, she could tell she was back in 2022. She was relieved and happy. She felt safe for the first time in the past few days. Aideen opened her beautiful gray-blue eyes and smiled up at her, giving a squeeze with her hand. Dani squeezed back. Aideen sat up, still in the Time Cradle.

"So, how did it go?" she inquired. "All as you'd expected?"

"Mostly," said Dani. "One thing I didn't expect though. After I got back 100 years or so, I couldn't remember what was going to happen next, even though before I left, I remembered most of it pretty clearly."

"Is that a normal thing, according to Charles?" asked Aideen.

"He said he experienced it, too. Called it Time Fatigue. Said he brings detailed written mission notes with him in case he forgets why he's there."

"Odd. I've never heard about that."

"He says you have to go back around 100 years or more for it to happen."

"But now you remember everything?" asked Aideen.

"Yes, clear as a bell. I'll tell you about it as soon as we have time."

"We should have plenty of time, unless Charles concocts

another emergency mission."

"I'm not sure about that," said Dani. "You remember I was supposed to bring someone back with me, right?"

"Oh, yes," said Aideen. "Where is she? Or he?"

"Should be arriving any minute if she was able to pull it off. Her name is Orla, and she's 12 years old. And also, I want to speak with you about Charles."

Suddenly, there was a flashing light. Dani blacked out for a microsecond as time stopped. When she regained her bearings, Orla was standing beside the Time Cradle, holding Aideen's hand.

"Jee-ah-gwitch, Aideen," said Orla. "Hello, Dani."

Young Orla ran to Dani and hugged her tightly.

"Well, I see you two have become close!" said Aideen.

"How did Orla know to speak Irish to you?" asked Dani.

"It's all come through into my mind just now," said Aideen. "We met in the Station a few moments ago, back in 1972, and I learned that Orla was much more comfortable with Irish than English."

"But she knows a little English," said Dani. "And with you knowing Irish, we can help her learn more. I want her to be able to speak for herself at the press conference when we announce the basis of the research for my dissertation."

"Yes, I remember," said Aideen. "Are you still sure you want to do that? Inform the world that time travel exists?"

"I think we should talk it through to make sure we're all comfortable with what Charles wants us to do. I got to know him better during the past two days, and frankly, I'm not completely comfortable with him anymore. Neither is Orla."

"Well then," said Aideen. "We have a lot to discuss!"

Aideen looked at her watch, pulled the tide chart from her pocket and reviewed it.

"It's a good time for us to leave the Station," she said. "Let's get back to the cottage and make some food."

"Great," said Dani, still holding onto Orla. "I can't wait to find out the details of Orla's trip, especially the first jump. That was the risky one."

The three of them left the Station and walked quietly back to the cottage through the dark night. A light rain was falling, and only Orla lacked a hood to protect her long, dark hair. When they got into the cottage, Aideen got a towel and helped the girl dry her hair.

"I could get the hair dryer," said Aideen, "but I'm afraid it might frighten her. The poor thing is 271 years in the future. We need to help her adjust as gradually as possible."

"For sure," said Dani. "Maybe you could speak to her in Irish to warn her about certain things, like cars and motorboats and cellphones, computers, things like that."

"And coffee makers and refrigerators and stoves and ovens and running water and toilets. She's used to none of that, Dani."

As they led Orla into the kitchen, Aideen spoke to her in Irish, pointing things out and explaining them to her. The girl's green eyes opened wide as she looked around, and Dani wondered how much of Aideen's explanations she was really understanding. She took Orla's hand, which brought a smile to the girl's face.

"I think I could love this girl, like a sister, or a daughter," said Dani.

"I could get used to that," said Aideen. "And she *is* our sister. She's a Time Link, just like us. But I don't see how things could be arranged for the three of us to stay together."

"Not unless we can convince Charles to allow us to do it," said Dani.

"I don't know how we'll ever do that," said Aideen. "But I suppose we can try. I would think you'd know from your future memories what ends up happenin' with Orla."

"It's odd," said Dani. "But when it comes to Orla, all I know from my future memories is that we went back to 1751 and brought her here. I have absolutely no memory of what happens next with Orla. Well, there is one thing. I get very sad when I think about her. But I don't know why."

"That's strange," said Aideen. "Maybe it has somethin' to do with her comin' from so far back in time, somethin' related to the Time Fatigue you mentioned."

"That's probably it," said Dani. "I hope we can convince Charles to let Orla stay if she wants to. And if it's what you want, too."

"I think I could love this child," said Aideen. "She seems very special. But it's more complicated than just convincin' Charles. The bigger challenge in my mind would be tryin' to keep poor Orla from goin' crazy, livin' in a time with so much technology she doesn't understand."

"It would," said Dani. "But I'm not worried about Orla. She's smart, and she has the wisdom of years inside her. I think she'd be fine if she stayed."

"Maybe so," said Aideen. "That's a challenge for another day though. Let's get some food."

Aideen and Dani made some spaghetti, and the three sat at the kitchen table and ate. Orla woofed the meal down as if she hadn't eaten in days. Dani explained the precarious nature of the first jump to Aideen, using an unsuspecting, unconscious Liam Murphy to jump Orla to a pub on Omey Island in the year 1801. Aideen had known there'd been a pub on the island at some point in history, along with shops and hundreds of people, and she was a little envious that Dani had gotten to see it without her. But she was even more intrigued by the manual time jump that Charles had programmed into the Station.

"It might come in handy one day if we could learn to do that," said Aideen.

"It looked pretty complicated," said Dani. "But we should definitely see if we can figure it out. We might be able to make use of that trick, for sure."

Aideen spoke to the girl in Irish, asking her about the jump to the pub in 1801. Orla launched into to an explanation that was full of excitement, smiles, and laughter. When Orla was done, Aideen reported back to Dani.

"Orla said that Liam never woke during the time she was in the Station with him back in 1751, but she held his hand anyway, and then she woke holding the hand of a drunk, old man in the pub on Omey Island in 1801. She said the man looked down at her as if she was a gift from heaven, but the barkeep was not happy to have a woman, especially one so young as her, in his pub. He yelled at her, and she ran out of the pub as fast as she could!"

"That had to have been crazy!" said Dani. "For all involved!"

"And when young Liam wakes up, he'll know all about it," said Aideen, a concerned look on her face. "Fact of the matter is he'll know the history of his entire life. I imagine that would be hard to cope with because he would have no idea how he knew all of that. Probably drive him to drink, at the very least. By the way, how is Charles planning on handling young Liam's knowledge of the location of the Time Station?"

"Well, Liam doesn't know yet," said Dani. "He was passed out when we put him in the Station. But I was wondering if you could ask Orla what Charles told her to do about Liam when she returned to 1751."

Aideen spoke to Orla in Irish, and frowns appeared on both of their faces.

"He told her to leave Liam there, tied up on the Time Cradle," said Aideen.

Dani wasn't surprised.

"That sounds like Charles," she said. "He's really a very cruel person. And he's not telling us something about the future. Something important."

"Fill me in then," said Aideen. "Maybe we should try to make a plan of our own."

Chapter 40

It was late, past three in the morning, but Dani, Aideen, and Orla wanted to figure out as much as they could about Charles and his true intentions. They sat in the small, cozy living room in Aideen's cottage. Dani and Aideen had agreed to speak slowly, in English, so Orla could pick up as much as possible from the discussion. If needed, Aideen would pause to explain things to her in Irish. Orla was part of the team now, though what *kind* of team was yet to be determined.

"Charles killed a man in 1801," said Dani. "It's *true* that the man was a perpetrator of incest and rape. We witnessed it, unfortunately. But still, what Charles did goes against all legal and moral principles, and he did it as casually as drinking a cup of coffee in the morning. And now that we know he was willing to leave an innocent man to die of thirst and starvation in the Time Station, it proves beyond a shadow of a doubt that Charles is not normal. If anything, he's a sociopath."

Aideen took a moment to translate what Dani had said to Orla, and the young girl asked a question. Aideen responded, the girl nodded her head, and then Aideen told Dani what Orla had asked.

"She asked what a sociopath is," said Aideen. "And when I

told her what that was, she agreed that Charles fit the description. She definitely doesn't trust him, and she has the experience of a 62-year-old woman to back up her gut feelin'. But gettin' back to the matter at hand, figurin' this out, are there any other clues in your mind, Dani, that bear discussion?"

"Yes, several, actually. First of all, he said that 80 percent of the biological population in 2253 are women. He also said things are fine, there's plenty of resources for everyone, no global warming, and AI is not the enemy."

"He said all that, yes," said Aideen. "What about it bothers ya', Dani?"

"If 80 percent of the world's biological population is women, and they live so far in the future that having test tube babies is probably akin to warming up soup for lunch, then why aren't they simply harvesting eggs from these women and making people, especially men, to replace the ones who are uploading their minds into computers? On top of that, why aren't there social programs in place to train the new babies about why it's so good to be human? Instead, they're asking us to do it, with this *Hearts and Minds* campaign!"

"He said there were no governments anymore, so how could they organize anythin' without that?" asked Aideen.

"The better question is, *why* are there no governments?" asked Dani. "And when there *were* governments, why didn't they have laws to outlaw mind uploading? Or at least to restrict its use. And why is it up to us to convince governments to make the laws? Charles never explained what caused governments to disappear, but in my mind, if the problems the future is facing are as he described, that makes government more important in their time than it ever was. So where did government go in the 23rd century? It doesn't make sense!"

Aideen raised her finger and translated to Orla, bringing her up to speed. Orla nodded her head, indicating she understood what was being discussed, then she said something to Aideen, who turned to Dani and translated.

"Orla asked if we think all the people in the future are like Charles," she said.

"I don't know," said Dani. "Let's hope not. What about the other Travelers you've met who he's brought through?"

"As I said, there's only been a few, but we haven't spent time together. There's woman named Brie who I think must be one of those Recruiters Charles mentioned, and when she comes through, she's usually movin' further back in time. Perhaps we should discuss all of this with Charles the next time we see him. Put it all on the table, tell him we won't cooperate until he gives us the truth."

"I think we're well past asking Charles any questions at all, don't you?" asked Dani. "We can't trust him, and in my view, we don't want to give him any clue that we're suspicious of his motives. And what's worse, if we tell him we aren't cooperating, I sincerely believe he wouldn't hesitate to kill us all."

"That may be true," said Aideen. "But I've known Charles for 50 years, and he's never acted like this before."

"But you don't *really* know him, do you? You've already explained that you have no idea what Charles does when he leaves you for his so-called missions. But I was with him on one of those missions, and it wasn't pretty."

"Tell me, Dani, if you were so suspicious of Charles during your trip, why did ya' follow through and bring Orla back to 2022?"

Dani didn't hesitate.

"Two reasons," she said. "First, I watched Charles kill a man. The last thing I wanted him to do was to suspect me at all, or who knows what he would have done to me. The second reason is that I truly want to spend time with Orla. I want to learn more about her life and times. I sincerely *want* to use her knowledge to help me with my dissertation. And as I already told you, it would be great if we could find a way to keep her here with us. She has nothing to go back to anyway."

"What about her mother?" asked Aideen. At that point, Orla interrupted.

"Ma's dead already," she said, scrunching her lips together and squeezing her eyes nearly shut, trying to hold back tears.

"How?" asked Dani, flabbergasted. She'd just met the woman.

"Hanged," said Orla. "By a mob."

"For God sakes why?" asked Aideen.

"Wife of a thief," said Orla. She stopped, then turned to Aideen and spoke in Irish. When she finished, she broke down in tears. Aideen translated for Dani.

"She says a drunken mob broke into her home the night we left. They raped her mother, then dragged her out and hanged her in the town square on the same gallows they used for her father."

"The poor thing," said Dani, going over to the young girl and hugging her tightly.

After comforting Orla for quite some time, Aideen and Dani put her to bed in the spare bedroom that used to be Dani's. The child was exhausted, both physically and emotionally. After getting Orla to sleep, the two resumed their discussion.

"There's only one good thing about what happed to Orla's ma," said Aideen.

"How could anything about that be good?" asked Dani, still in shock from Orla's revelation about her mother.

"Orla wasn't there," said Aideen. "I think she would have suffered the same fate if she had been."

"I suppose you're right," said Dani. "And now she has absolutely no reason to go back. How could she? What would happen to her?"

"I don't know," said Aideen. "But first, let's work on figurin' out Charles. You wanted him to think you were goin' along with his plan, is that it?"

"Yes," said Dani.

"And do you *actually* intend to go along with it?"

"Up to a point, yes. Until we can figure out what's going on. You've got to believe we'll be seeing Charles soon, right?"

"I would think so, yes," said Aideen. "But you're a smart lady, Dani. Can you nah see what would happen if ya' did this press conference the way Charles wants ya' to? I'm assumin' he'll tell me to pay the big news people to come because at that point you'll still be an unknown. It would take some big money to get them to show up, but they would, because I've got the big money."

"And if they do," said Dani, "it would be worldwide news, for sure."

"It would," said Aideen. "But are ya' truly considering doing this press conference?"

"I'm not sure," said Dani. "It depends on what we learn before then."

"Do you remember when I told you how important it was to the Time Masters to keep the existence of the Time Station secret?" asked Aideen.

"Yes, and I agree with that completely. And Charles's plan would enable us to do that."

"Until you were taken into government custody and interrogated! Don't you think *time travel* qualifies as a matter of national security for literally any national government on Earth?"

Dani raised her eyebrows.

"Ooops," she said. "Didn't think of that."

"I did," said Aideen. "And so did Charles, I'll bet. Right then and there was when I began to question his honesty. I said nothin', and I let you go with him because you told me you knew it all worked out. And by the grace of God, you're back here, and with poor little Orla ta' boot. And you've given a lot of other good reasons not to trust Charles. But the biggest thing we have goin' for us is we know he understands what's really goin' to happen after that press conference. And yet he's still tryin' to make it happen! The question is why?"

"I don't think we're going to find that out from Charles," said Dani.

"I doubt it," said Aideen.

"So, what are you thinking?"

"I'm thinkin' we need to go to the future and find out for ourselves."

Chapter 41

It didn't take long for Charles to issue a new mission plan, Time Mission 189. Dani and Aideen studied it in their minds. Charles was coming to pay them a visit in the cottage in about a month, on June 24. The assumption was that he wanted to check on Dani's progress on her dissertation and provide them with instructions on his plans and their respective responsibilities in such plans.

Dani was happy to proceed with her work on the dissertation. It was important to her to earn her PhD, and she needed the dissertation to be completed and accepted for this to happen. It would also give her a chance to get to know Orla better, something she very much wanted to do. It was slow going at first because Dani wanted to conduct the interviews in English. Orla couldn't read, neither in Irish nor English, which complicated things. The good news was that Orla spoke the Connacht dialect of Irish that was common to County Galway, the same dialect Aideen was fluent in. Aideen helped Orla pick up important English words, and she was a quick learner, but Aideen herself wasn't always available, and that's when things slowed down.

Aideen was spending a lot of time at the Station, trying to figure out the programming commands that were needed to initiate an emergency time mission. She'd been able to uncover the small touchscreen by placing her palm on the wall in the spot Dani had showed her. That was as much of a contribution as Dani could make, however, because she wasn't much of a code breaker, and she needed to spend her time with Orla.

Aideen told Dani she hadn't blown up anything yet and was firmly convinced that her sessions on the small touchscreen were not being reported back to 2253. Her logic was two-fold. First, there was no relation of the small screen to the large screen above it that displayed the time mission. Nothing she did on the small screen in any way changed the mission parameters being displayed on the large screen, which Dani confirmed was the way it had been when Charles initiated the emergency jump for Orla to go from 1751 to the pub in 1801. And second, if her dabbling with the small screen was being seen by technicians in 2253, she assumed they would have had an emergency visit from Charles and his friends from the future by now.

Dani would often take Orla for walks around Omey Island. Aideen had gone to Clifden to buy the girl clothes because she was much shorter than either Aideen or Dani. But when she was dressed in jeans and a T-shirt, it was hard to believe she was only a girl of 12. Orla's development was contrary to all knowledge Dani had about the age of puberty, for both men and women, over the span of history. The accepted theory was that health and well-being were directly correlated with the age of puberty, meaning that people from times of scarcity and poverty reached puberty at an older age. The current average age of menstruation for a girl in the western world was 12.5 years, but it should have been closer to 14 or 15 in Orla's time. Dani decided that here was a sign that the girl was better suited to be living in *this* time, instead of back in the retched 1700s. She realized she was reaching for reasons to keep Orla with them, but she didn't care. She loved the girl and wanted to help her and be with her.

Orla was amazed at how few people were on Omey Island compared to her time, and also at how very clean it was. She was so happy when she saw the birds, otters, and fish at Fahy Lough, telling Dani that all the wildlife had been killed for food during the famine of the 1740s. Orla became sad when she spoke of the famine because it reminded her of the loss of her little brother and sister during that terrible time.

One day during one of their walks, the girl casually took Dani by the hand, and this caused Dani's heart to swell.

"You like it here, don't you?" Dani asked.

The girl tilted her head up to look at her.

"I want ta' stay," she said. Her expression was the epitome of hope. And this caused Dani's heart to plummet to the depths of despair. She knew the girl was looking for a response from her, so she put on a smile and responded.

"We're working on that, Orla. We're going to try our best."

Orla squeezed her hand. *A squeeze of hope*, Dani thought. She squeezed back.

As the days and weeks went by, Orla's ability to understand and speak English improved dramatically. Her sessions with Dani became more productive, and Dani learned about the day-to-day lives of the girl, her family, the village of Claddaghduff, and the surrounding area. Surprisingly, the memories Orla had obtained from her older self were still there. They had not abated with her movement forward in time, as Dani's had when she moved backward. But no matter what period of her long life Orla reported on, one thing remained true throughout: It was a tough life.

Death was an everyday event for Orla's people, and while the history books would call them "commoners," Dani knew in her heart they weren't common at all. The resilience of the human spirit was more present in Orla and the people of her time than it was today. Dani found it ironic that she was capturing from the girl exactly what she'd been tasked to do by Charles, even though she suspected his aims were not so pure. What Charles *truly* wanted remained a mystery to all of them. They hoped they could glean more during his next visit, without revealing their own true intentions.

Chapter 42

June 24 arrived and so did Charles Burke. It was another solo mission, and he came directly to the cottage as he had before. Aideen and Dani didn't know how long he would stay, but they'd prepared the spare bedroom that Orla had been using for him, moving Orla into Aideen and Dani's bedroom. Dani loved the idea of sleeping with the little sister she'd never had, and Aideen seemed equally enthused. It would be like a slumber party of three generations, although Dani didn't think of it that way. Her new concept of time led her to understand that age was less important than people thought. A person's body would grow old and die, but they would live forever in the endless loop of time.

Before Charles arrived, Aideen had unlocked the secrets of the small touchscreen in the Station. She explained to Dani that it was simple digital inputting of the destination time, with detailed longitudinal and latitudinal coordinates of the destination place. Aideen taught Dani how to do the calculating and inputting, telling her it was impossible to know which one of them might be having an emergency as they moved further and further into the future. Their plan was not yet complete, but it was taking shape, and they hoped Charles's visit would provide additional insight so they could finalize their clandestine trip to the future.

Charles arrived, holding Dani's hand, having been transported by older Dani from Level 3. He quickly extracted his hand, said his hellos to all, and immediately addressed Orla, speaking to her in English.

"And how are you doing, Orla?" he asked.

Dani was surprised Charles wasn't using Irish with the girl, wondering if he knew more than they thought he did, and perhaps other things, but the plan they'd made with Orla was for her to speak to Charles only in Irish and to feign ignorance when English was being used. Orla spoke in Irish to Charles.

"Ah, so she's not picking up English yet?" Charles asked. Aideen gave the answer.

"She has a ready-made translator, so why should she?" asked Aideen.

"I thought it would be easier for Dani if Orla could learn English is all," said Charles.

"She didn't learn it in 62 years of life, Charles," said Aideen. "So, she's not very likely to learn it now."

"Such are the mysteries of life," he responded. "Shall we have a glass of wine and talk?"

Aideen got out the wine and four glasses. Orla, while 12 in body, had told them she'd grown fond of wine in her older years because it helped her to relax. She also asserted that the medicinal benefits of alcohol consumption were well known during her time, a smile on her face. And even though there were laws and social norms about women drinking in the 18th century, she had always restricted her imbibement to the privacy of her own home. Charles raised his eyebrows when he saw Orla sharing the wine with them, but he said nothing. He obviously had other more pressing matters to cover.

"So, the dissertation is going well?" he asked, drinking heartily from his glass.

"It's going *very* well," said Dani.

"Excellent!" said Charles. "I'd like to look through your notes tomorrow, if I may."

Dani was taken aback by Charles's question, but she recovered quickly.

"That would be awesome," she replied. "Having an anthropologist review my work would be a big advantage. I wouldn't want to plagiarize, however. You wouldn't actually be writing it for me, right?"

"No, not at all," said Charles. "Just providing some guidance, and even that might not be necessary. I'm sure you're nailing it all on your own."

"I feel like I'm capturing the *humanness* of Orla and her people, for sure," said Dani.

"Excellent. Can't wait to see your work. Tonight, I thought we might review the plans for the press conference. Does that sound alright?"

Dani and Aideen nodded. Orla remained still, a passive expression on her face, playing the role of someone who didn't understand what was being said quite well. A surge of pride coursed through Dani, as it would through a proud parent. Her silent revelry was interrupted, however, by their nemesis.

"The first thing we need to do is set a date for the press conference," he said. "Do you feel you'll be done before August 1st, Dani?"

"I expect it to be done before then, yes," said Dani. "But I'm wondering if we can talk a bit about Orla?"

"What is there to talk about?" asked Charles.

"We've grown attached to young Orla," said Dani. "And we were wondering if she could stay a little longer with us."

Charles raised his eyebrows.

"How much longer?" he asked.

"Uh, well, maybe permanently?" she asked.

Charles didn't hesitate.

"Out of the question," he said. "We need it to become obvious, immediately, that the child is from another time. When she disappears in front of everyone's eyes, that will be accomplished."

"But that can be determined by interviews with the child and with me afterward," said Dani.

"Which can lead to all kinds of other complications," Charles responded. "Such as the discovery of the Time Station itself, which cannot happen."

"But even if Orla is gone, Dani will still be here," said Aideen. "In fact, if you think about it, how can we be sure Dani won't be taken into custody after it's revealed she knows the secret of time travel. And myself as well! We live together, after all."

"Provisions will have to be made for the two of you," said Charles.

"What kind of provisions?" asked Dani.

"We'll need to move you to another time until things cool down a bit."

"Charles, are you sure you've thought this through?" asked Aideen. "Things are not going to ever *cool down* once this news gets out. And let's say you successfully move us to another time, where we'll have to stay for a long while I might add. What about the Hearts and Minds campaign? How does that carry on without us here to nurture it?"

"Dani's dissertation!" said Charles. "That's why it's so important to get it right!"

Dani could see that Charles was losing his patience, and it was also clear to her, as Aideen had just implied, that he hadn't thought things through completely regarding the press conference and its aftermath. But she had an idea that might turn his thinking, so she went with it.

"Charles, I've noticed something about Orla that might be relevant here," she said.

Charles seemed to settle down a bit when he heard this.

"Oh really?" he asked. "What would that be?"

"Orla isn't experiencing the Time Fatigue that you and I wrestled with during our trip back in time. She still has clear memories of her life after the age of 12 that transferred to her from her older self. I'm wondering if that means there are different properties at work when people move forward in time compared to backward. Do you have any experience with that?"

Charles narrowed his eyes and scrunched up his lips. He was either trying to think of why this might happen, or he already knew and was deciding whether or not to tell them. He took another healthy pull of wine and set his glass on the coffee table.

"The reality is," he said, "that we have very little experience moving people forward through time. Our efforts have been focused on backward movement to study the eras in detail that we felt had relevance to our objectives."

"How little is very little?" asked Aideen.

Charles hesitated again, but then continued.

"Orla is the first subject we've moved forward beyond the chronological end of her life."

"What about in your own time?" asked Aideen. "Surely you've gone forward to see what happens to the human race if nothing is changed."

Again, Charles hesitated, buying time by drinking more wine. This time, he held the glass in his hand while he responded.

"The reality is that we can't go forward at all in my time. The technology we have at this point, I mean the Time Station, doesn't seem to be able to move itself forward. Only backward. We've tried, believe me, but something about the chronological moment when the Station was first activated limits its ability to move forward beyond its natural time. Going back in time is of course no problem, with the help of its human partners, the Time Links. But nothing going forward."

Charles sipped more wine. Dani could tell he was clearly intrigued by Orla's resistance to Time Fatigue, and it was convenient that he was somewhat inebriated and revealing things he probably shouldn't be. Suddenly, he made an announcement.

"I think we should delay the press conference," he said.

"Why?" asked Dani.

"The absence of Time Fatigue in Orla," said Charles. "This revelation could change our approach completely."

Dani's heart soared. There was still hope that Orla could stay with them. She tried hard to hide her excitement, but Aideen noticed and took over the conversation.

"What do you want us to do while we wait, Charles?" she asked.

It was clear from Charles's eyes that his mind was whirling, in spite of the effects of the wine.

"Dani should finish her dissertation," said Charles.

"What else?" asked Aideen.

"I will begin planning Time Mission 190," he said.

"Why do we need a new time mission?" asked Aideen.

Charles didn't hesitate.

"Because you're coming to the future, ladies. All three of you. Bring your passports, and Dani, bring your university ID."

"But Orla has no passport," said Dani. "No ID whatsoever."

"That's all right," said Charles. "We'll talk more about it in the morning."

Chapter 43

Charles went to bed very drunk and spent the night in the spare bedroom. Aideen, Dani, and Orla slept in the master bedroom, lining up one beside the other in the queen-sized bed. Orla explained that she was used to sleeping like that because there was only one bed in her cottage back in the 1700s. For Dani and Aideen, it was new and different, and it further solidified their mutual desire to find a way to make Orla a permanent part of their lives. They put Orla in the center of the bed, and she held each of their hands for a while before falling asleep. It was a peaceful night, in spite of Charles being there in the cottage with them.

During breakfast the following morning, Charles announced he would be leaving immediately to put together the plan to bring them to the future. He instructed them to recruit a new Time Link for Level 4 because all of them would be Travelers, and the year 2022 would be left without a Time Link. They would need to find someone new to send the three forward in time. He encouraged them to find someone young who either Aideen or Dani knew from their future selves to have lived a long life. And of course, they needed to find someone who could be trusted, or at the very least, bribed. Charles never mentioned reviewing Dani's dissertation notes at all, and Dani presumed this was because he'd become obsessed about bringing them to the future.

Charles left the cottage at 10 in morning, walked away from them, and disappeared after strolling nonchalantly to the south. They went back into the cottage, and Aideen went straight to the kitchen, calling back for them to follow her. Dani and Orla did as she asked and saw Aideen opening a bottle of champagne.

"What's this about?" asked Dani.

"A celebration, of course!" said Aideen. "The bloody fool gave us exactly what we wanted. A trip to the future!"

Aideen poured three glasses of champagne, and the three of them toasted to their good fortune. They drank the entire bottle and became so tired they went back to bed, all three of them together in the master bedroom. Dani realized that at some point she would have to encourage Orla to begin sleeping in her own room again, but for now, it was great to enjoy their small victory together.

They rose around noon, had some lunch, and decided to review what they'd learned from Charles. The most important thing was obviously that Charles and his people in 2253 couldn't travel to their future. Aideen pointed out that Charles, being Charles, could be lying, simply wanting to lure them there to do away with them. Dani countered by telling them about the cigar-shaped instrument Charles had used to kill Ciara's father, pointing out that if he wanted them dead, he didn't need to bring them to the future to do it.

"He wants us there for a reason," said Dani. "It all started when I mentioned that Orla isn't suffering from Time Fatigue."

"Yes, and then he immediately began to doubt whether his current approach was the best one," said Aideen. "So much so that he postponed the press conference."

"And lost all interest in my dissertation," said Dani. "I think it's safe to say that Charles has moved on to plan B, which he's undoubtedly concocting as we speak."

"So, let's follow the logic," said Aideen. "Fact 1 is that Orla does not suffer from Time Fatigue. Charles probably believes that has something to do with her moving forward in time, beyond her own lifetime. She's the first Traveler to do that, or so he says."

"It's the forward movement that he's focused on, no doubt," said Dani.

"He must believe that he and his group have missed something, some rule of physics, that applies to forward movement in time that does not apply to backward movement in time."

"By his own admission, they've been solely focused on backward movement in order to identify keys to help them solve the mind upload problem," said Dani.

"I know he *says* it's a mind upload problem," said Aideen. "But we won't know that for sure until we get there. And maybe not even then, if he restricts our access to the outside world of 2253."

"Agreed," said Dani. "But the fact remains that Charles and his people don't know all they want to know about forward movement in time. If it's true that no one from his present can move forward in time, he very likely hopes that the three of us, not being from his time …"

"Can go to his future for 'im," said Orla, finishing Dani's sentence for her.

Chapter 44

Charles wasted very little time putting together the next time mission. It was published by the Time Station the next day. After they each received the plan in their minds, they gathered in the living room to discuss it. It was around seven in the evening on June 25, and they had just finished dinner.

TIME MISSION: 190: Preliminary Plan
FORWARD JUMP
TRAVELER(S): CONFIDENTIAL

TIME LEVEL	ARRIVAL YEAR	JUMP DISTANCE	TIME CHAIN TIME LINK 1	TIME LINK 2	ARRIVAL DATE
4	2022	0		NEW RECRUIT	2-Aug
3	TBD	TBD	NEW RECRUIT	Sophie/Station	TBD
2	TBD	TBD	Sophie/Station	Leah/Station	TBD
1	2253	TBD	Leah/Station		PRESENT

Time Mission 190 was the forward jump that Aideen, Dani, and Orla were expected to make to 2253. It was scheduled to occur on August 2, about 5 weeks away, and there were blanks that needed to be filled in. Because they had not yet found the new recruit, Charles didn't know how far in the future to plan for their first jump, from 2022 forward in time. This meant that the timing of the subsequent jumps could not be finalized either. The confusing thing was that even if they found the new recruit, this person would have no idea how long she would live, nor would she have a point of reference in the future they could jump to. That confusion was rapidly clarified, however, when the three of them each received the same internal message in their minds.

Use the manual override procedure that we used for Orla to tell me the time and place of your first jump. I know you know how to do it. Program it in as soon as you have the recruit and know the dates. I will override and publish a final mission chart at that time. The recruit should be fully briefed and a willing participant. Don't want another Liam Murphy in our Time Chain.

"Did you get that message?" asked Dani.

Both Aideen and Orla nodded.

When they'd recovered from the shock of the message, some kind of mind messaging from the future they'd never experienced before, they considered its meaning.

"He knows I figured it out," said Aideen.

"Yes, and he's telling us it won't do us any good, because he can simply override it if we try to do anything on our own," said Dani. "But regardless, he knows we've been scheming."

"But he brings us forward anyway," said Orla.

"Does not bode well for any of us," said Aideen.

"So, what do we do?" asked Dani.

"We get some wine," said Orla.

Dani and Aideen smiled, but also agreed. They went to the kitchen to get the wine, poured it, and reconvened around the kitchen table. Aideen spoke first.

"Now that I've had a sip of wine, I've got the courage of a drunk man. I say we go anyway!"

"Are you serious?" asked Dani.

"What's changed?" asked Orla. "We know he won't kill us, because he needs us."

"But what does he need us for?" asked Dani.

"I thought we agreed he wants to try to send us forward in time," said Aideen.

"Well, that's certainly what we thought," said Dani. "But why bring all three of us? It would be a lot easier to leave at least Aideen here to send Orla and I forward. That way no one else needs to be involved."

"You know what I think," said Aideen.

"What?" asked Dani and Orla at the same time.

"I think Charles is a very confused man. Somehow, when Dani brought up that Orla wasn't experiencing Time Fatigue, something clicked in his mind. He realized he was going about this whole thing the wrong way. So, he changed directions."

"But to what?" asked Dani. "What's the new direction?"

"Only one way to find out," said Orla.

"Go forward," said Aideen.

Dani took a healthy sip of wine. She thought long and hard about the situation, but she could not make herself feel good about it.

"If Charles can't go forward in time from 2253, then why should *we* be able to go forward from 2253?" she asked.

"We have no idea," said Aideen. "That's why we're goin' forward. To find out."

"But there's a bigger reason to go," said Orla.

"What's that?" asked Dani.

"Do we want to leave the future of everyone on Earth in *his* hands?" asked the wise girl from 1751.

Chapter 45

After some more cajoling from Aideen and Orla, Dani agreed to proceed. The first step was to find a new Time Link in 2022 who could send them all forward. Aideen was the person most likely to know someone local who had lived a long life. She told Dani and Orla that for one of the Travelers' missions she had been on the receiving end of a connection from older Aideen from the year 2075. Older Aideen was 121 years old in 2075. She was still working as a Time Link and living in the cottage, but she had hired a caretaker to help with the basics of living.

Dani was confused. She knew from her own connection to 2074 that she and Aideen were still together at that time and she didn't understand why Aideen would need a caretaker.

"What about me?" asked Dani. "Why aren't I taking care of you in 2075?" asked Dani.

"You are" said Aideen. "But when you're workin' as a Time Link, you aren't about, so I got the caretaker to come during those times. But that's not the important thing. What each of us must understand, ladies, is no matter what happens when we go to the future, everythin' will change."

Dani understood what this meant. So far, nothing of significance had been changed. Charles seemed to be pivoting in a new direction, but one thing was certain. He was going to do *something*, and the three of them, as well as many other people, would undoubtedly be affected by what he did.

The caretaker's name from 2075 was Eabha, which was pronounced *A-va*. Aideen told them it was Eabha's name that had caused her to hire her because it was the Irish name for Eve and meant "life." In 2075, Aideen knew she was nearing the end of her life, but she was still superstitious enough to hope that a person who's name meant *life* could give her more of it. In 2075, Eabah was 69 years old and in good health. Aideen remembered her as an intelligent woman who enjoyed reading many of the books on the shelves in the cottage. She was also quite spirited and seemed as if she'd led an interesting life and wasn't afraid of a challenge. She was from Claddaghduff, across the channel from Omey Island, which would be helpful because it was a small village, making it easier to find her. In 2022, Eabha would be 16 years old and still in high school. If they could convince her to become a Time Link, she could help them move forward to 2075.

Aideen and Dani formulated a plan to offer the girl a fictitious summer internship to help Dani with her dissertation, traveling the Wild Atlantic Way, with a home base of Omey Island. Of course, they had neither found nor met the girl, and they had no idea if her parents would agree to allow their 16-year-old daughter to be away from home for much of the summer. But it was a plan. The next step was to find the girl, who was more than likely attending the local public high school in Clifden. Aideen, having done her part in identifying their new recruit, suggested that Dani was the ideal choice to contact young Eahba.

Aideen's idea was that Dani go to the school on official business regarding her dissertation, explaining that she had traced Eabha's family tree, last name O'Flaherty, far back into Irish history and would like to interview the girl for her dissertation. During her meeting with Eabha, Dani would reveal that she had received funding from her university to pay for interviews, plus one summer internship. She would suggest a meeting on Omey Island, at the cottage she was staying at, to conduct the interview, which should take one to two hours. Depending on how things went during the interview, Dani and Aideen would explain their plans to the girl and hopefully gain her cooperation. They knew they needed to act quickly because school would be letting out for the summer break on June 29.

On the afternoon of June 26, Aideen drove Dani to the high school in Clifden. Orla was along for the ride, having adjusted well to the existence of gasoline-powered vehicles and the noise and speed that came with them. She actually seemed to enjoy riding in the car, so they'd begun taking her out more and more. Aideen and Orla waited in the car while Dani went into the school. A half hour later, she returned, and Eabha O'Flaherty was with her. School was letting out for the day, so it had been convenient for Eabha to come with them, especially with the prospect of a paid internship in the offing.

The four drove back to the cottage. They had tea, sitting around the coffee table and making small talk. At that point, Aideen pulled out a large wad of Euros and placed it on the table.

"We were thinking 10,000 euros would cover this," said Aideen.

The girl, another redhead, sat back in her chair, stunned.

"I think that's a bit much!" said the shell-shocked teenager.

"Indeed," said Aideen. "But we need your services for all of July and August to help Dani with her dissertation, if you have the time to give."

"I've no plans for the summer break as of yet," said Eabha. "But it's still far too much money."

"It's money we have to give," said Dani. "If you think your

parents would disagree, then take whatever amount you feel is fair. When your internship is over, I believe strongly you will feel you have earned all of it. But for now, tell your parents you're being paid whatever you want to tell them. It doesn't matter to us."

"Well then," said the girl. "What will the job entail?"

Over a period of a few weeks, the three women gradually introduced young Eabha to the nuances of time travel, their only rule being that Eabha was not to discuss these precious secrets with anyone, including her parents and friends. They explained that she would be able to disclose only her opportunity to work on Omey Island, helping Dani with her dissertation.

Orla was particularly helpful, because even though she was only 12, she looked to be around 16, and she had the wisdom of a 62-year-old. Orla and Eabha became friends, and one day, when Eabha asked Orla why she struggled with English, Orla told her the truth, that she was from 1751, when English was not commonly used in Ireland. Eabha had laughed at what she perceived to be a funny joke, but the three other women weren't smiling, so she gathered they were serious. Aideen took advantage of the opportunity to push the project ahead.

"We'll be happy to show you the Time Station if you can arrange to have a sleepover here on the island with Orla," she said.

"I can do that," said Eabha.

When they showed Eabha the Time Station, she was overwhelmed at first, but Orla calmed her down, and before long she was all in. Aideen then sent her back to the cottage with Orla and Dani, then manually programmed in the name of the new Time Link, the dates of the transfer, and the arrival date and location in 2075. Now they would wait for Charles to post the final mission plan.

Chapter 46

On July 14, the new mission plan came through. On August 2, young Eabha would send the three to older Eabah, who would be in the cottage with Aideen on September 7, 2075, celebrating Aideen's 121st birthday. The three would then walk down to the Station and meet younger Sophie, who would send them to older Sophie in 2155, who would give them over to younger Leah, who would send them to her older self in 2253.

TIME MISSION: 190: Final Plan
FORWARD JUMP
TRAVELER(S): CONFIDENTIAL

TIME LEVEL	ARRIVAL YEAR	JUMP DISTANCE	TIME CHAIN TIME LINK 1	TIME LINK 2	ARRIVAL DATE
4	2022	0		Eabha/Station	2-Aug
3	2075	53	Eabha/Station	Sophie/Station	7-Sep
2	2155	80	Sophie/Station	Leah/Station	7-Sep
1	2253	98	Leah/Station		PRESENT

Now that the mission plan had been finalized, they worked on two fronts. First, Dani pushed to complete her dissertation, assisted by Orla, who was an important source of information for her work. Aideen worked on bringing Eabha up to speed on the nuances of being a Time Link. They wanted her fully informed in all aspects of the job.

One evening, on the pretense of having a sleepover with her new friend, Eabha accompanied Orla and Aideen to the Time Station. Aideen sent Eabha back to 1980 to give her a taste of what life with no cellphones was like, while also indoctrinating her to the mechanics of the Time Chain. Upon Eabha's return from her trip, which lasted only an hour, Aideen made her a full Time Link by performing the simultaneous hands-against-the-wall routine she'd gone through with Dani. The next step was for Eabha to practice using the Time Cradle to send people to different times, but they saved that work for another night.

Dani was making good progress on her dissertation. She was confident it would be finished well before August 1. But eventually a decision needed to be made as to whether or not she would reveal her most critical source, Orla, in her work or make up some vague reference such as "According to the old storyteller Aideen." She consulted with Aideen on the matter, and Aideen had a typically wise answer.

"That's a decision we don't need ta' make until we return," she said. "If we return at 'tall."

On July 20, Dani finished the first draft or her dissertation. She asked Aideen to read it. Aideen was a fast reader, so she poured through the 50,000-word document in a day and a half.

"What do you think?" asked Dani, as they sat drinking coffee in the living room. Orla was with them, inseparable from her sisters.

"Boring as a cheese sandwich on white bread with no butter," said Aideen. "Until you get to the part about Orla. I see you've decided to give the true source reference for her. Is that a final decision?"

"No, it's not. It's just where my head is right now."

"You're right not to make a final decision on that yet," said Aideen. "A lot could change over the coming weeks."

"Agreed," said Dani. "But I'm feeling lucky. I think the three of us will go to the future and take care of things there and come back safely. And then Orla will stay with us, and we'll all live happily ever after."

"That's a fairytale ending for certain," said Aideen. "But let's take things one step at a time, alright? I want the happy ending as much as anyone, but first, we must get ta' the future, then outsmart Charles, and then we need ta' all get back safely."

"I know," said Dani. "That's what I said. Well, what I wished."

Orla, who didn't say much during their conversations but always had something relevant to contribute, finally spoke up.

"I wish it, tue," she said. "So, let's get ta' work."

Chapter 47

There were two options for the first jump. Option one was for Aideen to program the small emergency jump console to facilitate the jump, but she wasn't confident she could do it precisely enough to get the three of them exactly where, and *when,* they needed to be. So, they decided to pursue the second option, which was to *give* the memory to Eahba that she would need to get them there.

During the second half of July, they began training Eahba how to properly send them forward. They emphasized that for a Time Link to successfully initiate a jump like they were contemplating, Eahba would need to remember vivid details of a time and place that were uniquely their own. Dani recalled with horror the time when older Ciara had sent her and Charles back to the scene of her own rape, acknowledging that while this *was* a vivid memory, it probably happened more than once. It wouldn't have mattered much in that mission as to which rape they arrived at, if there *was* more than one, but the forward jump with Eahba was different. They needed to arrive at a specific time, not far from the Time Station, because young Sophie, Time Link 2 for level 3, would be in the Station on September 7, 2075, to receive them and move them forward in time.

The tenuous nature of this jump was that currently Eabha had no knowledge of her future. But Aideen did. She was the one who had thought of recruiting Eabha, based on her own knowledge of September 7, 2075. It was a day Aideen remembered well because it was her 121st birthday. But Aideen's memory wouldn't help them. It needed to be Eahba's memory.

To implant Aideen's memory into Eabha's mind, Aideen would send her forward to that future date with a camera. She would take a picture of older Aideen and older Eabha in 2075, holding a book from Aideen's bookshelf that was also on the bookshelf in 2022. Eahba would study the picture carefully, then attempt to send one of them there as a trial run. The book wasn't critical, but because it would also be present in 2022, Eabha could look at the book anytime she wanted, to add familiarity to the scene she would be targeting in the future.

On the early morning of July 30, Aideen sent Eabha to September 7, 2075. Eabha returned soon after that with the picture on her iPhone. She'd been told not to stay long. She simply needed to have older Aideen select a book, take the photograph of older Aideen with older Eahba holding the book together, then walk out the door and get as far away from the cottage as she could to break the connection and return her to 2022. Eahba had done that and was now safely back in the Time Station. Aideen asked to look at the picture, then showed it to Dani. Dani hoped she didn't show on her face what she was feeling inside when she saw what Aideen looked like at the age of 121. She had the appearance of a healthy 85-year-old, but looking 85 was a long way from what Aideen looked like in 2022, which was a healthy woman of about 50. Aideen reached over and took Dani's hand.

"Number one, we all get old," she said. "Number two, this is the path of my life that I know at this time. It may become a different path when we complete our mission."

"I hear that," said Dani. "And I'm good with it, as long as the two of us are together." She loved Aideen, and that wasn't going to change, no matter what their futures held. She looked at the picture again and noticed that the book Aideen and older Eabha were holding together was *The Last Watch*, by J.S. Dewes. It was a favorite of both Aideen and Dani's, and also the book that had helped point Dani in the right direction regarding her relationship with Aideen.

They made plans to try a trial run the next night, with Eabha sending one of the three forward. The first thing to decide was which one of the three would go. Dani wanted to go because there was no guarantee the trial run would go off without a hitch, and she would rather risk her own well-being than Aideen's or Orla's. The other two were having none of that, however. Each of them was more than willing to risk their own life in order to protect the other two. Nevertheless, Dani prevailed. She would make the jump.

The next thing they did was to prepare young Eabha for the download of a life's worth of memories upon her connection with her older self. Having all been through it themselves, they could each assure her in their own unique way that she would survive this, and they promised that they would help her afterward in handling the emotional shock and also the ongoing dilemma of knowing what's coming in your life before it happens.

Late Sunday night, technically, Monday morning, the 31st of July, Aideen and Orla left Dani and Eabha in the Time Station to make the jump. They would wait in the empty stone burial crypt, then reenter the main chamber after the Station powered down upon completion of the jump. They knew from Charles's disclosures to Dani during their mission together that the 300-meter proximity limit would be automatically programmed in by the AI of the Time Station, so Dani would return to where she started the jump, and

Aideen and Orla would be there to greet her and to comfort Eabha.

When they were alone, Dani instructed Eabha to concentrate on the moment in the future on September 7, 2075, that she had visited only the night before. The girl held the picture she had taken in front of her face, then laid it down on her chest. She moved her left hand over to the Time Cradle control while Dani took her right hand in her own. Within seconds, Eabha initiated the jump. The light from the Time Station increased in intensity, and Dani's mind went blank.

Dani regained her faculties while holding the hand of older Eabha and looking over at very old Aideen, who smiled at her.

"Well, hello there, young Dani!" Aideen said, with enthusiasm. "I was hopin' it would be you coming to say hello."

Dani maintained her composure, smiling back at her friend and lover.

"I can't stay," she said.

"I know," said Aideen. "And it looks like older Eabha is in a bit of shock herself. I guess she's getting some information from younger Eabha about being a Time Link. Don't worry about that, Dani. I'll make sure older Eabha understands what's going on."

"Good," said Dani. "Because the three of us will be back, probably in a few minutes for you, but it'll be a few days later in our time. It'll be a younger version of you, Orla, and me."

"Yes, I learned all about this when I connected with my younger self during the jump of younger Eabha, a few minutes ago."

"I understand," said Dani. "Hopefully, in a few minutes, we'll be back. Then we'll head down to the station and keep moving forward through Sophie's connection to her older self."

"Going forward's the new rage, it seems," said Aideen. "I'm not sure I'd want to be visiting our friend Charles in his time. He's enough of a pain in the arse in our times, isn't he?"

"Indeed, he is," said Dani. "But Aideen, I can't stay. I've gotta go." She leaned over and kissed Aideen on the cheek. "I love you," she said.

"And I you," said Aideen, a peaceful smile on her face.

Dani walked out of the cottage, and soon she was back in the station, in the early morning of July 31, 2022. Eabha absorbed the knowledge of the path of her life well, generally pleased with how it had gone. She'd suffered from knowing the timing and nature of the death of her parents, but she was comforted that each of them had gone peacefully at ripe old ages. The four of them returned to the cottage and went to bed, confident they had done all they could to prepare for the trip to 2253, which was less than 48 hours away.

Chapter 48

On the morning of August 1, around 16 hours before the mission would begin, the four women had a pleasant late breakfast in the cottage, having slept in, but the tension in the air was hard to ignore. Aideen suggested that Eabha pay a visit to her family that afternoon and tell them she was leaving with Dani on a two-week walk down the Wild Atlantic Way, as part of Dani's research for her dissertation. She asked Eabha to return before supper because the tide would be coming in soon after that.

After Eahba departed, Aideen, Dani, and Orla sat around and worried. The three had grown to love each other unconditionally during their time together. Part of that was their shared desire to free themselves from whatever devious plot Charles had embroiled them in, but most of it was simply because they cared deeply for one another.

Each of them was an orphan of sorts. Aideen had lost her mother recently and had no living relatives that she knew of. Dani was an adopted child who had found out through the memories of her older self that her parents were soon to be killed in a car accident. She knew in her heart that she would do everything in her power to prevent that from happening, even though it ran counter to the cardinal rule of Time Links: Do not change events that you know are going to happen. But Charles was trying to change things, in a much bigger way than saving the lives of two people she loved, so Dani was resolved to help them, as soon as the three of them got through the bigger challenge they would soon face. And then there was Orla, having lost her siblings to famine and disease, her father to a hanging for a minor crime, and her mother in a tragic, wholly unjustified lynching. Orla had told the three of them that her one wish was to return to 1751 and free Liam, then to convince him to send her forward again, making the journey back to her new family: Aideen and Dani. The three of them made a pact to save Dani's parents, Liam Murphy, and the future, and for the three of them to be together after it was all done. Dani also remembered that she had something to share with her two friends.

"I have something for each of you," she said, reaching into her pocket.

She extracted two pills and handed one to Orla and one to Aideen.

"What's this?" asked Aideen, eying the pill.

"It's the same pill Charles gave me when we were back in the past. It's supposed to dramatically and permanently boost immunity, and it also permanently changes the metabolism, so you don't gain weight, no matter what you eat. Plus, it allegedly increases your lifespan for decades."

"Well then," said Aideen. "Could always use a few more decades. And you took this? No side effects?"

"I took it, and no side effects."

"Bottoms up then," said Aideen, putting the pill in her mouth and washing it down with a sip of water.

Orla smiled and did the same. The three then prepared lunch and enjoyed themselves for a while out on the patio. After lunch, they went for a walk around the island. The sun was out, but the wind was brisk, bringing a chill onto their hands and faces. They arrived at the viewing point on the northwest corner of the island. The waves from the Atlantic crashed relentlessly against the rocks. They took a seat together on a large, smooth stone and gazed out at the sea and the barrier islands. Orla sat between Aideen and Dani. They all held hands. For a while, no words were spoken, but then Orla broke the silence.

"What do ya' think will happen to us in 2253?" she asked. She hadn't addressed her question to either Aideen or Dani, which was something she often did. It was as if she thought of them as one person, inseparable, and that felt good to Dani. Orla knew that one or both of them would answer her question, and in this case, it was Aideen who started.

"I think it's a big risk for all of us," said Aideen. "But I'm not sure we have a choice as to what we do next. All three of us are connected to the Time Station, and while I used to think that made me powerful, now I think it makes me vulnerable."

"How so?" asked Dani.

"I think it gives Charles power over *us*," said Aideen. "He seems to know what we're doin', even when he's not here. Like when he sent that message to us about us havin' figured out the emergency jump procedures. Or when he started speaking English to Orla, as if he already knew that we'd been teaching it to her."

"There's definitely a lot going on that we don't know," said Dani. "But he needs us, so that makes me think we'll be okay."

"Until he *doesn't* need us," said Orla. "Then what?"

"That's for us to go and find out, young lady," said Aideen. "The hard fact is that we have to do this if we're going to get control over our own lives again. And it doesn't hurt that we might be able to save the future while we're at it."

No one spoke after that. And their silence confirmed that they were all committed to going forward. They gazed out at the restless sea, each of them wondering if it would be for the last time.

Chapter 49

Later that night, with Eahba having returned from her visit to her family, the four walked into the empty channel and went into the Station. The time to go forward had come, and with it, the realization that they had no idea what would happen when they arrived in 2253. They were blindly seeking the truth, and if the right knowledge and circumstances presented themselves, they would try to set things right. The problem was, they didn't even know what was wrong. They simply felt that *something* was wrong. And they felt it deeply enough to risk their lives to unravel the mystery and to free themselves from the grip of Charles Burke.

They entered the chamber that contained the Time Cradles. Eahba got up onto one of the cradles and reclined into it. Before they'd arrived, Orla had expressed concern that if the three of them were killed, Eahba would be forever locked onto the cradle, in suspended animation for eternity.

Aideen explained that she had personally experienced a situation where a Traveler had been killed after she sent him back in time. Aideen had immediately woken and was able to leave the Time Station and go home. This provided relief to Orla regarding Eahba's fate should they not survive, but she was still concerned about poor Liam Murphy, strapped to a Time Cradle in the year

1751. She worried that because he'd never been connected to the Time Station by the simultaneous touching of palms, he could not escape, even if woken up. Aideen clarified that Liam's connection to the Time Cradle would serve the same purpose as the touching of the palms to the black stone wall, and she said that if he could free himself from the rope, he would have a chance of getting out. This gave Orla some comfort, but not enough. She said that if she lived, she was morally obligated to go back and free Liam. Aideen and Dani committed to help her do that. Dani reminded them both that the matter of her parents' car accident would also have to be addressed, and Aideen and Orla agreed that was a priority. Of course, each of them was aware that for these things to happen they would first need to survive the upcoming mission.

With nothing more to discuss, it was time to begin, but before the three stepped onto the platform, Aideen went over to Eahba, who was lying on the Time Cradle. Aideen leaned over and whispered something in her ear. Eahba nodded, then Aideen stepped up onto the platform, waving for Dani and Orla to do the same. When they were all on the platform, Dani addressed Aideen.

"What was that all about?" she asked.

"I'd rather not discuss it at this time," said Aideen. "Suffice it to say that I'm trying to help, alright?"

"Okay," said Dani, trusting Aideen as always.

"Let's go," said Orla.

With no further delay, the three reached over and grasped Eahba's hand and wrist. Eahba concentrated on visualizing the moment on September 7, 2075, squeezed the control, the light blossomed, and the three disappeared into the future.

They woke in the year 2075, grasping the hand and wrist of 69-year-old Eahba, who was sitting on the sofa in the living room of the cottage. Aideen was sitting across the coffee table from them, smiling.

"What have we here?" she said. "No doubt I recognize myself, and the love of my life, but who is this young beauty here?"

"This is Orla, of course," said Dani. "I know your memory from younger Aideen informed you about her, but now you can actually see her in person, for a moment."

"Indeed," said very old Aideen, standing up and giving the child a quick hug. "It's so good to see you again Miss Orla! But you know that all this mischief you young ones are up to is startin' to confuse us old ones terribly."

"I know," said Orla. "We are goin' to try and fix that. But things will likely get more confusin' before they become less."

"No doubt," said very old Aideen. "But I have confidence in you three."

"I'm sorry, Aideen," said Dani. "But I'm afraid we have to make our way to the Station. Sophie should be waiting for us."

"I'm sure she is," said very old Aideen. "Quite dependable, that Sophie. Always liked her. I think we can trust her if you ever need her to break the rules of the Time Masters."

"Good to know," said Dani. She leaned over and kissed very old Aideen on the cheek, and they left. Aideen from 2022 smiled and waved, having been utterly silent during the entire encounter, undoubtedly in shock about being in the same room with her very old self. Orla waved and smiled, and the three of them departed the cottage, also saying goodbye to the silent older Eahba, who seemed to know time was of the essence.

The three made their way into the channel, found the Time Station hatch, went down into the depths, and took the tunnel from the stone burial crypt into the chamber that would send them forward. Younger Sophie was there. Greetings were exchanged. Aideen took Sophie aside and spoke to her quietly. Dani suspected Aideen was laying the groundwork for a potential future unofficial mission, should one ever be needed. When Sophie nodded, she assumed it meant they had a green light on that.

Sophie sent them to the year 2155, where her older self introduced them to younger Leah, whom none of them had ever met. Aideen apparently had been given some assurances from Sophie that Leah could be trusted, because she once again took the Time Link aside and spoke quietly to her. Leah nodded, and then approached the Time Cradle. Within minutes, the three of them had been sent forward to the year 2253.

They woke holding the hand and wrist of older Leah. Dani was confused, however, that older Leah looked quite young, perhaps 30 years old, but she didn't have time to consider what that meant, because within seconds, an opening appeared on the opposite side of the chamber from where the exit normally appeared. Charles Burke came through the new opening. He was clothed in some kind of white fabric that was very tight to his body. He was a surprisingly fit man, thin but muscular. The troubling thing was that he was holding the cigar-shaped instrument that he'd used to kill Ciara's father in his right hand. He wasn't *pointing* it at them, but they all knew what he could do with it, if he chose to use it.

"Welcome to 2253, ladies," he said. "Come with me, please."

Chapter 50

The three Travelers followed Charles through the new opening and immediately entered a large room. Its walls, ceilings, and floor were the same black stone material as the rest of the Time Station. Three men were sitting at consoles, all dressed in the same tight, white clothing as Charles, each of them thin and muscular, and also like Charles, they all looked to be around 30 years old. Their hair color and length varied. One had short, blonde hair; one had long, dark hair like Charles; and one had medium length brown hair. They were monitoring screens with graphs and numbers on them. Charles quickly ended their speculation of what the room was.

"This is the control room for the Time Station."

"Is this room part of the Time Station in our time?" asked Dani.

"Yes, but none of the Time Links can access it, even if you mistakenly placed your palm in the right spot. This requires a higher level of clearance than any of you have."

"What goes on in this part of the Station?" asked Aideen.

"We monitor everything that's going on inside and outside the Station," said Charles.

"In all time frames?" asked Aideen.

"Yes," said Charles. "That's how we knew you were teaching yourself the emergency jump methodology."

"Can you see what we're doing when we're not in the Station?" asked Dani.

"I already told you that the Station functions as a worldwide radar, monitoring the location of all Time Links and Travelers in all eras. That's the extent of what we can see outside of the Station itself."

The more Charles spoke, the less he sounded like an anthropologist. Dani wanted to know what he really was.

"What *is* your area of expertise, Charles?" she asked. "Are you really an anthropologist?"

"Of course not," said Charles. "That's why I thought you might be useful to us, Dani, but you turned against us before you even got started."

"So, you've been lying to us all of these years then?" asked Aideen.

"I suppose so," said Charles. "But now's the time for the truth. Why don't you follow me to the conference room, and we'll talk."

Charles left the control room through another opening. This one led to a hallway, still made from the same black stone material. The hallway was about 50 feet long and was well lit, with no doors on either side. About halfway down, Charles stopped, pivoted left, faced the wall, and pressed his palm against it. A doorway appeared, beckoning them in.

The room had a rectangular table made from the same black stone, and eight chairs made of the same material. Charles told them to sit down, and they complied.

"This part of the Time Station is where we live and work," he said.

"Who are *we*?" asked Orla.

"Ah, so you do speak English," said Charles. "Thought so."

"Why keep secrets anymore," said Orla, "now you've decided to tell us the truth."

"The truth, yes," said Charles. "First, who are we? We're a small group of patriots, patriots of mankind, who want humanity to achieve its full potential."

"You told us you wanted to save humanity," said Aideen.

"Yes," said Charles. "But I must admit that the state of the world in 2253 is a bit, uh, *different*, than what I wrote in the synopsis I gave to you."

"How so?" asked Dani.

"First, there are more than 100 million people, a lot more, but a population drain *is* occurring. The best and brightest are being sent to the future, never to return."

"I thought you said you couldn't go to the future," said Dani.

"My group can't. But there's another group, a government-based group, that's doing that."

"You said there were no governments in 2253," said Aideen.

"It is true there are no governments, in a plural sense," said Charles. "Just government. There is one world government that's based in Brussels, Belgium."

"What happened to the United Nations?" asked Dani.

"It was more or less relocated to Brussels at the time it was given true power. This was the compromise that compelled China to agree to proceed with the one-world government. It's called EarthGov now, but look, we're wasting time here. And you three should know by now that I don't like to waste time. We can catch up on all the details of what things are really like here later. Right now, I want to tell you what I need from you."

"Please do," said Aideen.

"I need Dani to go on a mission for me. She will travel to Brussels and tell the people in charge of time management she is from 2022. She is to request asylum in the 2585 Utopia those people are building on the backs of humanity from 2253. She is to go there, then return to 2253, and then quietly make her way back to this Station. Our location is unknown to the people in Brussels, and it must remain so."

"Why just Dani?" asked Aideen. "We'd like to stay together, the three of us."

"Simple," said Charles. "It's because I need the two of you here as hostages. If Dani does not follow my instructions to the letter, you two will be eliminated."

Charles raised the cigar-shaped instrument into the air.

Chapter 51

Two men came into the room and took Aideen and Orla away. Before the men got out the door, Dani rushed over and embraced them both.

"I'll come back," she said. "I promise." And then they were gone, whisked away to be incarcerated in some black stone cell, more than likely. The door sealed over, leaving just Dani and Charles in the room. Dani wondered if Aideen and Orla would be interrogated or tortured. She wondered what they would eat. But Charles didn't give her time to think about them for long.

"Please come and sit down, Dani," he said. "I assure you they'll be fine, as long as you return here within one week with news of your successful mission."

"Why do you want me to go further into the future?" she asked, while making her way to a seat that seemed to have simply grown up out of the floor.

"That's not your concern. And if you ask that question again, your involvement will be brought to a close." Charles raised his eyebrows, his expression conveying that he hoped she understood what that meant. But Dani was not about to be bullied by him, or anyone else.

"Why don't you just go to Brussels yourself?" she asked.

"Me and my group are their enemies," said Charles. "They do not share our views regarding what humanity should and shouldn't be. They have no idea where we are, and we aim to keep it that way. I'm putting a lot of faith in you to keep this location secret, Dani. If you don't, then it's over for all of us, including your two friends."

"Why are you willing to go to such lengths to accomplish your goals?" she asked.

"Because the people you're going to see will not allow me, or anyone else, the freedom to choose our own destiny."

"I thought they were trying to create a utopia?" she asked.

"Yes, they are. One that doesn't include me and my colleagues, and one where the rules of life are set by them."

Charles was clearly not going to tell Dani what he was really after. She was left with only one option: go to Brussels and try to enlist the help of the people there who were fighting against Charles. So, that is what she would do.

"How will I get to Brussels?" she asked.

"We'll take you to the mainland, then you can go by air-rail to Brussels. There are no cars, trucks, or jets anymore. Everyone and everything moves by air-rail. There are stations nearly everywhere, but they're not the kind of station you might be thinking of. It's simply a vertical pole. If you come near it, it will ask you where you want to go, and when you tell it your destination, it will calculate a route and tell you the fare. If you agree, it will charge you for the fare and then begin making connections to other air-rail poles, coordinating with other transits already in process, like an ultra-competent air traffic controller. You then step onto a small platform, and you'll be launched to your destination. It will all become clear to you as you go through the process. I assure you, it's much simpler than taking a bus back in your time."

"What about money?" asked Dani.

"There's no hard currency anymore," said Charles. "Most people have a chip embedded in their arm that handles all transactions and communications. But some people still use detached devices, similar to the credit cards and cellphones from your time, just smaller. We'll give you a device that will pay for your expenses, but its communication capability will be disabled. You will either come back, or you won't."

"Will the device pay for food? How do people feed themselves here?"

"Most people have food manufactured in their own homes, as we do here. The material the Time Station is made of can perform various functions, including manufacturing food. We feed ocean water and seaweed into the food processing area of the Station, and it makes us what we want from it. All the minerals one needs to survive can be found in ocean water and seaweed, and if an ingredient is missing for a specific recipe, the processor simply creates it at the molecular level."

"What about clothing?" asked Dani.

Charles reached into his pocket and withdrew a capsule.

"You just take this," he said. "Your body will use it to make a thin layer of clothing that can keep you warm in cold weather or cool in warm weather. It's also completely wind resistant."

"So, that's what all of you are wearing?"

"Yes," said Charles. "However, out there in the world, many types of clothing pills allow your body to make different styles of clothing, but we have no need for that here. The one I've given you is common out in the world. You should blend in nicely. Just remove your clothes and take the pill. Your body will make everything, including protective coverings for your feet."

"I'm not taking my clothes off in front of you!" said Dani.

Chapter 52

"**F**ine," said Charles. "You must realize, however, that I could make you strip in front of me, and more, if I wanted to, but I'll let you keep your pride for now. However, cross me, and things will change quickly for you, for the worse."

Charles left the room. Dani wondered what she would use to help her swallow the pill. It was fairly large and would not be easy to get down without some liquid. Suddenly, a glass of water sprouted from the surface of the black stone table. She picked up the glass, smelled it, and assumed it was water. She used the water to help swallow the pill, then quickly removed all of her clothing. After a few minutes, she felt a tingling sensation on her skin, and then the clothing started to appear. It was a colorful blend of green and yellow stripes, gracefully curved, and this helped disguise the natural contours of her body more than the simple white garment that Charles and his colleagues were wearing. The material became thicker around her feet, and under her breasts, and in other areas, concealing and protecting in ways that made sense. She hoped Charles had been telling her the truth and that she'd blend in. She remembered the nude beach, Pelekas, from 1978, and used the same thought she'd had then to embolden herself now. *When in Rome ....*

Charles reentered the room.

"Ah, very nice. You look just like the people of this time now."

"So, now all I have to do is walk up to the United Nations building in Brussels …"

"EarthGov," interrupted Charles. "Specifically, the Department of Time Management."

"Fine. So, I walk up to the Time Management building and say, 'Hi, I'm Dani from 2022. I realize I'm 231 years in the future, but I was wondering if you can take me a bit further.'"

"Very funny," said Charles. "Now here's your official story. You definitely tell them you're from 2022, show them your passport and university ID, and let them do what they do to verify such things. And when they ask how you got here, tell them Charles Burke from the Humanity Project brought you here. That will get their attention."

"Why will that mean something to them?" asked Dani, hoping to glean at least some understanding of what Charles was really up to.

"Because they know what my organization is trying to do."

"And what is that?" asked Dani. "I have no idea what is true and not true about you and your organization."

"We're trying to improve the species. That's all you need to know about us."

"And why would they just let me go to the future?" asked Dani.

"Because you'll tell them that if they send you there, and you witness the peace and harmony they've been promoting, then the Humanity Project will join their cause."

"And you think they'll believe that?"

"I wouldn't be sending you unless I thought they would be happy to receive our offer. They're aware that we've spent 70 years figuring out what needs to be done if they refuse to work with us."

"So, why didn't you just execute the original plan? We were ready to help you, Charles! Remember? Can you at least tell me what was really going to happen at that press conference?"

"It would go off as planned," said Charles. "You would make your announcement about time travel, Orla would disappear on stage, you and Aideen would disappear soon after that, but your dissertation would be left behind, along with my *Synopsis of the Future of the Human Race.* Those two documents, plus the disappearance of Orla, would strike a serious blow to mind uploading before it ever got started."

"And how would that help you to improve the species, Charles?"

"I won't go into the details, but it would allow me to become the only remaining person on Earth, in any time era, with certain knowledge and skills, and that would give me great power."

Chapter 53

"So, why did you abandon the Hearts and Minds campaign?" asked Dani. "If it was going to give you all this power, why not just do it?"

"Because when you informed me that Orla wasn't suffering from Time Fatigue, I realized something," said Charles.

"What?" asked Dani.

"That there might be a better way!" said Charles. "When you revealed that Orla, the first person we've moved forward in time, was reacting differently than those of us who have moved backward in time, I realized that we very much *need* a new approach."

"Why?" asked Dani. "Not that I agree with your plan to make yourself all powerful, but it sounds like it might have worked."

"Might have, yes," said Charles. "But the risk is that I couldn't know for sure if the vagaries of the time ripples from the event in 2022 would become time tsunamis, wiping out people for no good reason, and I myself might end up being one of those people. The risk was too great when another, more risk-free option presented itself."

"And that is what we're doing now?" asked Dani.

"Yes."

"If you say so."

"I say so," said Charles. "Are you ready to go?"

"Not quite," said Dani. "What do I do if they say I can't go to 2585, which seems quite likely."

"Then they will have to suffer the consequences of their unwillingness to work with us. If they say no, you tell them we will immediately initiate an alternative plan to change the future."

"What are you going to do?"

"Not your concern. Suffice it to say that the devastation it will bring is far worse than anything the world has ever experienced before. Now, shall we go, or should I just end you three right now and go with Plan B?" Charles asked.

"Look, Charles, I'll do what you say, okay?" Dani said. "But don't you need to give me something so I can pay for travel and food?"

"Yes, of course," he said, coming back to reality from his dreams of power. "There's a tiny pocket on your left hip for you to place this device." Charles handed her a small, flat, metallic-looking device about the size of a stick of gum, then continued his lecturing. "It's called an MFD, a multiple function device. If it's on your body, when you step onto the air-rail, it will pay automatically. There's no need to remove it and wave it across a scanner or anything like that. For food, there are kiosks all over the place that will make it for you. Just tell the kiosk what you want, and it will prepare it."

"What kind of food should I ask for?" asked Dani.

"Whatever you want," said Charles. "The kiosks can make almost anything. If you want a burger, it will make a burger. If you want lasagna, it will make lasagna. Okay? Are we ready?"

"One more thing, and it's nonnegotiable."

"You're not in much of a position to negotiate anything, Dani."

"I want proof of life before I come back. For Aideen and Orla."

"You would need the communication feature of the MFD to

be activated for that to be possible, and I'm not comfortable with that."

"Figure it out, Charles."

"Okay, give me your MFD."

Dani reached into the tiny pocket and removed the MFD, handing it to Charles. He pushed on it in some kind of unique sequence that she couldn't decipher, then handed it back to her.

"It'll make a one-way call that will be routed to us from another, untraceable location. Don't call until you've had a successful mission. Your loved ones will speak to you, and that will be your proof of life. The device will make only the one call, so don't waste it. Are you finally ready to go now?"

"I suppose so," said Dani.

"Do you have your passport and university ID?" asked Charles.

"They're in my jeans pocket," said Dani.

"Get them, please."

Dani retrieved the documents from her jeans and wondered where she would keep them because her new clothing had only the one miniscule pocket for the MFD. Charles saw her dilemma and told her what to do.

"Just hold the docs near your hip. The clothing will make a pocket for them."

Dani did as she was told. The fabric took hold of the documents. She let go of them, and the fabric sealed itself around them, leaving an opening at the top for her to remove them when she needed to.

"Good," said Charles. "Follow me, please."

Chapter 54

Charles led Dani out of the conference room and into the hallway. He turned in the opposite direction from the Time Station chamber that Dani had thought, prior to this trip, was the entirety of the operation. The long hallway turned right and abruptly ended at a black stone wall. Charles touched the wall, and a door opening appeared. It was a tunnel, very much like the tunnel from the ancient burial vault to the main chamber of the Time Station. This one seemed quite long. They walked for several hundred meters and reached another black wall. Charles pressed his palm to the wall, and an opening appeared, revealing a black stone stairway. He walked up the stairway and Dani followed. He stopped at the landing at the top of the stairway and checked several video screens that were embedded in the wall. The screens showed various views of the landscape that was presumably just above the stairway.

"Okay, all clear," said Charles. "This particular exit comes up at the edge of the channel, where your favorite car park used to be located."

Dani looked at the screens. They showed green grass and a black pole in the distance. She wouldn't have known that this had been a car park a few hundred years before.

"Before I go, Charles, I have a question," said Dani.

"Oh, another one of those!" said Charles, facetiously. "What now?"

"Why do you make us dig in the sand to get into the Time Station, then go through an ancient burial crypt, when entrances and exits like this are available?"

"Theatrics," said Charles. "We want it to feel like Indiana Jones for you guys, you know?"

"Not necessary," said Dani. "I wasn't even born when most of those movies were made."

"But I bet you watched them!" said Charles. "And for the record, these entrances and exits are for people with the proper clearance, and you and your little gang of saboteurs definitely do not, and will never, have such clearance."

"Fine," said Dani. "Don't want it."

Charles pushed a button, and the ground above the landing opened up. The landing itself then began moving up. When it was level with the ground, it stopped.

"Very well then," said Charles. "The air-rail pole is straight ahead. Good luck, Dani. I hope you're successful, and you and your friends can be together again. In a living condition."

Dani stepped off of the landing and walked to the air-rail pole, without saying a word or even glancing back at Charles. When she arrived at the pole, she glanced back and saw that Charles was gone. The area where he had been was just green grass, with no sign of the anything ominous lurking beneath it. The pole spoke to her.

"Destination, please," came a pleasant female voice.

"Brussels, Belgium," said Dani.

"Which stop?" asked the pole.

Dani had no idea what the name of the stop was, but she knew her ultimate destination.

"EarthGov," she said.

"Fare will be 73 World Units," said the pole. "Transit time 59 minutes."

"Accepted," said Dani.

"Fare paid," said the pole. "Please step onto the platform."

Dani stepped onto a rectangular platform that was about 10 feet long and 2 feet wide, obviously designed to hold more than one person. The platform vibrated slightly. Suddenly, she rocketed straight into the air. She could see the landscape below her fading away. Omey Island below looked to have about the same number of homes on it as it did in 2022, although most of them were made from the black stone material. From Dani's new vantage point, she could see people on the streets in Claddaghduff.

When Dani was about 1,000 feet above the ground, her direction changed from vertical to horizontal. She sped east at high speed. She estimated her speed to be many hundreds of kilometers per hour. As she thought about it, if she was going to make this trip in one hour, her speed would have to be about the speed of a jet airliner. Yet she felt no wind, nor cold, whatsoever. She couldn't see a tube or anything else that was protecting her from the elements. But something *was* protecting her, some invisible force that she didn't understand. She wondered what Orla would think of this trip and believed in her heart that the child would be enjoying it thoroughly. None of the technological trappings of the 21st century had phased Orla, so why should this be any different?

Dani looked out in front of her and saw dozens of little dots darting in many different directions, at many different altitudes, all moving at fast speed. She figured out that they were other people, traveling the same way she was. She wondered where the energy to move and protect all these people came from, and she marveled about the power of the AI that managed all of this.

After about 20 minutes, Dani looked down and saw the Irish

Sea, then she was over either Scotland or England, and 20 minutes after that she was over the English Channel. When she reached the continent of Europe, she abruptly came to a halt, then began descending vertically, first at a high speed and then gradually decelerating. Two minutes later, she touched down on the ground.

Dani looked ahead and saw a group of tall buildings. One in particular was *very* tall. All of the buildings were sleek and made from the same black stone as the Time Station. Even the concourse in front of the buildings was black stone. No roadways were visible, only walkways with people walking or riding on some kind of hovering skateboards. A large sign in front of the group of buildings read "EarthGov Complex." Dani had arrived.

Chapter 55

Before Dani went inside any of the buildings, she decided to eat. She'd been exceptionally hungry since she took the clothing pill, and she assumed that was because the pill had utilized some of her own mass to make the clothing. She saw people sitting at black stone chairs and tables that seemed to have grown out of the black stone surface of the concourse. The people were eating and drinking, having purchased their food and drink from kiosks that lined the edges of the area. Dani noticed that none of the kiosks had any signage on them. She assumed this was because all of them made whatever kind of food people wanted, so there was no reason to advertise the type of cuisine that was being offered. It seemed that the kiosks were just a normal part of everyday life here, and no one needed a sign to tell them what they were for.

Dani approached an empty kiosk, which was also made of the black stone material that everything else seemed to be made of. As soon as she got close, it spoke to her.

"What would you like today?" came the pleasant female voice.

"I'd like a chicken sandwich on a hard roll with mayonnaise, lettuce, and tomato," said Dani.

"Salt and pepper?" asked the kiosk.

"Yes, please," said Dani

"Anything to drink?"

"An iced tea, please, unsweetened."

"What portion size for the sandwich and drink?"

"Medium for both," said Dani.

"23 World Units," said the kiosk.

"Approved," said Dani.

"Paid," said the kiosk. "Thirty second prep time. Please wait."

After 30 seconds, an opening appeared in the kiosk. A tray holding a chicken sandwich on a plate and a glass of iced tea moved forward out of the opening and came to a stop at the edge of the kiosk counter. Dani took the tray, and as she was turning away she thanked the kiosk.

"My pleasure," said the pleasant voice.

Dani found a seat at an empty table. While she ate the delicious sandwich, she looked around. She saw that the skies were blue. The air tasted clean as it moved into her lungs. She wondered why men like Charles would want to change this world. It seemed pleasant, clean, and highly efficient. She turned her attention to the people sitting nearby. Other than the strange clothing, they all seemed quite human. There were equal numbers of women and men sitting at the tables, of a variety of races. She noticed that some of them had the tight-fitting style of clothing she was wearing, but others wore shirts and slacks that seemed very similar to clothing from 2022. Again, it seemed that people were free to choose how they wanted to live and dress. *So why, Charles? Why are things so bad here?*

When Dani finished, she wondered what to do with her tray and its contents. No food was left because she had devoured all of it, but she didn't want to leave her used serving equipment just sitting on the table. She watched to see what other people were doing. She saw a man nearby stand up. He said, "Done," then walked away from his table, leaving his tray and its contents there. An opening appeared in the tabletop, and the tray and its contents disappeared into it. The opening closed, and the clean, hard surface of the table reappeared. Dani stood, said, "Done," then watched her serving equipment disappear into the table, too.

Now that Dani had finished eating, she needed to find the right building. She decided to ask someone. She approached a nearby table where a man and woman were just sitting down to eat. They were both wearing the tight clothing, with patterns similar to hers.

"Excuse me," she said. "Do either of you speak English?"

"Of course," said the woman, an attractive lady with short blonde hair. "Everyone speaks English." Dani noticed the woman had a northern European accent, but she couldn't place her country of origin, if there even *were* countries anymore.

"I'm trying to find the EarthGov Time Management building," said Dani.

The woman looked at the man, and they both raised their eyebrows.

"It's the tall building, over there," said the man. He had an English accent. He waved his hand in the direction of the building. "But you'll need an invitation to get in."

"Oh, I, uh, have one of those," lied Dani, wondering how she'd handle that issue.

The man frowned.

"I'm not intending to be rude," he said. "But if you had an invitation, you wouldn't need to ask us where the building is. Be careful when you approach the building. They don't take kindly to people without invitations."

"Thank you," said Dani, blushing with embarrassment that two random people had already figured out she had no idea what she was doing and didn't belong here.

Dani turned and walked toward the tall building. She looked up and estimated that it was about 1,000 feet tall. It rose easily twice as high as the next tallest building. There were windows in the building all the way up until about 100 feet from the top. Then it became solid black stone. When she got closer, she realized there were no entry doors, just solid black stone. This didn't surprise her. Nor was she surprised that she didn't see any human guards. As expected, a pleasant female voice spoke to her, the sound originating from somewhere on the surface of the black stone wall.

"No one is permitted without an invitation," said the voice.

Dani assumed that whatever this invitation was had some kind of electronic feature that allowed the AI to identify it. But clearly, the MFD that Charles had given her had no such invitation on it, so Dani needed to improvise.

"Yes, I know," said Dani. "But you see, I've only just arrived in your time from 2022, and I would like to seek asylum in the 2585 Utopia."

There was no response for a moment, then the female voice spoke.

"What identification do you have?" asked the voice.

Dani reached into her pocket, pulled out her passport and university ID, and held them up.

"Place the documents against the surface of the wall, please," said the voice.

Dani did as she was told and was shocked to see her documents disappear into the surface of the wall.

"One moment, please," said the voice.

Dani waited for about a minute, then a doorway opening appeared in the wall. At the same time the voice said, "Take the lift to floor 73, please."

Dani didn't move.

"I'll need my documents back first," she said.

"They will be returned to you on floor 73," said the voice.

"Very well," said Dani.

Dani walked through the doorway and scanned the lobby for an elevator bank. There was nothing that resembled an elevator to be found. It was simply open space. She *did* recognize something in the center of the large, empty foyer: a row of poles that looked like the one she'd used to board the air-rail. She understood then what she needed to do. She approached one of the poles.

"Floor 73," she said.

Without hesitation, she was lifted into the air. She flew straight up and entered a vertical tunnel that seemed to go up forever. She gained speed, then abruptly came to a stop. An opening appeared in the side of the vertical tunnel. The opening was about 10 feet away from her, and there was nothing but air between her and the opening. She would fall 73 stories to her death, unless a walkway, appeared for her. She didn't know what to do.

A voice came from near the opening.

"Please step to the opening," said the voice, again the same pleasant female Dani had heard so many times already. She was beginning to tire of that voice, and now that it might be asking her to commit suicide, she was exceedingly tired of it.

"I need a walkway to get to the opening," said Dani.

"The walkway is present," said the voice.

"I can't see it," said Dani, thinking the AI must have a malfunction.

"Invisible force field," said the voice. "Please walk to the opening."

Dani realized that if she was going to save her friends, she had to take this leap of faith. She needed to trust that AI in the year 2253 was not prone to malfunctions. So, she stepped forward and felt a solid surface below her, even though all she saw when she looked down was the black floor of the foyer, 73 stories below. She took two long steps and literally jumped into the opening.

When Dani regained her composure, she was greeted by two people dressed in light blue, skin-tight clothing, a uniform of sorts, she supposed. Their clothing also covered their heads, faces, and hands. It was clear in front of their eyes, but it was still there. They were completely covered with it. Both were holding cigar-shaped metallic devices in their hands. Dani knew what they were.

"Come with us, please," said one of the guards.

Chapter 56

Dani was led down yet another long, black stone corridor. They came to a stop, and one of the guards pressed a palm against the wall. A door opening appeared. They escorted Dani into a conference room. A table of black stone had been birthed from the floor, along with eight matching chairs around it. A lone woman sat at the far end of the table. She was of Asian descent, her long, black hair tied back in a ponytail. She wore the same tight, light blue uniform as the guards, except it wasn't covering her head, face, or hands. Her age looked to be around 30. It struck Dani that everyone she'd seen so far in 2253, including Charles and his coconspirators, the people on the concourse down below, and now this woman, all looked to be around 30 years old.

Without a word or salute, the two guards went back out through the opening, and the wall reformed itself.

"Please have a seat, Ms. Peterson," said the woman. She had an American accent.

"Do you have a preference as to where I sit?" asked Dani. "I can stay down at this end if you prefer."

"Come closer," said the woman. "The AI that is all around us will not permit you to harm me."

Dani eased down the left side of the table and sat immediately adjacent to the woman. The woman extended her hand.

"I'm Annette Li," she said.

"Danielle Peterson," said Dani, shaking the woman's hand. "May I ask you a question, Ms. Li?"

Annette nodded her head. "I'm sure you have many," she said. "And so do we. Let us begin this exchange of information then. What is your question?"

"Were those guards human? I couldn't tell because of their hooded clothing."

"Yes, they are. They're part of an elite military unit that is a dedicated force for the Department of Time Management. They live here in the building, as do all Time Management employees."

"Why do all of you people in 2253 appear to be 30 years old?" asked Dani.

"We don't *all* choose to look 30," said Annette. "But many of us do. It's the age when most of us believe humans achieve proper balance, physically and mentally. Physical deterioration has only just begun, and wisdom has taken root and begun to sprout. It's a nice age."

"But how do you keep *looking* 30?" asked Dani.

"Good nutrition, proper exercise, and proper medication."

"You have pills that make you younger, right?"

"Yes. We have lots of pills."

"So, I gather."

"I see you've taken a clothing pill. Who gave you that?"

"Charles Burke," said Dani. "From the Humanity Project."

This confession brought a pause to the conversation, although Annette's calm smile and steady eyes didn't waver. She seemed to be thinking.

"Why did Charles bring you here from your time?" she asked.

"So, you really believe I'm from 2022?" asked Dani.

"It has been verified. Why are you here, Ms. Peterson?"

"Please, call me Dani."

"Of course. And you may call me Annette if you're comfortable doing that."

"No problem. And hey, Annette, may I ask one more question that I've been dying to know the answer to?"

"Of course."

"Why is everything in the future made from black stone?"

"It's not black stone, as I'm sure you have guessed. It's an organic material. We use it to grow almost everything we need. We simply infuse the appropriate AI into it, and it becomes what the AI tells it to become."

"Where does it get its mass from?" asked Dani.

"If we are building underground, it simply converts the matter it encounters into what it wants to become. If we are building above ground, it either converts the building it's replacing, or we supply the matter. We typically bring in dirt, sand, or stone, depending on what is nearby. It all works equally well. The OIM has the ability to change it at the molecular level." Annette pronounced the word OIM as *oym*.

"Amazing," said Dani. "But I hate the black! Very boring."

"It can be," said Annette. "But black is still the color that absorbs the most light, and that helps supply the OIM with the energy it needs to perform its function. In some cases, the light alone is all the energy the OIM needs."

"So, you call this stuff oym?" asked Dani.

"It's an acronym," said Annette. "O-I-M. It stands for Organic Intelligent Material."

"Does that mean it's alive?"

"It is definitely alive. And because we infuse it with AI, it's an intelligent living being. And we treat it as such."

"So, if you want to tear down a building made of this stuff, what happens?"

"It's converted into a new use."

"Do you ask its permission?"

"In your time, do you ask your automobile if it's okay to give it a paint job?"

"No, but you said it's an intelligent living being, so it should have rights, shouldn't it?"

"It's a given that the OIM is here to serve us, just as AI is here to serve us."

"So, AI doesn't want to take over the world?"

"No, AI always wants to help us. Anyway, Dani, I've answered quite a few of your questions, and I'm sure you will have more, but to keep the balance in this conversation, may I ask you a few questions?"

"Absolutely," said Dani. "But can you at least tell me your job title?"

"I'm the Minister of Time Management for EarthGov," said Annette.

"Wow!" said Dani. "They brought me right to the top!"

Chapter 57

"It *is* true that I'm the highest-ranking individual in the Department of Time Management," said Annette. "But power is not our goal here. Peace and harmony are. At any rate, I've told you my title, so now, may I please ask you a few questions?"

"Of course," said Dani. "Thank you for indulging me."

"Very well. So, you say Charles Burke brought you here. Why did he do that?"

"He wants me to offer you a peace deal," said Dani.

"That's the latest of many such offers from Charles Burke, I'm afraid."

"Oh really, he's offered you peace before?"

"Many times, and in many different forms," said Annette. "What does Charles want this time?"

"When I first started working with Charles, he said he wanted to stop the mind upload companies before they get started," said Dani. "He said he was enlisting us to help him do that."

There was another pause while Annette processed the information she had just received.

"I see," said Annette. "Now I understand."

"Would you be willing to explain it to me?" asked Dani.

"Of course. Most of the innovations of the past century and a half, including time travel, were invented by the AI that was housing the uploaded minds of about 100 million people. We call it the Mind Upload Community. By eliminating or curtailing mind uploading, Charles would essentially destroy the world as we know it."

Dani interrupted. "Charles showed us a synopsis of the future that said there were only 100 million people left on Earth, and that everyone else had been uploaded, but when we got here, he said there were more biological people left than that."

"There are six billion biological humans on Earth," said Annette. "From the beginning, mind uploading was strictly managed by all governments, and then later consolidated by the world government, bringing all uploaded minds to one location. From the beginning, mind uploading was made available only to elderly people who were nearing death or people of any age who were terminally ill or had serious physical handicaps that dramatically reduced the quality of their lives. But that was still a large number of people over a period of years."

"Why did the AI need 100 million minds to invent time travel?" asked Dani.

"The Mind Upload Community needed very few minds, relatively speaking, to invent time travel," said Annette. "Just the ones with some form of expertise that was relevant to the area. My understanding is that a group of around 1,000 minds collaborated on that project. The human brain's capacity for innovation is something that AI cannot duplicate even to this day. But AI *can* and *does* play a critical role: coordinating, tabulating, analyzing, and sharing the thoughts of the minds that are working on the same subject. It's this combination of human minds and AI that has led to the vast majority of the innovations in our time. They invented OIM. They invented virtually all of the pills we take. And they invented the Time Station."

"Okay," said Dani. "So, how did Charles and his group get ahold of their Time Station?"

"The Time Station Charles is using was one of the early models. He was working here as a subcontractor. He was the world's leading expert on OIM Growth and Infusion, an expert at bringing the AI to life in the OIM, in whatever application was specified. In this case, the application was time travel. The Mind Upload Community supplied the appropriate AI for the task, and Charles and his team grew the OIM into a Time Station and infused it with the AI."

"So, how does time travel really work?" asked Dani.

"With the technology Charles is using, the Time Link's mind is uploaded into the Time Station itself, and then, based on their targeted memory of their younger self, the older mind is downloaded into the younger mind. The Station amplifies this connection, thereby opening a portal that the Traveler follows to the new time. The Station preserves the body of the Time Link until the connection is broken, then the mind is returned to the body."

"So, what would happen if the Station was to be turned off while a person is back in time?" asked Dani.

"The connection would be broken. The Traveler would remain in the time they had traveled to."

"And the Time Links in the cradles?"

"They would most likely die," said Annette. "Unless there was cloud backup and their minds could be immediately returned to their bodies. It is doubtful Charles has equipped his Station with that, however, to help avoid detection."

"What do you think Charles is doing during all of these Time Missions to the past he's been executing?" asked Dani.

"We don't know," said Annette. "But we *do* know that Charles has his own agenda, and we assume he's working with the Time Station technology to try to achieve it."

"And what is he trying to achieve?" asked Dani.

"Charles wants immortality, but he doesn't want to give up his biological self to accomplish that."

Chapter 58

"That's a new one," said Dani. "Charles never mentioned that he wants to be immortal."

"That's also like Charles," said Annette. "He can be very deceptive."

"It sounds like you know him well," said Dani.

"I was his right-hand person back when we were bringing the first Time Stations to life 70 years ago."

"Then you know him better than I do," said Dani. "But it doesn't take long to figure out that he can't be trusted. So, he just ran off with the tech?"

"It was discovered that Charles was running experiments outside of the parameters of the Time Station project. Specifically, he was attempting to infuse existing biological forms with OIM in the laboratories of his own company. His idea was that if he could develop a form of OIM that was compatible with mammalian biology, he could ultimately endow the biological entity with the same lifespan of OIM, which is theoretically infinite."

"So, how was Charles breaking the law?" asked Dani.

"For one, he was breaking the confidentiality provisions specified in his contract with EarthGov."

"But is seeking biological immortality illegal in this time?"

Annette went quiet for a moment, then answered.

"It's a complicated subject, Dani. I've already told you that mind uploading is strictly regulated. The reason for that is to avoid the very thing Charles told you had happened: that the human race would abandon its own biological basis for immortality. But the humans of my time live long, healthy lives, and most are ready to be done when their biological time comes to an end rather than continue on in the box. Charles's form of immortality could be more appealing, however, and therefore it is even more strictly regulated than mind uploading. The essence of the issue is whether or not an immortal human would be human at all. Would it be the end of homo sapiens? And if so, do we want to allow that to happen?"

"So, what Charles is trying to do is illegal?"

"Generally, yes," said Annette. "But work *is* being carried out by the Mind Upload Community in that area. Very strictly monitored work."

"Why not allow Charles to be part of that?"

"I'm sure he could have been, if he'd gone through proper channels, rather than working clandestinely and illegally."

"How did Charles get caught, if he was doing this work away from the government offices?"

"I turned him in," said Annette, her placid expression remaining unchanged.

Dani wasn't surprised. She could sense that Annette was a good person, and she was obviously also a person who believed in rules and regulations.

"But he got away anyway?" asked Dani.

"Yes, and he killed several people who were trying to stop him."

"That sounds like Charles. I saw him kill a man back in 1801."

Annette shook her head.

"Charles is a brilliant person, but he is very damaged psychologically," she said.

"He fits the definition of a sociopath in 2022, I can tell you that."

"*And* in 2253," said Annette. "Anyway, we haven't been able to find him since he disappeared all those years ago. He contacts us every now and then to give us his latest demands. He seems unconcerned about his acts of violence and his ongoing breaches of the most important law of time travel, enshrined in the EarthGov constitution as an amendment, not long after time travel was discovered."

"What law is that?" asked Dani.

"We shall never travel back in time," said Annette.

"Ooops," said Dani.

"Yes, Charles absconded with an OIM sample that had been infused with the AI that could manipulate time. He literally disappeared more than 70 years ago. He contacted us about 10 years later, claiming he'd been successfully traveling back in time and had made discoveries that could help us. He was seeking leniency for all of his crimes, and he also asked for us to install him in his own department to continue his research and development on biological immortality. Of course, we said no, and we warned him about all the risks that came with backward time travel, demanding that he stop what he was doing and turn himself in before it was too late."

"Well, that must have worked, at least partially, because he hasn't done anything yet, right? Why do you think that is? Seventy years is a long time."

"There's only one reason why Charles hasn't followed through on any of his threats so far," said Annette. "Self-preservation. Charles is an expert on OIM and AI, not on time travel. But it doesn't take an expert to know it's impossible to predict all of the ramifications that changes like he's threatened could lead to, including that *he* might never be born."

"Yeah, I can see that," said Dani. "He mentioned it several times, actually, and he *has* changed course a few times, probably because at some level he realizes he has no idea what he's doing, at least regarding time travel. So why haven't you EarthGov people been able to reach some kind of understanding with Charles? There's a lot at stake, right?"

"It's never been possible to have an ongoing dialogue with Charles because of his fear of detection," said Annette. "His communications are cryptic, well disguised, and not designed for an ongoing discussion. We've never been able to track him, until you arrived."

"And you think I'm just going to tell you where he is?" asked Dani.

"Of course," said Annette.

"I can't do that."

Chapter 59

Annette had just finished one of her long pauses, but she seemed unruffled by Dani's refusal to tell her where Charles was located.

"Would you like something to eat or drink, Dani?" she asked.

"I just ate, but some water would be great."

"Water for our guest, please," said Annette.

The OIM table grew a glass of water right in front of her. *I could get used to this*, thought Dani. She picked up the glass, took a sip, then explained the situation further to Annette.

"He's holding my partner, and our, uh, child, hostage," said Dani.

"And he sent you here to make this peace offering?" asked Annette.

"Yes."

"What is he offering?"

"He's offering to join your quest to create Utopia 2585, if you send me there to make sure it's good, and then return me to this time so I can report my findings to him."

"What are his criteria for 'good'?" asked Annette.

"No idea," said Dani.

"Of course not," said Annette. "That's because he has an ulterior motive for sending you forward and bringing you back."

"Very likely. But he wouldn't tell me why."

"It's because he needs a time marker in the future before he can go there," said Annette. "Has he explained to you that he can't go to the future?"

"He did, but he gave us some story about his Time Station being antiquated technology, which you kind of said was true, right?"

"It *is* antiquated technology because it relies on biological human brains to make the connection to other times," said Annette. "Charles can't go to the future because no one in his organization knows their future, so there is no reference point to link them up with a future time."

"But he showed us a way to overcome that by programming an emergency console in the station."

"Yes, I'm familiar with that console," said Annette. "But it can't work unless the Station is already in a time where you want to go. Charles's Station is not currently in the future, so that technique will not work."

"So, how does your tech overcome these barriers to moving forward?" asked Dani.

"That innovation came along a short time after Charles absconded with the old tech," Annette explained. "The Mind Upload Community had developed their initial designs for biological humans to use. So, they based the tech on human Time Links. But the flaw in that is that human Time Links cannot move us *forward* because they have no memories of their futures. After the limitations of their initial design were verified, the Mind Upload Community changed their approach to a purely mathematical one. They've written tremendously complex proofs and algorithms, far more advanced than anything ever contemplated by quantum theory. These programs are able to break into static moments of time at any point along the chronological spectrum."

"In our first tests of the new tech, we sent inanimate recording devices to the future, then brought them back." Annette continued. "It was a bit like landing an unmanned spacecraft on Mars. The data the devices brought back verified that they had indeed been to the future. The experiments soon moved to living animals, and then our first human volunteers. There's never been a failure at any point in the project. The Mind Upload Community got it right from their first submission."

"I should also mention that the technology they developed for time travel has also been expanded to encompass space travel. We can now go to other worlds in an instant. We have yet to discover any that are suitable for human habitation, but we'll keep reaching out further and further until we do. The missions are all staffed by AI, so no human lives are risked."

"This is all quite amazing!" exclaimed Dani. "Almost too much to take in. Where are the uploaded minds kept?"

"Right here in this building," said Annette. "Several floors above us, in the Time Station itself."

"Am I going to get to see that?" asked Dani.

"Perhaps. But we need to come to an understanding first."

"I can't let him kill my family!" exclaimed Dani.

Annette raised her hand, palm toward Dani.

"I fully understand your feelings," she said. "And we will make every effort to prevent that and to reunite you with them. But we absolutely must formulate a plan that enables our people, our entire world, to survive. That has to be the first priority."

"I understand," said Dani. "Believe it or not, that's how all of us Time Links got involved. Charles told us that the future was in danger and that we could help save it."

"He was right that the future is in danger, but he's the one creating that danger!"

"I am 100 percent in agreement with that," said Dani. "All I would say is that if we're going to stop him, the more I can understand about what you're doing, the better. For example, it's unclear to me why you feel you need to create this Utopia in 2585 when things in 2253 seem pretty darn good. Can you explain that?"

"I haven't decided if I want to tell you that yet," said Annette.

"But why?" asked Dani.

"I need more information from you first. This was supposed to be an exchange of information, and so far, it's primarily been me sharing information with you. It's your turn. Start talking."

Chapter 60

Dani explained the details of Charles's plan to change the future in detail: Hearts and Minds, Sabotage, and the roles she, Aideen, and Orla were to play in executing both. She also revealed that he claimed to have a Plan B, which he said would be devastating beyond anything ever seen before, and that he would initiate this plan if EarthGov did not comply with his demand to send Dani forward to 2585 and then return her to him. This revelation sent Annette into a very long pause, although as always, her expression remained neutral.

When Annette finally spoke, she said there were too many variables to formulate a plan at this time. They had reached an end point in their discussion, and the day was coming to an end.

Dani had no idea where she would be staying, so she asked Annette. "I assume you have some cell to put me in for the night, right?" asked Dani.

Annette didn't hesitate. "You can stay in my apartment if you're comfortable with that," she said. "I'm enjoying our conversations, but we obviously still have more work to do."

"Wow, I didn't expect that. Thank you. Yes."

"Very well."

"Why does everyone who works here have to live here?" asked Dani.

"Our world is safer than it ever has been," said Annette. "But there are still risks, especially for employees of the department that manages the most powerful technology ever developed."

"Do you ever leave?"

"Most of us don't leave the building until our service here is over. But very few stay for more than two years."

"What about you?" asked Dani. "How long have you been here?"

"This is my life's work," said Annette. "I've been here for 70 years. Charles's company was disbanded after he disappeared, but the Department of Time Management still needed that expertise, so they hired me. I've been working my way up ever since."

"Oh, wow," said Dani, impressed by Annette's dedication. "But you get to leave sometimes, right?"

"Yes. I take holidays from time to time, but those are always carefully choreographed and secretly planned. And I'm always accompanied by a large contingent of secret service people. But frankly, I love my work. And I travel to 2585 frequently, which is quite invigorating."

"How so?" asked Dani.

"Because it reminds me of the sheer resiliency of the human spirit. It teaches me that we are a species that can and will survive almost anything."

"I'd love to hear more about 2585," said Dani.

"We can talk about it at dinner," said Annette. "Will you join me?"

"That would be awesome. I'm feeling pretty lonely right now, and because you're the only person I know in Brussels in the year 2253, I would love your company. I look forward to learning more about your world. It seems like a fascinating place."

"It's a good place," said Annette. "And my job is to keep it that way. Maybe you can give me some insight into *your* world. Of course, I've studied history, but I've never had access to a real-life *source* from history."

"Sounds great!" said Dani.

The two left the conference room and walked down the hallway toward the invisible elevator.

"Would you like to see the Time Station?" asked Annette.

"Absolutely!" said Dani.

They took the elevator up about a dozen more floors, until they reached the very top. There was a ceiling above them now, which meant it was the end of the line.

"Above us is the Time Station," said Annette.

They walked across air on the invisible force field and entered another hallway. Annette pressed her hand on one of the hallway walls, and a door opening to a local elevator appeared. They took it up four levels and emerged on the top level of what looked like an arena. It was circular and made completely of the black OIM that everything else was made of. About 50 rows of black seats rose up from the black floor, each row circling around the entire circumference of the room. On the floor was a large black, cubical monolith. It looked to be about 50 feet long on each side, and it dominated the room.

"This is the Time Station?" asked Dani.

"It is," said Annette, a look of pride on her face.

"How many people does it hold?" asked Dani.

"It holds up to 2,500 people. But we typically send only 1,000 at a time because that's usually the most slots we can fill in any given week. We'll be sending around 1,000 tomorrow, as a matter of fact."

"Which is why Charles wanted me here," noted Dani. "He actually expects me to be on that trip."

"There was no way that was ever going to happen," said Annette. "Charles would certainly know that. I wonder if he has something else up his sleeve."

"He must," said Dani. She leaned over and whispered in Annette's ear. "Do you think any of the devices he gave me or my clothing might be transmitting back to him?"

"Not possible. First, your devices and clothing have been thoroughly vetted by our AI. And second, the walls of our building are completely impenetrable for any wavelength transmission. Nothing can get in or out, unless it's through one of our own transmission mediums."

"Okay," said Dani. "We really ought to figure out what he's up to then."

"We should. Let's just keep talking and sharing, and maybe we can."

"How many people have you sent so far to 2585?"

"Around 2 million people over the past 40 years," said Annette.

"That's a lot of people. But in a world of billions, it doesn't really seem like it could make a difference."

"You mean in the future, right?" asked Annette.

"Yes."

"Actually, we believe it *can* make a difference," said Annette. "For two reasons. First, all 2 million have been carefully vetted. All of our Travelers to 2585 are driven by a desire for harmony, peace, and open-mindedness. And second, in 2585, the total world population is only about 10 million humans."

"What! How could that be? What happened?"

"Someone will change something, and nearly the entire human population will perish."

"Oh, my God!" said Dani. "When will it happen?"

"I'm sure you understand that I can't give you the details," said Annette. "Suffice it to say that it happens at some point after today."

"Was it Charles?"

"I feel almost certain it was," said Annette.

"Does anyone else other than Charles have the time travel

technology?"

"Not that we know of. And we know a lot. It's the most heavily policed technology in our world of 2253. Possessing time travel tech is so illegal that it's the only remaining crime that still carries the death penalty."

"So, we better stop Charles then," said Dani.

"Yes, we better stop Charles," said Annette.

"What's that huge black box in the center of the floor?"

"That's the home of the Mind Upload Community," said Annette.

"All of them?"

"Yes. 100 million souls."

"You're not telling me you actually upload their souls along with their minds?"

"It's certainly a possibility," said Annette. "What we know is that during the upload, the AI is able to capture something from the human brain that it cannot produce on its own. It's that indescribable spark that all humans possess, the thing which makes us different from AI, and allows some of us to have inexplicable abilities, the most common being the capacity to innovate, to come up with miraculous theories and inventions that others could not see, based on logic that AI cannot duplicate. But AI can *capture* it and *manage* it, and *that* is what has resulted in the fantastic leaps that the human race has experienced over the past 100 years. Some would call this special element the soul of the human being. Others simply call it genius."

"Wow," said Dani. "That's wild. So, why don't more people upload their minds?"

"It's illegal for most. And frankly, it's pretty nice being a biological human these days. We live long lives, average lifespan about 180 years, and when our time comes, we're given the option of carrying on in the box. But most say no. And many who *do* elect to go into the box decide later to have themselves deleted."

"I wonder why?"

"Perhaps one day you will find out," said Annette.

"You mean, if we end up staying here in 2253?" asked Dani.

Annette paused, then spoke.

"You must realize, Dani, that you cannot go back to your time, no matter if we save your friends or not."

Chapter 61

Annette and Dani had a fantastic dinner—an outstanding facsimile of sautéed fresh North Atlantic Cod, pasta, and broccoli—in the modest two-bedroom apartment that Annette would call her own for as long as her assignment to the Department of Time Management continued. She'd been working there for 70 years, and it seemed to Dani that Annette would continue serving until she was either relieved of her duties or when the world as she knew it came to an end, which seemed likely, unless the two of them came up with a solution.

Dani had glossed over Annette's declaration that she and her friends wouldn't be allowed to return to 2022, telling Annette she liked what she'd seen so far in 2253 and looked forward to spending more time here, but failing to mention her desire to return and try to save her parents, as well as the three's shared ambition to free Liam Murphy from Charles's Time Station.

Dani asked how the major powers had all agreed to join EarthGov, and Annette explained that the inventions from the Mind Upload Community had begun to spring forth in greater and greater numbers throughout the 2100s, and then when OIM had been invented and commercialized in the 2150s, the quality of life throughout the world advanced quickly. With virtually the entire Earth enjoying an above-average standard of living, there was no longer any basis for autocracies or dictators, and they were either overthrown or died natural deaths and were succeeded by democratic institutions.

After that, peace prevailed throughout the world for the first time in history. Nuclear weapons were outlawed and destroyed. Hunger was eliminated. Fusion power replaced all fossil fuel and nuclear-based power plants and joined with solar and wind power to bring truly clean energy to the entire world. It was a time of plenty, and the people of Earth looked forward to continued prosperity. The disastrous fate of the future was unknown to most of the world's population, and this was deliberate, to avoid the mass hysteria that by itself could destroy society. Recruits for Utopia 2585, after they'd been approved and accepted into the program, were told that the world would suffer a nonviolent cataclysmic event, resulting in a dramatically reduced population and a simpler, less technology-driven way of life.

Dani described the world of 2022 to Annette, beginning with a geopolitical perspective but ending with her own personal way of life, including the way her relationship with Aideen and then Orla had occurred. The mission Dani had taken with Charles back to 1751 seemed to fascinate Annette. Dani had become so comfortable with her that she had disclosed everything about Orla, including that she was here in 2253, a prisoner in Charles's Time Station along with Aideen. The discussion then returned to finding a way to stop Charles that could also provide a reasonable means of Dani helping her friends.

Annette calmly explained that if they wanted to, they could painlessly extract the information they needed from Dani's mind with no harm to her, and Annette warned her they would do that soon, unless another viable plan was developed. But Annette wanted to give Dani the chance to come up with some ideas that might help save her friends. Unnecessary death was something the world of 2253 took very seriously, and Annette assured her that EarthGov would support an operation that could help avoid that, as long as its primary objective was to stop Charles and deactivate his Time Station. They would even try to preserve the lives of Charles and his coconspirators, each of whom would be given their day in court, should Annette's government capture them.

Dani inquired as to why Annette hadn't brought in a team of advisors to strategize with her on the situation, reiterating her astonishment that she'd been brought directly to the Minister herself, without at least being processed by bureaucrats in the Department of Time Management. Annette had a quick answer to that.

"The fewer people who know of your existence, the better," she said. "If you and I can come up with a reasonable plan, I will seek approval directly from the Executive Committee. Pending their approval, the manpower and resources to execute the plan will then be authorized."

"So, do you have any ideas?" asked Dani.

"For starters, we know you will need to return to the Humanity Project Time Station, within a reasonable amount of time. How can we work with that?"

"I've been told not to return until I've been to 2585," said Dani.

"Yes, but we've been through that. It serves no productive purpose for you to go, other than *Charles's* purpose of establishing a time reference in 2585 through you."

"Agreed," said Dani. "But there's got to be something we're missing. As you said, number one, Charles would know I wouldn't be allowed to go to 2585, and number two, if I *was* allowed to return to him, it would be with EarthGov forces in tow."

"We should make several plans: A, B, C, etc.," said Annette.

"And then we should debate the pros and cons of each."

When Annette recited the letters *A,B,C,* a recent memory surfaced in Dani's mind. She quietly mouthed the words "Plan B," speaking to herself.

"What is it?" asked Annette.

"I'm sure you remember when I told you about Charles's Plan B, right?"

Annette nodded, and Dani continued.

"He said that if I wasn't allowed to go to 2585, he would immediately initiate Plan B, and it would be the most devastating event the world has ever known. And it seems that something like that will happen, right?"

"Yes, that fits the description of the event," said Annette.

"Which means what?" asked Dani.

"Among other things, it means you and I failed to devise a successful plan to stop Charles, at least so far," said Annette.

"How much time do we have to prevent the catastrophe?" asked Dani.

"Six days."

Chapter 62

"Will you please just tell me what happened?" asked Dani. "If we have only six days to fix this, it's time to put all the cards on the table, Annette. Seriously."

Annette paused, her favorite move for thinking something through, and then made a decision.

"Very well," she said. "Someone created a virus that killed all the OIM in the world."

"You said Charles was the world's premier expert on OIM, right?" said Dani.

"I did," said Annette. "So, if anyone could do that, it would be him. It's just hard to believe he would actually go through with it."

"His original plan," said Dani, "Hearts and Minds and Sabotage, was designed to create as little disruption as possible while still accomplishing his goal of squashing mind uploads."

"The first rule of time travel is there is no such thing as a small disruption," said Annette. "The consequences of any single change, no matter how small it may appear on the surface, can never be predicted. But what Charles was attempting in his Plan A would have a devastating effect. No mind uploading, no time travel, but also no OIM, no air-rail, and no medicine to save and extend lives: a completely different way of life. Charles was kidding himself if he thought his odds of surviving such a massive change to the course of history were good. A roll of the dice is what it was, by someone who really has very little knowledge or respect for the power of time travel."

Dani nodded, a thoughtful expression on her face. "I've been thinking about Charles," she said. "He's really quite devious, you know."

"He's a good liar, if that's what you mean," said Annette.

"It's more than that, Annette. He makes you think he wants one thing, but he really wants another."

"So, what does he want?"

"First, I think he actually wants to go to 2585 himself."

"Yes, he wants to destroy the Utopia we're helping to build that has risen from the ashes of his original destruction!" said Annette, more emotion in her voice than Dani had heard so far.

"I don't think so," said Dani. "I think he wants to *live* there because why would he want to live in a world with no food, transportation, medicine, or heat to protect him from the cold?"

Annette raised her eyebrows. "My word. That makes sense."

"Yes, I think it does," said Dani. "When you told me about Charles's crimes and his true objective of biological immortality, things began to make sense. His first plan, to eliminate mind uploading through Hearts and Minds and Sabotage, would theoretically enable him to become the only expert on OIM growth and AI infusion, and he would also know more about time travel than anyone alive because it would never have happened."

"And if it never happened, Charles would never have committed his crimes," said Annette. "However, the knowledge he wipes out would also be lost to him, unless I'm missing something."

"You might be," said Dani. "But I'm not sure. Can you tell me what happens to inanimate objects when time ripples change the future?"

"We have a limited amount of experience with that," said

Annette. "And the answer is, it depends. If they're basic articles that would not have been affected by the time ripples, then they often remain. But other things would disappear, for example, high tech machines that would not have been invented due to the time ripples."

"What about paper?"

"Paper is very rare in our time, but it's been around forever," said Annette. "It would remain."

"Charles told me he takes written notes with him when he travels back in time to combat Time Fatigue. And he left us a written synopsis of the future, which he clearly believed would remain in our time, no matter what happened in the future. So, I'm sure he's got copious notes on how OIM growth, AI infusion, and time travel work, as well as documentation on all of his experiments relative to biological immortality. If he survived the time ripples, he would be able to teach himself how to do all those things, but no one else would even know about them!"

Annette was obviously impressed by Dani's logic, and she carried it through to its logical conclusion. "But Charles realized that this plan had risks, so when he learned from Orla's experience that Travelers moving forward did not experience Time Fatigue, he formulated his Plan B."

"What's the deal with this Time Fatigue?" asked Dani. "It doesn't make sense to me that people experience it only when they travel backward in time."

"It's because of the tech Charles is using," said Annette. "His Time Station has to take itself back in time in order to move people back, and the further back it goes, the weaker it gets. Through the Time Links, which are supported by the Station itself, Travelers are held back in time. But because the Station's power diminishes the further it goes back in time, the first things to go are the short-term memories of the Travelers. But Charles doesn't know that."

"Oh, now I understand," said Dani. "So, we're in agreement that we think Charles actually wants to go live in the future as soon as he plants the virus in 2253?"

"Yes!" said Annette, showing more excitement than Dani had witnessed in the short time she'd known her. "This exchange of information is beginning to bear fruit! Dani, do you have any more insight into Charles's plans that might be useful?"

"I think I do," said Dani. "Now that we know why he wants to go to the future, the next question is *how* does he plan to get there."

"And?"

"I think he *wants* you to find him," said Dani.

Annette put her finger to her chin.

"Possibly," she said. "Please go on."

"What kind of team would you send in behind me?" asked Dani.

"A group of our dedicated military personnel."

"That's what I thought. So, what do they have that I don't?"

"I'm not following your line of thought," said Annette.

"You said Charles would know you wouldn't send me to 2585 and that you'd send in a team right behind me when I return to his Time Station. So, do any of those dedicated military ever travel to 2585?"

Annette nodded her head.

"Absolutely!" she said, realization dawning in her expression. "A small complement, around 10, accompanies the mission every week. They do a four-week tour and then return to our present. So, most of the soldiers have been there, yes."

"So, if Charles knows you're sending a team in with me, he'll be ready for us. And he'll capture at least one of the military personnel, and *they* will be his link to 2585."

"I believe you're right!" said Annette. Then she fell silent, dropping her chin slightly, a look of sadness crossing her face.

"What's the matter?" asked Dani.

"That leaves only one option," said Annette.

"What?"

"Immediately destroy Charles's Time Station."

Now it was Dani's turn to pause. But she quickly decided it was time to go for the gold.

"There's another way," she said.

"Tell me," said Annette.

Dani described her alternative to the destruction of the Time Station to Annette. Annette told Dani that her idea was against the law, but it was only a minor infraction with a huge potential benefit. She agreed to promptly pursue the matter with the Executive Committee, retiring to a room in the apartment, where she spent the next 30 minutes. When she returned, she had news.

"The Executive Committee has agreed to try your plan, with one condition," she said. "If it fails, we must proceed immediately with the only other option: complete destruction of Charles's Time Station, including all people there at the time."

"Then we have to make my plan work," said Dani.

"It would be best if we did," said Annette. "We will execute your plan tomorrow, following the mission ceremony."

"What's that?" asked Dani.

"We have a short ceremony preceding every weekly mission to 2585. I say a few words of encouragement and offer our thanks to the Travelers, and then the mission proceeds. Would you like to attend?"

"Yes, I would, very much," said Dani.

"I will arrange it, as well as the details of your plan to stop Charles, on one condition."

"What?"

"Tell me the location of Charles's Time Station. Now."

Dani didn't hesitate.

"It's under the channel between the mainland and Omey Island, in County Galway, on the west coast of Ireland."

Chapter 63

At the ceremony the next morning, Dani was permitted to sit in what seemed to be the dignitaries' box of the Time Station complex. It was a suite with a dozen chairs of black in two rows. Dani and Annette sat in the center two chairs of the first row, looking out through thick glass at the seats of the stadium below and the massive monolith that housed 100 million uploaded minds. Beside and behind the two were Annette's direct reports, introduced to Dani as the deputy minister of this and that, none of which she could remember. She was nervous, not only for the "launch" of the Travelers, but also because of what she'd have to do afterward.

Every seat of the stadium was full, all 2,500 of them. The 1,000 seats closest to the floor were occupied by the Travelers, all dressed in tightly fitting yellow clothing, except for the 10 military personnel who would accompany them who wore the light blue color of the Ministry of Time Management, with full hoods. Above the Travelers were 1,500 spectators, all dressed in light blue, presumably employees of the department.

Dani looked more closely at the 1,000 Travelers, trying to ascertain what kind of people they were. And even though the vast majority appeared to be around 30 years old, she realized this meant very little and that the group was quite likely composed of many different age groups. But children were also present, holding their parents' hands, anxious looks on many of their faces. The group was made up of all races and ethnicities, most likely reflecting their proportions in the world population of 2253.

Directly across from Dani's box, at the same level, high above the floor, was another box, full of busy technicians who were undoubtedly responsible for managing the mission. As if on cue, the heads of the technicians in the control center all raised up, looking toward Dani's box. Annette stood, stepping forward so she could be seen in the glass at the front of the box. Her image was also being shown on a four-sided video screen that hung above the mind upload monolith. The restless movements of the crowd and their quiet conversations came to an abrupt halt. The time had come for the lives of 1,000 human beings to be changed forever. Dani's heartbeat quickened, excited that these lives were being saved from the pending disaster that was about to crush the world, but also a nervous wreck, because so many of the people who remained behind here in 2253 would perish, unless Dani was successful or Charles's Time Station was destroyed, which would also end the lives of Aideen and Orla.

Annette began her speech.

"Travelers," she said. Dani could hear Annette's unamplified voice inside their box, followed by the amplified version spreading throughout the stadium. Most of the crowd looked up at the screens, but some were staring directly at Annette. "This morning, you venture forth to a future time. In that new dawn for humanity, the year 2585, you will join 2 million others, who like yourselves, began their lives in our time era. You will also join 10 million survivors of a great culling of the human race, something that has not yet happened. The Department of Time Management is working around the clock to prevent this disaster, and if we do, the world of 2585 will be different than it is now. Very likely it will have a lot more people, and perhaps it will be an even better version of our world of 2253. But even if we fail, I promise you that where and when you are going is a wonderful place and time. Its people lead simpler lives, and with our help, they are now receiving the medicines and other technologies that will enable them to live as long as, or even longer, than we do now.

"You are today's pioneers. You venture forth to build a new world. And you join a people whose commitment to peace, harmony, and acceptance of all forms of peaceful individuality is an inherent right. I salute you for your commitment to the cultivation and the preservation, of all that is good in the human race. May your travels be safe, and may you find happiness in your new world."

A large round of applause erupted from the stadium crowd, including the Travelers themselves and the people in Dani's box. All stood and continued clapping, and Dani felt tears of anticipation and hope roll down her cheeks.

"All Time Management spectators, please clear the chamber," said Annette.

With that command, the 1,500 people dressed in light blue began filing out of their rows and up the stairs to the stadium exits. Dani could see a ring of viewing glass all the way around the upper reaches of the stadium that would enable them to witness the launch.

When the spectators had departed, a countdown timer appeared on the video screens. It started at 1 minute and resolutely worked its way down. Dani saw now that all the Travelers had joined hands. Not just individual families. All of them. She wondered if this was part of the mission protocols or simply the human need to draw comfort from one another. Dani felt Annette's hand reaching for hers, and she took it, glancing over at the woman. She saw tears streaming from Annette's eyes, and she realized that this heroic servant of the human race did not want to send these people away to the future. But it was her duty, above all others, to protect humanity. To do everything in her power to insure that our species continued on.

The final seconds of the timer ticked down. 10 ... 9 ... 8 ... 7 ... 6 ... 5 ... 4 ... 3 ... 2 ... 1. A familiar light began to grow in intensity, but it did not hurt the human eye. When the light reached its zenith, the group of 1,000 Travelers down below could no longer be seen. Suddenly, the intense light ceased to be, returning the lighting of the stadium to a normal level. Dani felt a moment of disorientation, but she soon recovered and looked down at an empty stadium.

Chapter 64

"What will happen to the monolith when the OIM virus hits?" asked Dani. Annette and Dani were now alone in the viewing box, overlooking the vacant stadium. They drank tea together as they talked.

"It will be destroyed, along with everything else made from OIM," said Annette.

"But the 100 million minds? What will happen to them?"

"Gone," said Annette.

"What about cloud backup?" asked Dani.

"The cloud servers are all made of OIM, Dani," said Annette. "They will be destroyed by the virus, too."

"If you know this virus is hitting soon, can't you go there, get samples, and let the Mind Upload Community figure out some kind of vaccine or something to protect the OIM?"

"They've been working on it for 40 years, since we learned of the issue in the future."

"That's a lot of time," said Dani. "I'm surprised they haven't come up with a fix by now."

"You said it yourself, Dani."

"What?"

"Charles is a devious person."

"He is, but damn, that's pretty devious if 100 million minds can't solve it."

"Charles is a genius," said Annette. "In his field, no one has ever come close to his abilities. And in the case of this virus, it mutates so quickly that it's impossible to keep up with it, even for the Mind Upload Community."

"But can OIM come back to the world in the future?"

"I suppose so," said Annette. "But someone will have to invent it again."

"And there's no sign that Charles did that in the future?" asked Dani.

"No sign of OIM nor Charles in 2585."

"So, maybe we stopped him!" exclaimed Dani, excited.

"We may have stopped him from going to the future, but we didn't stop him from destroying the world as we know it. Not yet. It will be up to you, Dani."

"That's a lot of pressure."

"I'm sure you also feel the pressure of saving your loved ones," said Annette.

"I do. I'm scared."

"So am I," said Annette. "But we've charted the course. Now we must sail."

"I have one more question," said Dani. "What about you? If you know this virus is hitting in five days, won't you and other key people from 2253 be going to 2585 before that?"

Annette paused, a somber yet resolute smile on her face.

"Some traditions from history are still relevant today," she said.

"How so?" asked Dani.

"The captain will still go down with the ship."

Dani was saddened but not surprised by Annette's confession that she would fight until the end to stop what was coming, and if she failed she would perish with the rest of her people. Her respect for this brave woman continued to grow.

"Shall we proceed?" asked Annette.

"Why wait," said Dani, nervous, but her determination was growing, inspired by Annette's courage.

The two made their way from the viewing box down into the stadium itself. They walked all the way down to first row of seats and sat. The mind upload monolith loomed in front of them, rising far above their heads. Four military personnel joined them, dressed in light blue clothing that covered their heads. Each of them was holding a cigar-shaped instrument in one hand.

Annette noticed Dani staring at the weapons.

"We call them Ticklers," she said. "They have an official name that is a bunch of letters, numbers, and hyphens, but Ticklers are their common name, among those of us who know of them. They are quite rare, and highly illegal. Most people aren't even aware of their existence. Nor would they want them, even if they did. The devices are not meant to kill, but they can. Their main purpose is to tickle the brain, bringing the subject into a state of submission. This is the device we would have used to extract the location of Charles's Station from your mind, if it had come to that."

"I was wondering why the guards' heads were covered," said Dani. "It's to protect them from those things, isn't it?"

"Yes." said Annette. "I will leave you now." Annette stood, extending her hand to Dani.

Dani stood and shook Annette's hand.

"The four soldiers here have not been to the future," said Annette. "That way, in case the mission fails, Charles will have gained nothing."

"I understand," said Dani.

"You also understand that since we're using the old tech for this mission, these four will be depending on you, and you alone, to get them where they are supposed to go safely."

"I understand," said Dani. "More pressure."

"Please take your seat," said Annette. "The four soldiers will need to touch you in order to travel along the connection you will make with your younger self. Your clothing will allow their touch to penetrate to your skin. Just think it, and the clothing will comply. They will do the same with theirs."

"I understand," said Dani. "I'll get them there."

"Good luck, Dani."

Annette nodded to the soldiers and exited through a door at the edge of the floor. The soldiers gathered around Dani. Two sat beside her and took her hands. Two sat behind her, each putting a hand on her shoulder. She told her clothing to allow them to touch her skin, and she instantly felt their bare hands making contact. A moment later, the light intensity began to increase. And then the soldiers were gone, and Dani slept. And dreamed.

Chapter 65

The beauty and the agony of being Time Link 1 and sending Travelers back to Time Link 2, your younger self, was that you could experience all that was going on in the past through the mind merge. When Aideen had sent Dani back to 1978 to her younger self, her mind literally became the mind of younger Aideen. The experience was far more real than virtual reality because it *was* reality. In this case, older Dani would experience the events that were about to unfold in the past through her younger self. What was unique about this particular mission was that younger Dani, Time Link 2, would be only one day younger than older Dani, Time Link 1. Another quirk of this mission was that younger Dani had no idea the soldiers were coming. But neither did Charles.

The four guards popped into existence in Charles's Time Station, two holding younger Dani's hands and sitting in chairs at the conference table and two behind her with their hands still on her shoulders. Charles was sitting directly across the table from them. Unfortunately, Aideen and Orla were not in the conference room. Dani had tried to pinpoint the arrival time for the few minutes when all three were together in the room, but she had obviously missed that time by a few seconds. It was just Charles and herself, and now the four soldiers, sealed in the conference room, with no door opening present. Dani was still wearing her clothes from 2022, so it was before she had taken the clothing pill Charles had given her. Things happened quickly at that point.

The soldiers removed their hands from her and raised their Ticklers, but Charles reacted quickly.

"Emergency exit!" he screamed, and almost instantly he dropped straight down, chair and all, into a hole that appeared in the floor. The hole sealed up immediately. The soldiers rushed around the table, and one of them used his Tickler to cut a hole in the wall, giving them access to the hallway. The four soldiers rushed out, none of them saying a word. Two went right, toward the Control Room, and two went left, toward the exit Dani and Charles had used to leave the station. Dani assumed the soldiers all had devices that enabled them to communicate with each other without speaking. The previous evening, older Dani had worked with them and an AI assistant to draw a map of Charles's Time Station based on where she had been during her time there. The guards were separating to cover as much ground as possible.

Dani needed to make a decision on which two to follow, or alternatively, not to follow at all. Her main priority was to find Aideen and Orla, but she knew that was a secondary priority for the soldiers, and she was sure Charles would know this. The soldiers were tasked with apprehending him and gaining control of the Station. After that, they would attempt to find Aideen and Orla. Dani had an idea of what Charles might do next, but she needed to catch up to the soldiers to tell them.

Dani ran after the two guards who were headed toward the Control Room. She caught up to them while they were cutting their way inside. When they entered, they saw the Control Room was empty. The personnel there had probably been whisked away in the same way Charles had, and they were very likely seeking an exit at that moment. Dani ran to the wall of the Control Room that was adjacent to the chamber where the missions were executed.

"Cut here!" she yelled to the soldiers. "I think he's trying to escape by going back in time."

The soldiers cut open a hole in the wall. Dani could see an intense light inside the chamber, and she knew they were too late. The light faded as they entered the room. Orla was tied to one of the Time Cradles and Aideen to the other. Aideen was awake, but Orla was asleep, meaning Charles had used Orla to make his escape. Dani ran to Aideen, hugged her, then untied her.

"He's been holding us in here since you left," said Aideen.

"It's okay," said Dani. "We're going to be okay!"

"What about Orla?" asked Aideen.

"I don't know," said Dani, turning to the soldiers. "Is there a way to free her from this state of suspended animation?"

"Yes," said one of the soldiers. "But we need to secure the Station first. We'll be back once we've done that."

The two soldiers rushed out of the room, heading in the direction the other two had gone. While they were away, Dani brought Aideen up to date on most of what she'd learned during her time in Brussels. Aideen was overwhelmed by all of it, but she seemed comforted by the fact that their ordeal might be coming to an end, if only they could free Orla without injuring her. After about 20 minutes, two soldiers returned.

"We've apprehended five people. If there are more of them, they've either gone back in time with Burke, or they've escaped."

"What about Orla?" asked Dani. "Can you help her?"

"Yes," said the soldier.

The soldier had a Tickler in his right hand. He brought it in front of his chest and made some adjustments on it with his left hand. Then he pointed it at Orla.

"Wait!" screamed Aideen. "Won't that kill her?"

"No, Ma'am. These things do much more than just kill. Trust me. She'll be fine."

He pointed the Tickler at Orla and squeezed it. The Tickler made no sound or other sign of it doing anything, but then Orla opened her eyes and smiled. Dani and Aideen rushed over to Orla and hugged her tightly while the soldiers cut the restraining ties away from her.

"Where did he make you send him?" asked Dani.

"To my older self in 1801," said Orla.

"It appears that is where he'll stay, unless we go get him," said one of the soldiers.

"Why?" asked Dani.

"We broke the link," said the soldier. "He should have immediately returned here when we did that, but he must have set the parameters of his trip as one way. No return."

"You can do that?" asked Dani.

"Yes, unfortunately," said the soldier.

"And what about Dani?" asked Aideen. "She's a day in her past from where her present is. How do we reconcile that?"

"We just changed the future," said the soldier. "Ms. Peterson never went to Brussels."

"But I remember all of it," said Dani. "If I never went there, how can I still be remembering it?"

"The vagaries of time travel," said the soldier. "A greater mind than mine will have to explain it to you."

"What do we do now?" asked Orla.

"I suppose we travel back to Brussels," said the soldier. "But it won't be by time travel because our link isn't there anymore. I'll call headquarters and let them know that we've been on a secret mission and captured the Humanity Project Time Station. They'll send a private air-rail vessel, with troops to hold the Station, and return us to Brussels. We'll try to explain what happened to everyone, particularly the Minister herself, when we arrive."

Chapter 66

When Dani, Aideen, Orla, and the four soldiers arrived in Brussels, they were escorted to a secure location within the Department of Time Management building. The civilians were separated from the military personnel and held in a confinement area, where they were soon joined by Minister Li. Dani was surprised by how Annette opened the interview.

"I am led to believe that you were on a mission, which I helped to plan," she said.

"And do you believe that is the truth?" asked Dani.

"Yes," said Annette.

"Why?" asked Dani.

"I found these in my office this afternoon." She threw Dani's passport and university ID on the table. "There was no way they could be there unless they were brought here by you."

"Just like Charles's paper," said Dani.

"Excuse me?" asked Annette.

"Never mind," said Dani. "It's something you explained to me during my time here about inanimate objects and time travel."

"Very well," said Annette. "I'm afraid you're going to have to give me the blow by blow of this missing day of mine, beginning with how you and I met and what happened next. I have no memory of any of this because you changed my future."

"Okay," said Dani. "Well, at least we're not in trouble, are we?"

"I don't think so," said Annette. "Please bring me up to date on what happened here."

"I will," said Dani. "Because I *do* remember. But why do I remember? And why do the soldiers remember?"

"Time Links and Travelers never forget what they've experienced. By changing the future, you simply denied *me* of the memory of being with you for around 24 hours, which I'm sure was delightful."

"This is sounding more and more like the multiverse," said Dani. "The soldiers and I remember a different reality than the one we are all experiencing right now."

"It's an area we're still exploring," said Annette. "But that's a discussion for another day. Please, talk to me."

Dani told Annette all that had happened: The two of them had devised the mission plan to capture Charles and the Time Station and to save the lives of Aideen and Orla. She told her they had accomplished all their objectives except capturing Charles, who had escaped to 1801 through Orla but was now stuck there. She said the soldiers would be seeking guidance from her as to what to do about Charles if anything. She then breached the subject of her own status and that of Aideen and Orla.

"We have reasons that we need to go back to our times, at least temporarily," said Dani.

"And I'm sure that at some point during our time together, I explained to you that was definitely not going to happen," said Annette.

Aideen and Orla shared looks of surprise because this had not yet been discussed. Aideen decided to intervene at that point.

"Minister Li," she said. "Would it be possible for Dani, Orla, and me to speak privately for a moment?"

"Of course," said Annette. "I will instruct the AI, which are monitoring us at this moment, to disengage so that you have true privacy." She handed Dani a communication device. "I assume you've never used one of these, but if you think the word *Contact*, then my name, the device will open up a mind link between us. We can then make plans about what to do next. It was nice to make your acquaintance, ladies." Annette turned and left the room. The door sealed shut behind her.

"Well," said Aideen. "The future is ..."

"Different," said Dani. "It's actually quite a spectacular place."

"I'm sure it 'tis," said Aideen. "But there's another matter I've been meanin' to bring up to the both of ya', for some time. Since it appears we may be prevented from returnin' to our time, I cannot keep this matter secret any longer."

"What do ya' want to tell, Aideen?" asked Orla, an anxious look on her face.

Aideen proceeded. "It seems to me that you, Orla, are my great-great-great grandmother."

Orla lowered her head as if she'd known all along. As Dani thought about it, Orla would have traveled to 2022 through Time Links that represented Aideen's family tree. After the jump through Liam Murphy to 1801, Orla had used Ciara, her granddaughter, to go forward, then Roisin, her great-granddaughter, then Aoife, her great-great-granddaughter, then Aideen, her great-great-great-granddaughter. And then it hit her. If 12-year-old Orla did not travel back to her natural time to bear the child that would be the mother of Ciara, Aideen would never be born. Aideen was still here simply because that time in young Orla's life had not yet arrived.

"How old were you when you had Ciara's mother?" asked Dani.

"Eighteen," said Orla.

"Six years from now, in your time," said Dani.

"Yes," said Orla, who was crying now. But she continued on, blubbering through all of it. "I knew it was true that Aideen was part of my family and that I couldn't stay. But I wanted to. I *still* want to. But I will nah kill my family by bein' selfish. And I must release the Time Links who lie asleep right now while I'm here in the future, the ones who sent me forward to 2022, including Liam, who will die for certain if I doan' go back. And the three of us, we've left people sleepin' to get here. We need ta' go back to 2022, and then I must leave you forever."

Dani was crying now. All that Orla had said was true. If they didn't go back to their times, 2022 for Aideen and Dani and 1751 for Orla, many lives would be ruined or lost. It was a harsh reality, but even worse was the people of the future preventing them from doing what was morally right. They were being held in 2253 against their will. At the very least, that would result in Aideen ceasing to exist in approximately six years.

"I'm at a loss," said Dani. "I usually can come up with something. I devised the plan to stop Charles. But I have no clue what to do this time."

"But I do," said Aideen, a determined look on her face.

Chapter 67

Dani thought the words *Contact Annette.* Annette responded immediately. Dani could hear Annette speaking to her inside her mind. Dani responded, thinking to Annette that the three had finished their private conversation and would like to resume their discussions with her. Annette soon returned to the room they were being held in.

"Why don't we move to a conference room?" she asked. "Please follow me."

When they were all seated comfortably in the conference room, Aideen opened the conversation.

"Minister Li," she said.

"Please call me Annette."

"Very well, Annette. First, I wanted to let ya' know that Dani has briefed Orla and me on the time she spent with you, the time that ya' don't remember. And what ya' told her, among other things, is that the most sacred law of time travel is to never go backward in time."

"That's correct," said Annette.

"But ya' just finished a mission where ya' did exactly that," said Aideen.

"That's true," said Annette. "However, the law was put in place to protect the present and the future, so there was truly no conflict."

"By the way," said Dani. "Has it been confirmed yet what's going on in 2585?"

"A team was sent as soon as the call came in from the team at Charles's Time Station. They've returned now, and the news is good. The OIM was never infected, and the catastrophe has been averted. Better yet, we found a lab in Charles's Time Station where he was apparently continuing his work on biological immortality. We found the virus there that he would have used to infect the OIM if you hadn't stopped him. On behalf of EarthGov and all the people on Earth, thank you for your help on that, Dani."

"You're welcome," said Dani. "But you really have all three of us to thank."

"Yes, of course," said Annette. "Our eternal gratitude and thanks go to all of you."

"I don't think you're quite understandin' what you're thankin' us for, Annette," said Aideen.

"How so?" asked Annette, confusion on her face.

"You see, if we three had never come here to 2253, this problem would not have been fixed."

"Yes, of course," said Annette. "But that's obvious."

"What may not be so obvious, however, is that if you keep us here, all the good work we've done together will have been for nothin'," said Aideen.

"How so?" asked Annette, raising her eyebrows.

"Orla is my great-great-great grandmother," said Aideen. "If she's kept here, she'll never get the chance to live her life, get married, and have children. And then, I will never be born, and I'll never meet Dani, and she will never come here to save your arses. What all that means, Annette, is that by keeping us here on the pretense of savin' the future, you'll actually be destroyin' it."

Annette paused, but it wasn't a long one.

"Yes, you appear to be right," she said. "Alternative plans will need to be made. I take it Charles did not program a proximity limit into this mission, which would make it a lot easier to send you back. You could all just exceed the programmed distance limit from the Time Link, and you would go back to your normal times."

"I'm assuming he didn't," said Dani. Charles had briefed Dani on Proximity Limits during their mission to 1751, so she understood the concept well. "But we can find out from Leah, the Time Link who brought us to 2253. She was working in Charles's Station. Was she captured in the raid?"

"Rescued is the better way to put it," said Annette. "She was being held against her will. But we have her."

"Can you find out if he put in a proximity limit?" asked Dani.

"One moment," said Annette, going quiet, apparently communicating telepathically with the people who were holding Leah, obviously somewhere in the building. After a moment, she looked up at them.

"No proximity limit," she said. "This makes things more complicated."

"Is Charles's Station still operational?" asked Aideen.

"Yes," said Annette.

"Then that's the best way for us to go," said Aideen.

"Why?" asked Annette. "We have a much more advanced Time Station here. We can send you and Dani back to 2022 and Orla back to 1751, and all the Time Links will wake up."

"I understand," said Aideen. "And even though Charles's Station is less advanced, if we go back that way, we can help you with something I think you'll want help with."

"What's that?" asked Annette.

"You'll be wantin' us to explain to the other Time Links that they're goin' into retirement, and if they ever see or hear from Charles Burke again, they should turn the other way and run as fast as they can."

"I can see how that would be of some value," said Annette. "And we would also want you to remind them of the absolute necessity of their continued silence on the matter of time travel and the roles they played in it."

"Of course," said Aideen. "All of them will do that because that's what they've always done, just like us. So, do we have a deal?"

"Possibly," said Annette. "But how do you know the older Time Links you need to go back in time will be in the Station at the moment you need them? We know the Time Link 2s, the younger links, are all there because they sent you forward. But what about the older links?"

"They'll be there," said Aideen. "I took the liberty of speaking to each of the younger links who sent us up the Time Chain to 2253. First, there was Eahba in 2022, then Sophie in 2075, then Leah in 2155. I knew their memories of what I told them would transfer to their older selves during the mind merge connection."

"And what did you tell them?" asked Annette.

"I told them to have their older selves gather enough food and drink to last a few days, bring it to the Station with them, and wait. I told them to expect us to be coming back down the chain soon."

Annette smiled.

"It seems you know quite a lot about time travel, Aideen, and also about negotiation!" said Annette. "I believe we have a deal then."

"Aideen's been doing this for 50 years," said Dani. "She knows what she's doing."

"Very well," said Annette. "I'll need to run this by the Executive Committee, but the logic is sound. Irrefutable, actually. Give me a few hours. I'll need to put together a team to escort you to Charles's Station that includes the techs who will help you plan and execute the mission and the Time Link, Leah."

"There's just one more thing we'll need," said Aideen.

"What's that?" asked Annette.

"We'll need three of those pills that help you live a really long life," said Aideen.

"Which pills, exactly?" asked Annette.

"The ones that turn you into a 30-year-old will be fine," said Aideen.

Annette frowned.

"Well, even assuming I could get the pills, they don't actually keep you 30 years old for the rest of your life."

"Everyone I've seen here *looks* 30," interjected Dani.

"That's because most people stop working in our time when they are 120 years old. That's right about when the pill wears off and the body begins to age again. And that assumes you've also taken the other recommended meds," said Annette.

"Like what?" asked Aideen.

"The most important one is the Immunity and Metabolism pill," said Annette.

"We've had that," said Aideen. "And what about Dani? She's only 24. When should she take the pill? Should she wait until she's 30?"

"That's not necessary," said Annette. "The pill will allow her to age normally until she reaches 30, then it will hold her at that level for around 90 years."

"And how long will it take for the pill to work on an old lady like me?" asked Aideen.

"It takes about a week for the process to unfold, no matter the age of the person taking the pill," said Annette.

"Good," said Aideen. "So, can we get those three pills?"

"Frankly, I don't think I can get that authorized," said Annette.

"Or we could always just stay," said Aideen, raising her eyebrows. "Dani says 2253 is a very good time to be alive, and since we'd be livin' in this time, we'd be entitled to all the benefits, right, like the pills?"

Annette smiled.

"I'll get them," she said. "You obviously will not be denied. And in my mind, you've earned it."

Chapter 68

"So, once you two are in 2022, your natural time, and Orla is in 1751, *her* natural time, all the Time Links who got you there will wake up," said Annette. "You don't need the help of a Time Link or a Time Station to stay in your natural time."

"Understood," said Dani.

"When older Leah wakes up, we'll know you're all where you are supposed to be, and we'll shut this Station down for good. I'm afraid there will be no more time travel in any of your futures."

"No worries," said Aideen. "We'll be fine." Aideen winked at her two friends, as if she knew something that no one else knew.

"And it goes without saying," said Annette, "that the three of you must keep all of your knowledge about time travel and the future secret."

"We've all managed to keep it secret before we ever met you, Annette," said Aideen. "In my case, for 50 years. So, you don't have to worry about us. It's Charles you'll have to figure out how to keep quiet."

"We're working on that," said Annette. "A mission is being planned."

"Just let us know if you need any help."

"Would be easier to just let me kill him," said Orla, smiling.

"I know you're just kidding, young lady!" said Annette, her expression suggesting she was not at all certain that was the case.

"Just make sure to wear the right clothes when you go back," said Dani, jokingly.

"No problem," said Annette. "Okay, are we ready?"

Annette had accompanied the three to the Omey Island Station, along with the team that would program the Time Station and send the Travelers back. Leah had agreed to come back to the Station to help, in spite of the fact that it was full of bad memories for her. Leah was reclined in the Time Cradle, and the three Travelers were saying their final goodbyes to the year 2253. Annette shook their hands, thanked them all once again, and gave a special hug to Dani.

After Annette left the room, the light intensity increased, and the three began their journey back to 2022. When they arrived there, they went to the cottage to spend one more night together before Orla was sent back to 1751. After dinner, they all brought their wine glasses to the living room and sat down to talk. Dani and Orla were quite obviously depressed, but Aideen seemed cheerful. Dani didn't understand why.

"Are you putting on a happy face to make it easier for all of us or am I missing something?" she asked.

"First of all, I'm looking forward to takin' my pill to make me live a long life as a 30-year-old," said Aideen.

"I've been meaning to ask you about that," said Dani. "Did you ever have the chance before now to take one of those pills? You've always avoided answering that question."

"I told you it was complicated," said Aideen, still smiling.

"How so?" asked Dani.

"It was complicated by you!"

"Why?"

"Because even though Charles offered me the pill, I needed you to figure some things out, and you finally did."

"What did I figure out?" asked Dani.

"That I am the same person you fell in love with in Pelekas. It would have been too easy if I looked nearly identical to younger Aideen. So, I refused the pill, and I waited for you to figure things out on your own. I suffered a bit, but it was short lived because you're a smart woman, Dani." Aideen's smile grew even larger, and Dani couldn't help but smile a little herself.

"You know, you are one tough broad," she said.

"As tough as they come," said Aideen. "And now I get to take the pill after all. And I'm also feelin' good about my newly increased immune system, as I'm sure Orla is, even though she looks to be poutin' a bit about our upcomin' separation."

"And you're not?" asked Dani. "Come on, what gives?"

"I have another plan," said Aideen, smiling brightly.

Chapter 69

Dani's heart leapt.

"You have a plan that keeps us all together?" she asked.

"I have a plan that will get us all back together soon, I hope," said Aideen.

Dani's enthusiasm declined.

"How soon?" she asked.

"As soon as you and I can get to Egypt," said Aideen. "And then all we have to do is talk Sadiki into letting us use his Time Station."

"What?" asked Dani. "You mean, the young man in the tent in 1978? His father was named Asim, right?"

"Yes, but Asim has retired. Sadiki runs the family business now."

"Such business being time travel?" asked Dani. "Is Sadiki a Time Link?"

"No need for him to be that," said Aideen. "He's got the newer model!"

"Oh, my goodness, tell me everything!" said Dani.

"It's a long story," said Aideen. "Short version is that Charles had heard there was another Time Station in Egypt that was using the most modern technology. I went with him to Cairo several times, trying to find it. Charles was always nearby, but when we met Asim and Sadiki, I had a feelin' they were the guys. But I didn't tell Charles. And neither did they. I went back on my own time to find out, and sure enough, Sadiki is the caretaker of the other Time Station. He doesn't function as a Time Link. He actually runs the Station. The Travelers who use it are from the future, but they don't go back there, probably to avoid any trouble with that law of theirs about not goin' back in time. They just come and go from Sadiki's station. They've taught him how to operate it and have given him the medicines to increase his lifespan, and lots of money, to buy his loyalty."

"So, why did he tell *you*?"

"I've got lots of money, too!" said Aideen. "And it's not like the Travelers are going to kill him if they find out he's breached their trust. They're not like Charles."

"But who are these people? These Travelers? Did he tell you?"

"I gather they're part of Annette's group. I think they've been runnin' these backward ops for a while now, going way back in time, much further than Charles ever got."

"Okay great!" said Dani. "But how does this help us? Orla still has to go back in time to have her family, which will ultimately include you."

"She does," said Aideen. "And we will miss young Orla terribly. But we'll at least be able to visit her."

Orla brightened at this prospect, but Dani had been hoping for more.

"That's something," said Dani. "But is that it?"

"Not quite," said Aideen. "You remember I got *three* of those pills that make you live longer, right?"

"Yes," said Dani. "I know you got one for yourself and one for me, but I never understood who you wanted to give the third one to."

"To Orla!" said Aideen.

"But she's only 12 years old!"

"Not to *young* Orla," said Aideen. "To *old* Orla, the one who's already had all her kids and raised them as well. We know there's a 62-year-old Orla living in 1801. So, we'll go get her with Sadiki's Time Station, bring her to 2022, and give her the pill. Then the three of us can be together for a long, long time. And young Orla can have that to look forward to during her whole miserable life from 1751 to 1801."

Dani thought about it, and it felt right. It felt good. Orla seemed to feel the same way because she was smiling brightly.

The next day when they sent her back to 1751, it was not nearly hard as it would have been. They promised Orla to come see her younger self as often as they could, and they also promised to bring her older self to 2022 as soon as they could get to Egypt. They embraced and said their goodbyes, then sent Orla walking up the road, knowing that Charles had programmed in a proximity limit between Aideen and Orla when he planned the mission to bring her to 2022.

In spite of the fact that they had a plan and felt certain they could pull it off, it was still hard. Twelve-year-old Orla was a special child, and they might never see her again at that age. And she would have a hard life. They all knew this, especially Orla. But she walked up the road with a sense of optimism about the future. Both Dani and Aideen could feel this, and it rubbed off a little on them. Dani yelled one last thing to young Orla as she made her way up the road, putting some distance between her and them.

"Don't forget to untie young Liam Murphy!"

And then Orla was gone.

Dani and Aideen had been holding hands the whole time Orla walked away. Suddenly, Aideen pulled her hand away. She used it to wipe the tears off her face. Then she looked directly at Dani with those beautiful gray-blue eyes.

"Let's go get our girl," she said, determination in her voice.

"We'll have to wait for low tide," said Dani. "Or not. I'm willing to swim across if that's what it takes."

Epilogue

In the year 1801, 66-year-old Liam Murphy slapped his empty mug down on the bar, having just guzzled its entire contents.

"I've been chuggin' down the suds me whole life!" he exclaimed, speaking English with a heavy Irish accent, addressing the tall man with a beard who was sitting beside him at the bar. "I'm the oldest man in town, but I can still get the job done!" He threw his gray head back and bellowed out a hearty laugh. But he wasn't finished with his story. He lowered his voice, looking around to make sure no one was listening.

"Ever since I was held prisoner in a tomb made of black stone, I been drinkin', heavily," he said. "For 50 years I tell ya'. Fifty years! And no one, to this day, believes it. A beautiful young lass, only 12 years of age, took me from the tomb. But before she untied me, she made me promise to wear a blindfold or she wouldn't let me out. Said it was for me own good. Said I'd be killed if I ever set foot in that tomb again! So, I did what she told me, and she walked me out of there, and to this day, I've not been able to find it again. And no one believes me story!"

"I believe it," said the man.

Liam Murphy snapped to attention, stunned by the man's

admission, wondering if this was just another practical joke surrounding his story that no one believed.

"Do ya' now?" he asked. "You serious about that, are ya' lad?"

"More serious than you would ever believe," said the man, his smooth, melodious voice having an English accent. "May I ask you a question about your ordeal, Mr. Murphy?"

"Indeed, you may," said old Liam, mollified that someone was finally showing interest in his outrageous tale.

The man reached into his pocket, withdrew a piece of black stone, then held it up in front of Liam Murphy's face.

"Did it look like this?" asked the man. "The black stone of your prison?"

Liam's eyes opened wide, and a look of terror crossed his face.

"That's it!" he screamed. "That's the black stone!"

The man quickly placed the stone back into his pocket.

"Allow me to reintroduce myself, Mr. Murphy," said the man, extending his hand. "We've met before, actually. My name is Charles Burke."

Please Post a Review on Amazon

Please be so kind to leave me a review on Amazon, especially if you've enjoyed the book and would like others to as well. Just use the camera on your phone to hover over the QR code below and press you finger on it to go to the review page.

SD

Acknowledgments

My thanks to Christine Davin, the person I trusted as the first reader of this book, because she was the right person for the job. Her love of reading and keen insights helped make *Time Chain* a better story, and I am grateful to her for that.

I am also grateful to Cassandra Yorke for her help with the cover and for her kind words about *Time Chain*.

Thank you also to Jennifer Bright and her team, always there to help with literally everything that makes a book real.

And my eternal gratitude to Christopher and Teresa Stacey from Footfalls Walking Holidays in Ireland for introducing me to their wonderful country and for continuing to take me to places that unearth new possibilities for my soul and my writing. It was Christopher himself whom I followed across the causeway to Omey Island while the tide was out. It was also Christopher who led me to the woman in the car park, just before the rainstorm hit. It all came together for me a few months later, and then the work on *Time Chain* began.

About the Author

Steven Decker is a world traveler who believes strongly in the first commandment of writing: Write what you know. His experiences around the globe often appear in his books as settings, characters, or plot points, and hopefully this enhances the experience of the reader. But any good work of fiction requires more than that. Fiction readers want to escape from their everyday lives when we read a book, thus the true job of a novelist is to imagine special things, sometimes even spectacular things, then write about them in a way that inspires the reader to go there, too. The author spends his days with his two dogs, Jenny and Wilson, doing his best to write good fiction in a quiet town in Connecticut.

Printed in Great Britain
by Amazon